She ⋯ *vatching.*

She missed sex. The thought popped into Jillian's head, and for once, she didn't push it away immediately. Acknowledging the truth—to herself, in private—lightened her step just enough to catch the rhythm of Cade's martial arts workout.

Yeah, she was aroused. And she loved it. The illicitness of desire, the heat of untamed need reminded her that she lived and breathed and responded like the hot-blooded woman she was. Life pumped through her veins, and it was now riding a wave of lust and need *this* man inspired. *This* man, who had no idea he had an audience...

Jillian recognized the Tae Kwon Do forms Cade practiced, having learned most of those moves during her own quest for a black belt. But following him—letting him guide her—was like stretching her muscles for the first time.

Arms. Legs. Stomach. Chest. Lungs. She felt his influence everywhere. She tried to concentrate on mirroring his movements, but all she could think about was the unfulfilled ache spreading through her body.

She wanted to make love...with Cade. Stranger or not.

Blaze™

Dear Reader,

MIDNIGHT FANTASIES...secret thoughts lurking in shadows, waiting until the lights are out to slip into your mind and wreak havoc with your dreams. What a thrill to be a part of this fantastic miniseries!

When I wrote my first Blaze novel, *Exposed* (August 2001), I toyed with the idea of voyeurism. My hero and heroine, experimenting with lovemaking in sexy San Francisco, had no idea that someone was watching them, preparing to expose their affair.

The idea fascinated me...so much so that I decided to go further—but in a different direction. What if the heroine watches the hero without him knowing, long before they exchange one word? What if she learns intimate things about him, things she can use to seduce him?

And what if, in the course of their red-hot affair, he ends up watching her?

Please stop by my Web site, www.julieleto.com, to let me know how you enjoyed *Just Watch Me*.... You can also read an excerpt from my next Temptation HEAT novel, where Cade's partner, Jake, finally tangles with the sexy mystery writer who's driving him nuts in this book! Or you can write to me at P.O. Box 270885, Tampa, FL 33688-0885.

Enjoy...

Julie Elizabeth Leto

Books by Julie Elizabeth Leto

JUST WATCH ME...
Julie Elizabeth Leto

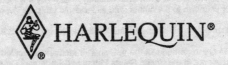

HARLEQUIN®

TORONTO • NEW YORK • LONDON
AMSTERDAM • PARIS • SYDNEY • HAMBURG
STOCKHOLM • ATHENS • TOKYO • MILAN • MADRID
PRAGUE • WARSAW • BUDAPEST • AUCKLAND

For Marilynn and Charles Klapka, the best in-laws
a girl could have! Thank you for sharing your family, your
son and your time—particularly to "watch" the Princess.

ISBN 0-373-79033-3

JUST WATCH ME...

Visit us at www.eHarlequin.com

Printed in U.S.A.

1

"MAN, OH, MAN, talk about your major job perk."

Following her best friend's line of sight, Jillian Hennessy cast a glance at the house across the street. Or, more pointedly, at the man who apparently *lived* in the house across the street.

Man, oh, man was right.

Wearing nothing but a cropped T-shirt and cutoff jean shorts, he walked around the corner of his wraparound porch and down the front steps with a slight hitch—so slight, an untrained eye or overly romantic heart might mistake his movement for a confident swagger à la John Wayne. Jillian, however, simply considered herself an expert on the quirks and ticks that made someone unique—an essential skill in her line of work.

And from this man, her talent for observation picked up pure male power in a body built for sin. Broad shoulders. Flat stomach. Arms and legs taut with muscle and sprinkled with fine, dark hair over an outdoorsman's tan.

But gorgeous as he was, he was no John Wayne. Her father had been a certified authority on the Duke. Her earliest memory was watching *Stagecoach* and *Rio Bravo* on her father's lap during Saturday afternoon breaks from her brothers' baseball games or her sister's dance recitals.

John Wayne? No way.

Mel Gibson? Robert Redford? Close, but still…different. Whoever her new neighbor was, he had a distinct presence that demanded the attention of any and all women in a ten-mile radius.

The last type of man she needed right now.

She hadn't uprooted her entire life so a man could distract her. She'd moved here with a job to do, a job that required one hundred percent of her attention, twenty-four hours a day. A job that demanded she blend into the neighborhood quickly and without garnering too much attention. Not that Jillian was easily knocked off course by her hormones, but it had been known to happen.

Yet, so long as the bright Florida sun gave her a reason to keep her sunglasses on, Jillian surrendered and freely joined Elisa's openmouthed stare, though she *did* manage to keep her lips pressed firmly together.

She watched every move as her neighbor paused next to a lamppost twined with fragrant jasmine. As he bent to snap a few weeds from the base, Jillian's entire nervous system hitched, as if another kick-start would send her into complete overload. She had a god of a man living across the street, a libido that hadn't felt so primed since Luke Hamilton coaxed her to second base on her sixteenth birthday and every reason in the world to act as if her sexy neighbor didn't excite her in the least.

The contradictions made her dizzy.

Elisa pulled her ever-present lollipop out of her mouth with a smack and stepped down to meet Jillian at the bottom of the porch.

"I don't suppose he's the guy you're supposed to watch?"

Jillian dropped the sealed box on the porch, glad she'd just carried an undamageable carton of clothes from Elisa's car rather than any of her cameras or computers. She turned toward her rental house in Tampa's revitalized south-side neighborhood of Hyde Park and watched her neighbor sort his mail in the reflection from her glass front door.

If only.

She swallowed the dreamy reply, guessing Elisa would expect her to be instantly enamored. Doing the expected was never much fun in Jillian's estimation. "Does he look like a bespectacled weasel extorting money for bogus injuries?"

"Oh, we're buying into stereotypes now, are we?"

"What stereotype? I've seen Stanley Davison. Trust me, he's a weasel."

"Then who's this guy?"

Jillian turned just as the hunk in torn clothing looked up, squinted, then gave a friendly wave in the style of a casual military salute. She resisted the urge to wave back, leaving the geniality to Elisa, who wiggled her fingers in his direction and flashed one of her best smiles. Jillian wasn't moving in to this rented house to consort with her neighbor. She had a job to do—and too much at stake to let anything or anyone stand in her way.

Especially a dark-haired hunk in strategically ripped attire, though she couldn't deny that he was a physical manifestation of her perfect fantasy lover. He wore his black hair cropped close to the nape of his neck, yet just long enough in front to look freshly tousled by a lover's fingers. His build, athletic and tanned, bespoke a man who wasn't afraid to sweat.

Jillian bit back a sigh.

Her neighbor returned Elisa's greeting with a broader smile, but despite the good twenty-yard distance between his mailbox and her front porch, Jillian sensed the exact instant his attention turned to her. His squint narrowed. A corner of his mouth tilted up in, what? Approval? Interest?

She couldn't tell. She didn't want to tell. If he found her attractive...well, great. That she found him attractive right back was an inconvenience at worst and an affirmation at best. It had been so long since she'd wanted a man in her life, since she'd even allowed a member of the male gender to turn her head, she'd started to wonder if the divorce she claimed to be "over" wasn't still subconsciously controlling her decisions. She had an active social life thanks to her friends and family, but dating? No time. Too much business to attend to. Too much ambition to feed.

Yet up until this moment, the only job perk she'd experienced in twelve years of working for her uncle's investigation firm was that the tech team had installed all the surveillance equipment in the upstairs bedroom the day before she arrived and saved her the hassle and heavy lifting.

Now she also had a handsome neighbor to anonymously ogle during her off-hours. If she had any off-hours. While on the job, she'd reserve her watching to the weasel who lived one house over. Once she succeeded in proving Stanley Davison was a fraud and an incorrigible con man—something two P.I. firms, a judge and a bevy of lawyers had failed to prove so far—she'd get all the special attention she needed as the new CEO of the Hennessy Group.

Born smack in the middle of five children, Jillian had learned early on that she had to bust her tail for any and all recognition. She started her P.I. career in the mailroom during summer breaks from junior high and worked her way up through every department. She now knew all facets of the Hennessy Group, the deceptively bland corporate listing for the South's most illustrious investigation firm—well, almost all facets. Though she'd sat in her uncle's chair on more than one occasion, usually in a last-minute bid to undo some mishap her uncle's growing carelessness caused, the chair was still his.

Until he retired and turned the worn leather swivel chair over to her. Or to her brother.

That thought made her turn completely away from her hunky neighbor with the midnight hair and incredible shoulders. She loved shoulders. Especially wide ones, curved just right between the pec and collarbone to invite her face to press against him.

She shook her head. This was a distraction she couldn't afford. She picked up the box and took it inside, dropping it atop five others stacked at the bottom of the staircase. By the time she returned, her neighbor had disappeared.

"He's got a great ass," Elisa declared.

Jillian bit the inside of her lip. Elisa, her best friend and the Hennessy Group's head bookkeeper, had been a bona fide date-a-holic before her uncle hired Ted Butler to head up the tech team. Just a few months later, Elisa and Ted were one hot item. Her friend worked fast, and this time, perhaps, for keeps.

It was nearly enough to convince Jillian that true love did still exist in the world. Just not for her.

"I don't think Ted would appreciate you rating another man's ass," Jillian said.

Elisa shrugged and took another long suck on her

lollipop, which was coloring the inside of her lips Blow Pop purple. "Ted has a *perfect* ass. Your neighbor's is only great." She returned to the porch and draped herself across a wicker chaise, patting the spot next to her so Jillian would take a break.

"Perfect, huh?" Jillian glanced at the open trunk of Elisa's car, now empty, and decided a short break wouldn't hurt. Maybe talking about Ted's ass would distract her from the fact that she'd just transported the entire contents of her daily life in five medium-sized boxes and a hanging bag.

She hadn't really seen her neighbor's butt long enough to make an honest comparison, but if the rest of his body was any indication, Jillian was certain her nameless hunk across the street would give Ted and his perfect ass a serious run for their money.

"Oh, yeah," Elisa reaffirmed. "Ted used to play baseball. Baseball players have the best backsides. Haven't you noticed?"

Jillian's gaze wandered to the front window of the house across the street. She thought she saw the front blinds flutter, but shook her head, sure she was mistaken. Even if her neighbor was peeking, he was more than likely looking at Elisa. Though they were probably equal as far as attractiveness went, Elisa possessed a natural vibe that arrested men's attention the moment she made eye contact.

Jillian, on the other hand, worked long and hard at sending out a vibration that said, "Back off, Bub." She didn't have time to waste on romantic entanglements. She'd wasted it all in a bad marriage. Now, she wanted one thing and one thing only—the keys to the executive washroom in her uncle's office, even if she had already mastered the art of picking the lock.

"Obviously not," Elisa quipped.

"Huh?"

"Baseball? Butts? Never mind. You should check that guy out." Elisa eased her tanned legs onto the chaise and stretched as if she'd done all the carrying and carting of twenty boxes, not a measly five.

Jillian grinned. "I'm here to check out Stanley Davison, and that's what I plan to do."

"Twenty-four/seven? The guy isn't home all day. And if I know you, and I do, you've assigned a second team to tail him when he leaves the house."

Jillian dug her hands into the pockets of her short denim skirt and nodded. Though this was her first field assignment, she'd organized the operation for maximum efficiency. Assigning more than one agent to watch Stanley day and night was expensive, but would pay off if they obtained the proof they sought.

Just a month ago, Stanley Davison had won a high-profile lawsuit against the Tampa Police Department. Claiming he was incurably injured after being knocked down during a police foot chase, he'd received over two million dollars in compensation for soft-tissue damage to his neck and spine. Jillian had first followed the case out of curiosity. Because of Stanley's publicized claim, the TPD had been inundated with charges of careless disregard during other pursuits and was fighting off a rash of pending lawsuits.

A subsequent interview with the police department's insurance carrier stimulated Jillian's nose for finding new business. The spokesman for First Mutual Insurance bemoaned the rash of bogus claims plaguing the industry. The company had its fraud investigators working overtime, but claimants were getting down-right professional in fooling doctors and juries.

Jillian had read into the comment a clear implication that the insurance companies were falling behind. She made a few inquiries and learned that First Mutual was looking for a private investigation firm to put on retainer, to help out their in-house staff. Jillian had immediately convinced Uncle Mick to submit a business plan, but she wanted to add something more—something that would separate the Hennessy Group from the rest of the pack.

Something like proving that Stan Davison, the recipient of the most notorious claim to date, was a certifiable fraud. Not only could catching Stan help her bring in a huge client for the firm, she could prove to her uncle that *she,* not her brother Patrick, deserved to run the company.

"If they're following my schedule," she admitted, "Stanley Davison won't pick his nose without someone from the Hennessy Group making a note. On the road, Jase and Tim have him. When he's home, he's mine."

"Stan's not a homebody. What will you do with all that time in between?"

Elisa's question was fraught with expectations of boredom—expectations Jillian preferred not to think about. She'd been in the office every day of every week of every year, except usually Christmas and Easter, since she'd graduated from college. She arrived before 7:00 a.m. and never left before 7:00 p.m. Her hobbies included studying old investigations, double-checking the accountant's work on the books and making sure none of the employees realized her uncle made errors in his investigations from time to time.

But here, in the field and away from the daily grind, she had nothing but a lying weasel to occupy her time.

And, perhaps, Mr. Cutoffs across the street.

"I suppose I'll catch up on my reading," Jillian decided.

"Sexy spy novel?"

"Case reports."

"Bor-ing." Elisa sang the two syllables.

"Maybe, but a sexy spy novel isn't going to help me get what I want." She wasn't about to admit that she had the latest bestselling suspense novel tucked into a box of clothes. She did have an image as a no-nonsense, no-private-life-to-speak-of businesswoman to protect, even with her best friend.

Elisa laughed and stood, smoothing her hands over her skintight jeans after fishing her keys from her pocket. "Maybe not, but it will most definitely point you in the direction of what you *need*."

"Don't start the 'you need a man' thing again. I had a man. And a marriage. And a divorce. I even got to enjoy the gift of another woman...or twelve," Jillian said, trying to inject humor into the reality that still stung. "Now, all I want is a company to call my own."

"A company doesn't keep you warm at night, sweetie."

"I've got blankets. And this is Florida. It doesn't get that cold."

Elisa frowned, but backed off. They'd had this conversation enough times to know that neither of them would budge or compromise. Also Jillian would never admit, even to her closest friend, that she was lonely as hell.

Elisa had skipped down the porch before Jillian registered that she was leaving.

"I don't suppose you want to pick up dinner at Cesare's and go over the Anderson case with me tonight?" she asked.

Stopping to glance over her shoulder, Elisa grinned. "Review a closed case with you over Italian food—" she held out her left hand as if weighing the possibility, then did the same with her right when she voiced her other option "—or making out with Ted during his stakeout of the Rinaldo estate?"

She paused, allowing Jillian to draw her own conclusion.

"I'll call you in the morning," Jillian said.

Elisa slid into her car, rolling down her window as she backed down the drive. "You've got everything you need while your car's in the shop?"

Jillian nodded and waved, remembering, even if she didn't want to, when she and her ex-husband Neal had once had sex in the back seat of his car when he was supposed to be working on a case. At the time, the experience had been thrilling, forbidden, exhilarating. Now, it was a bitter reminder of how gullible she'd been.

Oh, and how much she missed thrilling, forbidden, exhilarating sex.

As if she needed reminding. Especially since she was apparently now living across the street from a man who had stirred her interest while hardly acknowledging her presence. What she wouldn't give for a quick, clandestine glance into his house. His bedroom, perhaps. At midnight. That magical time each night when fantasy and reality often melded into Jillian's sinfully erotic dreams.

She threw up her hands and padded to the front door, determined to get that thought out of her head by doing what she did best—work. She had boxes to unpack, schedules to study and calls to make before Stanley Davison got home and she would start her official surveillance.

But before she pulled open the squeaking screen door, a shiver crept up the back of her neck, stopping her cold. The sweat gathering between her breasts from the outdoor heat froze like icicles.

Someone was watching her.

Someone nearby.

Slowly, she cocked her head to the left, catching a movement across the street in her peripheral vision. Blinds fluttering. Could be his air conditioner. Could be a pet.

Or it could be him.

Watching her.

The heat that had deserted her body an instant before flamed in the center of her belly and then licked out and down like tongues of fire—straight to the now tingling flesh between her thighs. Just one thought—an errant possibility that *he* was watching her—conjured sensual scenarios and pyrotechnic possibilities that flushed her skin from the inside out.

She corralled her forbidden musings by reminding herself that she knew absolutely nothing about the man who may or may not have peeked at her through the blinds. Maybe he was a wacko. Maybe he was just nosy. But Jillian preferred to think he simply liked what he'd seen earlier and wanted another look.

But that's all he'd ever get to do—catch a glimpse, perhaps a brief perusal. At the most, they'd exchange a wave when neighborly politeness forced the issue, maybe a quick hello.

What would happen if he actually spoke to her? Jillian didn't want to imagine, but the rush of hedonistic possibilities assailed her before she could push them away. A man like him would probably have a voice that could melt chocolate.

Ooh, and what she could do with melted chocolate.

But she'd do those things one place and one place only—in the realm of her midnight fantasies. It might not be as satisfying as the real thing with a real man, but Jillian already knew from experience that dreams were a whole lot safer.

WHEN THE BEEPER-SIZED cell phone clipped inside his pocket trilled, Cade Lawrence jumped. He jangled the blinds, then swore at the possibility that he'd given away his secret vantage point. The stunning redhead stopped and tilted her head to the side as if she could sense him from across the street, watching her, wondering about her. Wanting her in a way he hadn't wanted a woman in a long while—especially a stranger he'd never even seen up close.

Still, there was something about her, something he couldn't name, yet his blood thrummed through his veins as if he were in his old cruiser with sirens blaring and squad cars speeding to the scene. She sent out a cool, aloof vibe, but the rhythm in her walk, the mystery behind her guarded grin, had him more than just intrigued or interested.

He was straight-up turned on.

Slipping two fingers through a slit in the blinds, he had widened the strips of plastic so he could watch her retreat. Her ponytail brushed against pale, bare shoulders. When she stopped toward the door, the abbreviated length of her skirt allowed him a flash of white thigh. Pausing, she turned and looked straight in his direction. She didn't smile. She didn't frown.

But she had looked.

When his phone rang the fourth time, he swore again and backed away, feeling like a crazed Peeping Tom. He flipped open the tiny mechanism and answered.

"What do you want?"

"Oh. I see the undercover blues have already gotten to you, and after only two weeks. You're losing your edge, Lawrence."

Cade growled. He wasn't losing his edge. Just his patience with his partner, who called every day like his father used to when he first went off to college. He was also frustrated with this case, which was taking too damned long to break. The fact that a gorgeous Irish beauty had moved in across the street broke the monotony in a big way, but rather than alleviate his stress, this possible diversion made him ache for a dalliance he couldn't afford.

Cade marched into the kitchen and grabbed the last sweet roll in the paper bakery box. Mouth full, he continued. "Did it ever occur to you that your call could interrupt some important police work?"

"It's nearly noon. Davison is off to his daily lunch at the diner, I'm sure."

"Maybe Davison isn't all I'm watching."

He thought of his new neighbor. Thick red hair twisted into a haphazard ponytail. Slightly athletic build on a body not quite short enough to be called petite, but decidedly feminine with all those luscious curves—curves meant to fit a man's palm. He swiped sweat and sugar from his fingers onto his shirt and decided he was completely pathetic. She hadn't taken off her sunglasses or even smiled in his direction. She was cool, in control.

With his fascination growing by the minute, Cade

wondered if he'd been on this case and out of circulation for too long. He'd never had a long attention span, which had always gotten him into trouble. Coupled with his healthy male libido, trouble and women usually came as a package deal. He should know better than to even toy with the idea of introducing himself to the new occupant of the house across the street.

And yet...he toyed.

Jake's bark on the other end of the phone reminded him that he had more pressing matters to deal with. "Davison sure as hell better be the only person you're watching or Mendez will serve your ass to Internal Affairs along with my head. I pulled in a favor getting you back on duty, Cade. You'd best not screw this up."

Unable to erase his new neighbor's cocky little strut out of his mind, Cade slipped back into the living room and took one last peek out the front window. She was gone. With no car in the driveway, it looked like she wasn't leaving anytime soon. He could salivate later. For now, he had to give his report like a good little soldier.

A good little soldier with nothing interesting or usable to report.

"Yeah, yeah. I'm so grateful, I'm weepy-eyed. I don't suppose you could pull some strings and get Davison to slip up, maybe do a cartwheel for my camera so we can prove he's faking?"

Jake snorted his less than amused response. "If I could do that, I'd be the lieutenant's darling instead of you. Nothing yet, huh?"

Cade returned to the kitchen and shoved the empty pastry box in the trash. "The guy's good, I'll give him that. I started up a conversation with him finally last night. Seems he's a Buc's fan."

"Can you get him to toss around a pigskin? That ought to prove his injuries don't warrant a two million dollar judgment."

Cade frowned. The fact that the department, or more accurately, the department's insurance company, had had to shell out such a huge amount to a con and thief chafed Cade's butt worse than the time he spent on motorcycle duty as a rookie ten years ago. When Stanley Davison stepped in the way of a police foot chase during the annual Gasparilla parade, got knocked over and then sued for disability, wrongful endangerment and a plethora of other bogus charges, no one in his right mind thought the man would see his day in court, much less win a multimillion dollar lawsuit. But apparently, no one in his right mind sat on the jury either. Without evidence to prove otherwise, the city had been forced to start paying out.

But the new mayor didn't like the hikes to his premiums, not to mention the bad public relations. He'd instructed the department to prove that Davison's injuries weren't as severe as he claimed. The city attorney, worried about the legal implications of an official investigation, advised the brass to proceed with discretion. Cade, assigned to routine desk duty after he'd fired his gun during the apprehension of a murder suspect, suggested an undercover sting. After all, he was one of their top undercover detectives. Why waste his talent behind a desk? Jake, the partner with the unblemished performance record, had made the official proposal to the brass. In one of the quickest cuts of red tape Cade had ever heard of, he'd landed the assignment.

Potentially tossing a football with a scam artist like Stanley Stuart Davison wasn't the most appealing work, but Cade would do anything rather than fill out forms and shuffle piles of paper, even for one day.

"I'm working on him," Cade continued. "At least he acknowledged my presence this time. The guy is incredibly suspicious."

"I would be too if I was pulling off such a huge scam. I just don't get why he stays in town. You'd think he'd take the money and run."

Cade had noted that peculiarity himself. He figured old Stan wasn't just a con man, but a con man with an incredible ego. He wanted to rub his win in the face of the cops for a while. Even the diner he frequented every day at noon catered to officers on the downtown beat.

"Not his M.O. Stan's not going to be an easy nut to crack," Cade admitted.

"*Nut* being the key word?"

"No, he's smart. Too smart to be crazy."

"Sounds like you've got your hands full."

In more ways than one. Not only did he have to crack this case as soon as possible, he had to do so while trying to keep his mind and hands—heck, his whole body—off his enticing new neighbor.

"Sounds like," Cade answered.

"Your kind of case, huh?"

Cade chuckled. *Yeah, exactly my kind.* The kind no one else wanted since the collar looked impossible. And in this situation, Cade wasn't even looking to make an arrest. Since he was officially off active duty, his job was only to gather legal, useable-in-court evidence to prove that Stanley had either faked his injuries or severely overstated them. Charges for fraud would come later, when Cade was off on some other, hopefully more dynamic, investigation.

After chewing the fat with his partner for a few more minutes, Cade slipped his phone back in his pocket and checked his watch. Stanley would be arriving home in about twenty minutes if he stuck to his usual schedule. Lunch at the Blue Star Diner. Coffee with the other independently wealthy, unemployed types that hung out there. Then home for a siesta, either outdoors in his backyard hammock on a clear, warm afternoon or inside on his custom-built waterbed when a thunderstorm rolled through.

Luckily for Cade, the weather looked clear and sunny. If he parked himself in his own backyard, conveniently subleased by the city shortly after Stan moved in next door, he might get another opportunity to strike up a conversation and worm his way further into Stan's confidence. Stan needed to feel comfortable, off-guard, before he'd make any significant slip that might break the case open.

And since Cade had learned that Stanley appreciated good gardening, albeit that which required the lightest amount of work, he'd gone to the hardware store yesterday and purchased three buckets of American Beauty roses and shoved them in the ground near the fence that separated his yard from Stan's. With any luck, he'd find another topic of conversation they could share. Another in—since *in* meant *out* of this ridiculously slow investigation.

Cade grabbed the bucket of gardening tools he'd left on the back porch and headed into the yard, once more glancing over his shoulder at the suddenly occupied home across the street. He wondered if his sexy new neighbor would lust after a man who got his hands dirty, even if only with potting soil.

Knowing gardening wasn't on the top ten list of

grunt-and-beat-your-chest activities, Cade preferred to believe she was too busy unpacking to notice his new hobby. He shook his head, wondering what line the real estate agent had used to sell her the junker. Though the house looked just as renovated and pristine as the rest of the eighty-year-old homes on the oak-lined brick street, the department had taken one look at its leaky roof and antique air conditioner and opted to call in a favor from the owner of the house he now occupied.

She must be loaded if she shelled out the exorbitant asking price. Hyde Park was prime real estate. She wouldn't be the first person to pay too much money for a parcel of Tampa's history, even for that money pit. And she'd hired a top-notch mover to boot. The day before, he'd watched a crew arrive with what seemed like two housefuls of boxes and furniture. By the time he returned home with his flowers, nearly every box had efficiently been moved inside.

When she arrived this morning, she'd only lugged in five cartons and a suitcase, none looking very heavy nor requiring she do much bending or twisting to ac-commodate their size—much to his very male chagrin. He wondered what she did for a living. What brought her to this part of town.

What kind of panties she wore.

Cade shook his head, looked up at the clear after-noon sky and decided if the sun wasn't getting to him, boredom obviously was. He didn't have time to dally with the neighbor, no matter how hot she was with all that thick red hair and quick little walk or how hot that hair and walk made him. He had about another week or two to get something on Stanley before he was scheduled to return to active duty. And as much as he looked forward to returning to the street, he didn't like the taste of doing so without settling this case first. To accomplish that feat, he needed the full breadth of his easily distractible interest.

And that meant no flirting or talking or interacting of any kind with his new, gorgeous neighbor. No matter how snug her derriere fit into the sassy denim skirt she wore. Or how round her breasts looked beneath her tank top. The image of her thick auburn hair, loose and mussed, spilling over bare, dark-nippled breasts flashed in his mind, renewing the hard-on he'd experienced when he'd first seen her.

He let out a string of four-letter words that belied his fascination. If she could stir his lust from a distance—without even trying—he could only imagine the magic she'd weave tangled in his sheets.

Cade grabbed the garden hose, turned the spigot and sprayed his new roses until they drooped beneath the water. He'd need a cold shower of his own if he didn't put his mind back on his case where it belonged.

2

JILLIAN GRABBED THE note tucked between the wall and the thermostat. She recognized Ted's handwriting and briefly wondered what her tech team director and her best friend, Elisa, were doing right now in the back seat of Ted's car.

Don't go there, Jillian. Not when she knew they were having way more fun on their surveillance assignment than she was on hers.

She read the directions aloud. "Turn air off, then on. Wait five seconds. Repeat. Flick red arrow twice and the air should kick on. If not, wait ten minutes and try again."

Some "high tech" team her uncle employed. They could wire a house for sight and sound with completely unnoticeable cameras and microphones. They could break in and set up their wares without tripping alarms or garnering the least notice from nosy neighbors or wary homeowners. But they couldn't fix a simple air conditioner?

Jillian followed the regimen for the second time that evening, sighing a silent prayer of thanks when the thirty-year-old monstrosity kicked in with a not-too-subtle hum.

She checked her watch. Five minutes after eight o'clock. She'd eaten dinner two hours ago in the front parlor's window seat, hidden by the slats of wood blinds while she waited for Stanley to go inside. She itched to go upstairs and test out her surveillance equipment, maybe catch Stanley working out or doing heavy lifting.

The man was good at perpetrating fraud. He didn't slip in public and though he'd been suspected of swindling insurance companies in the past, no one had ever proved his deception. Luckily, the Hennessy Group employed tactics that, while not entirely legal, could at least get the goods. Like the secret surveillance. Jillian often wondered if she'd become too complacent about using any and all means to prove a case, but this was her first field assignment—and an important one at that. Stan was a pro. And, according to Uncle Mick, the only way to catch a true con man was to lure him onto a level playing field.

Hence, the cameras and microphones. But in order for Jillian to use them, the man had to go inside, where he felt safe, unwatched.

Instead, Stanley had spent the better part of the afternoon chatting over the four-foot fence with her sexy neighbor across the street. From the looks of things, they were talking about flowers. Roses, to be exact. About thirty minutes into their conversation, Stanley was directing her hunk in the frayed denim cutoffs while he reinforced his flowers with twine and trellis. When the conversation went on longer than she imagined any two straight males would ever spend discussing flora, she dug her binoculars out of a carton and read their lips—a studied skill she rarely had the opportunity to use behind her desk.

She learned three things. First, Stanley Davison considered himself a complete and total expert on the subject of gardening, not to mention other topics like travel, diner food and apparently, football.

Second, she learned her neighbor's name was Cade. Thankfully, Stanley spoke the name several times, verifying that Jillian hadn't misread his lips.

Cade. She'd never heard the name before. Was it a nickname? A shortened version of a family moniker handed down from generation to generation? Mystery upon mystery added layers of intrigue to this man with the dark, wavy hair and to-die-for body, causing Jillian's naturally curious and sensual sides to merge together—a powerful combination.

"Cade." She'd said the name aloud and heard a breathless wanting in the sound that made her skin tingle and her cheeks flush. She imagined saying his name while he kissed her neck or brushed his lips over her temples—and that was before she learned the third thing that nearly drove her into a cold shower fully clothed.

Cade had incredible lips.

Not just run-of-the-mill sexy lips. His were particularly expressive. Thick and pouty, always holding a hint of a smile and surrounded by a square jaw and darkened by rugged, tan skin and afternoon stubble, his mouth was as male as they came.

She wondered how he kissed. She ran her hand over her mouth, noting the enhanced sensitivity while she pondered the possible flavors clinging to his lips. He'd been drinking iced tea all afternoon. Would the essence of stirred sugar make his mouth sweet, or would his kiss bite hers with the tangy tartness of lemon?

Let me taste you.

She wondered what his voice sounded like. Deep and throaty? Baritone or bass? She traced the shell of her ear with a tentative finger, wondering…and remembering the thrilling warmth of a man's breath brushing her skin. Was he the type to whisper sweet nothings? Or spicy somethings—words that tore straight to a woman's hot center and forced her desire out in a wild rush?

She'd eventually gotten so wrapped up watching his mouth for purely personal and sensual delight that she'd forgotten to decipher what he was saying.

When she finally regained control, she had to dart to the kitchen to refill her drink. She added extra ice and pressed the cold glass between her breasts and to her forehead to cool her overheated skin.

She'd never reacted to any man with such innate, physical force—not even to Neal, her ex, who'd lured her into marriage by skillfully disguising sex as love. But Neal at least had had to work on her. Growing up in a family peopled with cops and private eyes made her naturally wary and suspicious. She'd resisted him for over a year until his charm and her libido proved impossible to fight. Once they'd become lovers, she'd given him her heart. And once he had that, he cheated. Her only conciliation was that Neal had scammed everyone else in his life, too, including the ''other'' women.

But that didn't lessen the humiliation of an unfaithful husband, particularly one who waylaid a career she'd been working at in varying degrees since age eleven.

So the minute she'd shown Neal the door, she'd locked her needs away and denied the loneliness she grappled with constantly, especially during those long, hot nights when her fantasies seemed more real than even her sweaty sheets and lumpy pillows. In her dreams, she was safe, untouchable. And since Neal she hadn't met anyone who'd even tempted her to risk her heart again, even if just for a one-night stand.

But this Cade turned her inside out without even knowing, without even realizing she was watching.

She'd returned to the window, binoculars in place, and discovered that Cade knew zip about flowers. His mother had apparently brought over the plants to spruce up his yard, and he couldn't just let them die. He also couldn't ask for mother's help unless he wanted her sniffing around his house and yard day and night—an idea that both he and Stanley found intolerable in that "I'm a man and I don't want my mommy around" sort of way. Anything Stan could teach him, well, he'd owe him a six-pack.

So Cade and Stanley talked about roses and soil and sunlight until Jillian couldn't stand watching them any longer. Or, more accurately, she couldn't stand watching *him*. She'd used up too much energy reminding herself that *Stanley* was the object of her investigation—energy she might need later. So she abandoned her post, unpacked her measly collection of personal items and waited for the sun to go down.

She checked the locks on the doors one last time then tugged her tank top out of her waistband as she climbed the stairs to the second floor. The air grew warmer and more humid on the way up, but she shivered when she entered the master bedroom. Situated on the top floor, facing the decidedly quiet street, Ted and his tech team partners had filled the large space on the wall farthest from the window with more electronic equipment than a small video store. They'd installed a window-mounted cooling unit to ensure the circuits didn't overheat. She went through a practiced mental checklist, flicking on surge protectors, video monitors,

CD burners and a slim laptop computer that controlled the countless wiretaps, microphones and cameras planted surreptitiously throughout Stanley Davison's home.

Shivering, she padded to the window and adjusted the thermostat until she could hear only the sputter and whir of the untrustworthy attic unit. Curious, she lifted the shade. The lights inside Stanley's house were indeed on.

And so were the lights next door.

She drummed her trim, self-manicured nails over the glass, wondering what Cade, handsome and lusty even while chatting about aphids and fertilizer, was doing home alone on a Friday night. His driveway was empty. No visitors—yet. She knew next to nothing about him—had never even heard his voice or seen the color of his eyes. Yet he most definitely didn't seem the type to spend the first night of the weekend in front of the tube or, as she usually was, curled up with a book or a pile of boring reports.

Maybe he was a night owl, a social vampire who didn't venture out until midnight. The type who caused a stir when he arrived late, who restarted a dying party just by entering a room.

She flicked the shade closed and marched over to the monitors. According to Stanley's file—which Jillian had practically memorized—he rarely went to bed until after the late show, so she popped open a caffeine-loaded soda from the small refrigerator beneath the desk and tapped on her computer keyboard. Three video monitors, each providing alternating views of rooms in Stanley's house—living room and kitchen, garage and attic, then all three bedrooms—came into focus. She used the mouse to turn the cameras to her preferred position.

Then, she wondered where he was. Tapping back into the master bedroom, she angled the camera so it caught the reflection of a mirror, giving her a decent view into the master bath.

He wasn't there either.

A shadow of movement caught her attention when the monitor to her left flipped automatically to the attic. She entered commands so the main monitor displayed that view. She hit the record button on the VCR and adjusted the brightness as much as she could. The image on her screen flickered.

Candlelight? In the attic?

With a minor adjustment, she finally caught sight of a man striking matches around the room. For the briefest instant, she wondered if Stan was about to sacrifice a chicken in his attic.

Then he stepped closer to the camera.

He wasn't Stan.

He was her neighbor across the street. Mr. Cutoff shorts. Cade with no known last name. Except he'd abandoned his cutoffs and traded them in for loose fitting, hip-hugging white pants—the bottom half of a martial arts *gi*. The torn T-shirt was gone as well, but he hadn't bothered to replace it with anything. Jillian watched him light the rest of the candles—bare-chested and bathed in warm flickering light—until her eyes grew itchy because she'd forgotten to blink.

She shook her head to clear the reinvigorated lust away long enough for her to figure out what the hell was going on. He was at Stan's house? Wearing next to nothing? Lighting candles in the attic?

She most definitely did *not* like where this scene was

going. She pulled up the operating system window that controlled the sound, then searched the rest of the house for any sign of Stanley Davison. She flipped back to the garage.

What the...?

Sure her neighbor couldn't see from the attic, she called up the controls that would activate the garage light from across the street. She slapped her forehead, but forced herself to process what she saw. The car in the garage wasn't a silver, four-door Mercedes-Benz sedan, the transportation of choice for Stanley Davison.

It was a truck. Big and tough and bulging with automotive muscle.

Just like her neighbor.

They'd wired the wrong house!

Jillian pulled the file on Stanley from the slot beside the video recorder. She flipped through the paperwork, searching until she found the inter-office wiretap order her uncle filled out for Ted's tech team. She ran her finger down the handwritten entries, then found the address she searched for: 807 Park Side Drive.

Except that Stan lived at 809.

She closed the file and buried her face in her hands.

Uncle Mick strikes again.

Jillian swore, berating herself for not double-checking all the paperwork on this case. Usually, that was her main responsibility as Mick's second-in-command. But she'd gotten caught up in the thrill of her first real, on-location, down-in-the-trenches assignment. She'd spent her time developing the operation plan, renting the house, assigning shifts for tails when Stanley puttered around town and, lastly, organizing her affairs so she could leave her studio apartment unattended for as long as it took to break this case.

Mick insisted he help. As president of the company, he *was* lead detective on all cases, after all. The least he could do was supervise the tech team's installation, especially with all the new toys he and Ted had purchased at their last convention in Las Vegas.

Glancing up, Jillian acknowledged that they had done an impeccable job. The views were clear. The sound crisp and free of static. She heard the precise moment Cade flipped on his portable CD player, filling the attic with the delicate sounds of Korean shaman music. Only problem was, instead of watching and listening in on a suspected con man, her vision focused on Cade's tapered back, slim hips and most incredibly perfect backside. The one she'd watched nearly until sunset. The one she'd promised herself she would avoid. The one she couldn't tear her gaze away from.

Cade stood in the center of the room, tall and broad and completely still. Then with a quick, noisy inhale, he pulled his arms in front of him, steepled his hands and breathed. She couldn't help but watch as air filled his lungs, pumping his pecs to perfection, flattening his washboard stomach so his pants slipped a quarter of an inch lower than they had been before. When he breathed again, so did she—and the reality that she hadn't taken in air dawned slowly, like a summer sun that rises and grows instantly hot.

Jillian, you're in big, big trouble.

"No!" She twirled her chair away around so she faced her bed rather than the screen. *I can't do this. I can't watch. My heart can't take it. My body won't survive.* She switched off the screen without looking, without allowing herself to think.

"Business, business," she chanted.

She glanced at the clock at the bottom of her laptop

screen. Too late to do anything about this screwup to-night. Too late to even call Ted, whom she knew was on a surveillance assignment on the other side of Or-lando, nearly two hours away. She had no way of sal-vaging this operation until tomorrow. Her logical, prac-tical mind toyed with the idea of turning off the rest of her equipment and getting a good night's sleep.

She'd clicked off the visual, but the sound echoed through the six-inch speakers on either side of the dark-ened main viewer. Even, calm, male breathing became sharp whooshes of air. He'd completed his stretching and had begun his workout. The rough stuff. The real, sweaty, muscle-bulging, body-flinching part.

Rolling her eyes at her own weak will, she clicked the screen back on. Who was she kidding? This man wasn't someone to be turned *off*. She couldn't tear her-self away, even if she wanted to.

Which she didn't. No matter how much Jillian told herself that watching Cade practice his forms for tae kwon do was wrong—professionally, morally, even spiritually if she opted to open that can of worms—she couldn't look away.

She wanted to look closer. Without trying, he reached the emptiness inside her and offered her a brief break from being alone. From hiding that part of her that made her a woman—the part that sought an inti-mate joining with a man who would stroke her soul to ecstasy. His anonymity made him safe. With this stranger only known by his first name, she had no real reason to reign in her fantasies or censor her increas-ingly X-rated thoughts.

What the hell. Who was she hurting? She'd never meet the guy, he'd never know she was watching and she promised to turn off the video recorder the minute he did anything too personal or potentially embarrassing.

"Okay, Cade. This is my first night on a stakeout and I'm watching the wrong guy. Make it worth my while."

She typed in the commands to suspend the surveillance of the bedrooms and living areas, tuning all three monitors to the workout in the attic. The center screen, twenty-seven inches of fascinating maleness, held her complete attention.

His muscles rippled with each jab, starting at his shoulders and undulating down to his taut fingers. His gaze, slightly narrowed, seemed to envision an opponent. She saw the bloom of antagonism. The slightest hint of anger. Then, amid his pure concentration, a smirk broke through. A slant of confidence. In battle, he knew he'd win.

She slid her soda closer, wiping the condensation from the can across the base of her throat to cool the burning. Leaning back in her chair, she slid the keyboard onto her lap.

"You'd win, all right. What would you take as spoils?" she asked with a sigh, giving herself permission to talk aloud to the screen and say whatever popped into her head, whatever she'd never dare say if he could actually hear.

She imagined herself as his opponent. She imagined him pumping her up, trifling with her, stalking her in a circular pattern, closing in on her and then taking her down. To the ground. On the floor.

Did he have a lover? And if he did, did he allow her to watch him work out? Jillian couldn't think of a more potent aphrodisiac. His moves were sleek and com-

manding, his body honed, his attitude bold and domi-
nant in a way that thrilled rather than intimidated.

She explored different angles with the cameras,
zooming in on his stomach, watching his abs ripple like
an undulating washboard, her belly clenching with brazen need to feel the purl with her own hungry hands.
She closed in on his eyes. The lighting didn't allow
her to discover the color of his irises, but she saw the
completeness of his concentration and wondered if he
was just as centered when he was making love. She
imagined her face inches from his, body heat to body
heat, drinking in every ounce of his overpowering
strength.

By the time he was kicking the air, blocking or
punching his arms in practiced slices that would break
bones if they made contact with another human body,
Jillian was unconditionally enthralled. With the precision of his movements, the economy of his energy. No
breath was wasted. No kick unfocused.

She stood. Clothed in the same short denim skirt and
tank that she'd worn all day, she wasn't exactly dressed
for a workout, but she couldn't resist imitating his
movements as best she could, anything to clear her
brain of the more erotic images that relentlessly assailed her. She flattened her bare feet against the cool
wood floor, spreading her legs and adjusting her stance
until she'd attained perfect balance. Her skirt rode high
on her thighs. A leftover chill from the air conditioner
in the window kissed the flimsy material of her panties.

Startled, she stopped. She was wet, warm, aroused.
Her nipples flared and chafed against her lacy bra.
From just watching.

I miss sex.

The thought popped into her head and for once since

her separation from Neal, Jillian didn't push it away immediately. Acknowledging the truth—to herself, in private—lightened her step just enough to catch Cade's rhythm and mirror his workout.

Yeah, she was aroused. And she loved it. The illicitness of desire, the heat of untamed need, reminded her that she lived and breathed and responded like the hot-blooded woman she was. Life pumped through her veins, riding the wave of lust and need this man inspired.

All from watching.

She knew the forms he practiced, having learned most of these moves during her own quest for a black belt. But following him—letting him guide her—was like stretching her muscles for the first time.

Arms. Legs. Neck. Stomach. Chest. Hips. Lungs. She felt his influence everywhere and she didn't bother to contain her grunts or groans when her body protested the movements she hadn't done in far too long. She tried to remember her last workout, but all she could think about was her warm, wet, unfulfilled body. How she wanted to make love. With Cade. Stranger or not.

She'd never been indiscriminate or easy, but Jillian had always resisted buying into the belief that women shouldn't enjoy sex. Though she'd learned with Neal that the implied intimacy of making love could be the ultimate deceit, she missed being touched by a man, caressed, pleasured.

And she was going to have to continue missing it. Better to expel her energy this way—with Cade and his tae kwon do.

Or just with Cade.

Jillian stopped, winded. She balanced her hands on her knees and took deep breaths to push the thought—

no longer a fantasy, but a possibility—from her mind. But the music, an alluring blend of *kayagum* strumming, and Cade's even breathing drew her gaze back to the screen. His skin shimmered with sweat. His eyes were narrow slits of utter concentration and his expression betrayed a man who drove himself to the limit with thoughts best kept to himself.

Anger. Frustration. Passion. And yet he never moved without precision or even slightly lost his balance.

His sheer power drew Jillian back to her chair. She ran her hand over the main viewer, imagining the sensation of sliding her palm over the smooth skin on her neighbor's chest. Though the light could be deceptive, she didn't see much hair to hamper a slow, tactile exploration. He was hot. He was hard. Would the aroma of his sweat turn her off or would the combination of musk and man enhance her desire?

She paused when her hand passed over the image of his pecs. She wondered about the beat of his heart, wanting to measure the rapid pounding against the wild cadence of her own.

Jillian shook her head and pushed her chair back. She was losing her mind, obviously, conjuring fantasies about a man she knew nothing about, and never would beyond what she learned in her clandestine observations.

Observations she couldn't tear herself away from.

BY THE TIME HE finished his workout, they were both desperate for breath. When he grabbed a towel from where he'd hooked it on the back of an old chair and started wiping the sweat from his neck, Jillian suddenly felt the dampness beneath her hair, down her sides. Lower.

He blew out the candles, shut off the music and left, sending Jillian scrambling for her keyboard to reactivate her views into the other rooms. She checked the bedroom first, but he appeared in the kitchen. After chugging a carton of juice straight from the refrigerator, he dried himself off one last time, tossed the towel on the washing machine tucked into a nearby closet, then opened his back door.

Jillian jumped like a child with her hand caught in the cookie jar until she remembered that the back door faced Stanley's house, not hers. She scrambled with the cheat-sheet card Ted normally slipped under her laptop and punched in the codes for the porch and backyard views. Just as she did, he went back inside, holding the largest cat she'd ever seen.

She zoomed in a bit closer, thankful she could concentrate on anything but the empty yearning Cade had unknowingly stirred. Soon her body cooled, but her mind raced with thoughts she'd denied for a long time. She missed sharing a home, a bed. Her marriage to Neal had been less than ideal in reality but, for a time at least, she'd enjoyed the illusion of completeness.

She'd settle for the illusion again, so long as it didn't interfere with her goals. She wouldn't consider anything permanent, of course. Marriage was out of the question. Been there, done that.

An affair, perhaps?

She watched Cade stroke the cat between the ears then drop it on a dinette chair before he rummaged through the refrigerator for a carton of coffee cream. He poured a generous helping into a cereal bowl, paused, then pulled out a second bowl, filled it with Cheerios, drowned them in milk and the two of them sat down to a quiet, late dinner with the newspaper.

Jillian listed Cade's positive attributes as if she were checking off an inter-office form. He works out. He likes animals. He grows roses because it would hurt his mother to let them die, and he grins almost all the time, even at smarmy con men like Stanley Davison. No wonder she was interested. The guy was every woman's dream.

Watching him eat would only draw more of her attention to his mouth again, so she took the opportunity to take a quick shower and change into her favorite cotton drawstring pajama pants and a pilfered FBI T-shirt, two sizes too big.

As she pulled her shirt over her head, she glanced over her shoulder. He was rinsing his bowl in the sink. When he finished, he turned and scanned the kitchen. Searching for other dirty dishes, perhaps?

Then, for the briefest instant, his gaze made contact with her camera lens.

She snapped the T-shirt to her bare chest before she remembered he wasn't looking at her. And she was fairly certain he hadn't spotted the camera, either. The lens was the size of fiber-optic wire, and Ted and his tech team were the best in the business when it came to hiding their wares.

But common sense didn't stop the chill that chased up her spine, twirled around her neck, then reached the tips of her breasts.

What if her equipment could work both ways? What if he was watching her...?

3

"I'M GOING TO HAVE an affair with him."

Jillian made her announcement to Elisa over coffee and croissants. She waited for her friend to show the least inkling of shock or surprise, but Elisa only smiled knowingly and took another sip from the flaming red ceramic mug she'd brought that said When I'm Bad, I'm Better in swirling pink type.

"I'm assuming you're not talking about Stanley Davison."

Jillian dropped her pastry, her stomach suddenly nauseated. "Ew."

Elisa's reaction was much more animated. Tongue out and gagging reflexes simulated, she made them both dissolve into girlish giggles. Jillian wondered when she'd last felt so incredibly vibrant, so inherently female. She figured it was sometime around midnight, after she'd finished her nightly routine and returned to her monitors.

She'd found Cade in the shower. Her fingers had hovered over the keyboard. Should she? Though her firm drew the line at following their subjects into the bathroom, the bedroom camera was still angled into the dresser mirror, providing a fairly decent shot into the shower stall. Steam was billowing from the open door. He liked his showers scalding hot. Everything about this man was hot.

She'd tried to waylay her voyeurism by digging into the secret of his identity. She accessed her Internet connection and then tapped into the office database and did a search by address. The house, owned by a real-estate corporation, was currently listed as a rental. She did several searches to pull up the full name of the latest leasee, but came up empty.

She tried newspaper delivery records, phone records and courier files. No luck. She keyed back in to the garage view, but the angle of the camera didn't allow her to see the license plate number on the truck. She'd considered sneaking over to get the number herself when the sound of running water from the speakers on the main viewer had ceased.

She had the good intention of turning away, or disconnecting the video monitor entirely to give him some privacy, but these options became impossible the minute he stepped out of the stall. Jillian swallowed deeply. The mirror in the bedroom was hazy from steam, but his image, all male, all tan and muscular and wet, begged for her complete attention. A cloud of humid air swirled around him. Her fingers seemed to tap the zoom command all on their own.

She watched him towel off. He rubbed the terry cloth first over his arms, then his neck, chest and back. His movements were brisk, efficient, down to business.

If she'd had the towel, her technique would have differed entirely. Without doubt, she'd start at his feet and work her way up. He had incredible legs. Powerful and strong, but more slim than bulky—like a runner or a swimmer.

As if he sensed an intrusion on his solitude, he turned his back to the mirror as he dried himself just below his waist, but not before Jillian looked her fill.

Even lax, he was impressive. Followed by a glorious nude view of his backside, she couldn't stop the incredible thrill that coursed through her, a jolt of pure lust. In time with the increasing pounding of her heart—spurred by desire, guilt, and complete, unhampered sexual titillation—a throbbing between her legs made her squirm in her seat. Hardened nipples rasped against the inside of her T-shirt. She had grabbed her tepid soda, drank until the dryness in her mouth subsided, and watched until he hung his towel over the top of the shower stall and slipped into a pair of navy boxers that did little to hamper her view.

When he slid into bed with the latest bestselling spy novel—the same one she had tucked into the drawer beside her own bedside—Jillian knew she was in over her head. This man, this stranger, had intrigue and sex written all over him more than any published work of fiction. When she chose watching him read over sleep, she accepted the inevitable.

This man was a mystery she had to investigate. He was the key clue that could unravel the puzzle of her empty personal life—one that she wanted him to fill.

"So...what's his name?" Elisa asked, not popping the erotic image out of Jillian's mind so much as causing a gentle fade-out that left a grin lingering on her lips.

"Cade." She spoke the single syllable long and raspy, cherishing the decadent sound on her tongue.

"Mmm. That's different. Cade what?"

"Don't know yet."

"Is he interested in you?"

"Don't know that yet, either. Give me a break, 'Lise. I only made my decision this morning."

Elisa nodded, completely understanding the lack of

logic that accompanied a spontaneous decision since she made them all the time herself. Of course, Jillian's resolution hadn't really been as impulsive as she was leading her friend to believe. She'd decided on the affair this morning, yes—around 3:00 a.m. when she abandoned the warm comfort of her bed to switch on her equipment again and watch her neighbor sleep.

When she woke at sunrise slumped over her keyboard, weary and cranky and yet unable to resist watching him rise and dress and demolish an entire box of chocolate doughnuts and pot of coffee, she knew she wouldn't be able to concentrate on her job so long as he remained a mystery.

She'd called Ted and instructed him to wire the right house during Stanley's daily lunch at the diner, but she declined his offer to disconnect the devices in her other neighbor's home. Too risky, she insisted. They'd take care of it after the job was done, when there'd be no risk to the investigation.

All the danger was to her own sanity.

"Just how long did you watch him once you realized Mick had the wrong house installed?" Elisa asked, having already heard Jillian's carefully censored version of her night's activities.

"None of your business."

Elisa's grin would have really annoyed Jillian if she weren't still reeling from her clandestine observations.

"How do you plan to seduce him?"

Jillian wrapped her hands around her warm mug and bit her lip. Good question. Despite her occupation, Jillian Hennessy was no Mata Hari. She'd never seduced anyone in her whole life.

"Do I need a plan?"

"Jillian Hennessy without a plan? Can that happen?"

Jillian sipped her warm chocolate and cream-laced coffee and fought the urge to smirk. Elisa knew her very, very well.

"It's going to have to. In fact, it's best this way. No plan means no screwups. I'll just go with the flow. The only planned outcome is sensual satisfaction. I'm sure there are lots of interesting ways to get there."

Elisa suddenly sat up straighter in her chair, her eyes wide and round as she peered over Jillian's shoulder toward her side kitchen door.

"Interesting way number one is standing on your stoop," she informed her.

Jillian glanced over her shoulder, nearly choking on her last swallow of coffee when she saw her very sexy, very live-and-in-person neighbor peeking through the gingham curtains on her half-glass door.

Cade's smile was pure sin. His lips were full, but drawn in a crooked grin that reached into his eyes.

They were green. Lord, were they green.

Jillian's heart paused a full beat before Elisa's kick beneath the table restarted her breathing and made her stand. She wiped her hands down her khakis, forced a smile and opened the door.

"Hi, I'm Cade Lawrence, your neighbor," he nodded his head in the direction of his house, "across the street."

Jillian swallowed her initial, instinctual response. *Yeah, I know* sounded entirely too desperate.

She took a deep breath and held out her hand, forcing her fingers and muscles to relax so her grip would be lighter and more girly than her usual all-business shake.

"Jillian. Jillian Hennessy."

Before he touched her, before he took her palm in his and squeezed with subtle pressure, he glanced down at her proffered hand then back into her eyes. She felt instantly naked, exposed. As if he knew things he couldn't possibly know. As if he wanted things she couldn't possibly give.

She almost didn't realize that he'd taken her hand until his body heat created a trail of sensation up her arm like a gentle caress. She nearly pulled away, but his jade-green gaze held her steady. His grin didn't change. His eyes revealed none of the swagger or ego that a man usually displayed when they knew they had a woman instantaneously mesmerized. Either he was completely unaware of his effect on her or he was the coolest operator Jillian had ever encountered.

She'd have to match his cool if she was going to pull off the seduction she had envisioned while brewing her coffee and waiting for Elisa to arrive.

She disengaged her hand and glanced down at the frilly basket dangling from his grip. "Are you the Welcoming Committee?" she asked.

His laugh was guttural and deep, like his voice. Pure Southern charm, but without a hint of accent. And most definitely baritone.

"No, ma'am. Someone delivered it on my porch this morning. It has your address."

He lifted a white wicker basket wrapped in clear cellophane. Inside, a decorative carafe, two tall glasses, a small bag of sugar cubes, a dozen plump, sunshine-yellow lemons and a handheld squeezer made up a clever gift to accompany the handwritten note dangling from a ribbon around the handle.

Congratulations on your new home. Here's your chance to sweeten the situation.

Jillian glanced over her shoulder at Elisa, who gulped her coffee and read her horoscope as if the secrets to her future were indeed printed amid the morning news.

She hefted the basket onto the counter to better read the numbers on the tag. "That's my address, all right. I don't see how anyone could make such a mistake."

She glanced at Elisa again, knowing well the story of Elisa's seduction of Ted. She'd invited him to help her move into her new apartment, then lured him to stay with ice cold lemonade and her hot tub. So, her friend's hand in this was perfectly clear. Even if Jillian hadn't decided to have an affair with her neighbor, Elisa had taken steps to make sure she at least met him.

He leaned onto the doorjamb with confident ease and slipped his hands into the pockets of his jeans—snug around the hips, but just loose enough around the backside and thighs to qualify as comfortable. "This isn't so bad as far as mistakes go. Gave me a chance to say good morning, and welcome to the neighborhood."

"Would you like to come in?" Jillian asked, trying not to think about how the fit of his jeans allowed just enough room for a woman to slip her hands into the waistband. "The pastry is fresh."

"You have company," he answered.

"Me?" Elisa piped up, standing to take her half-full mug to the sink. "I'm not company. I'm just a pal delivering baked goods. I have to go anyway. Don't want to be late for work. My boss is a real bitch sometimes."

She winked at Jillian, who gave her a tilted smile. Bitch, huh? She'd remember that come bonus time.

Elisa grabbed her purse from atop the kitchen counter and squeezed between Jillian, the doorjamb and Cade, the neighbor who lingered just outside her doorway and yet still managed to fill the entire kitchen with his presence.

Elisa paused briefly to gaze up at him. Her round, brown eyes betrayed every ounce of her innately feminine appreciation for his very male presence. Cade had the decency to blush, which caused Elisa to sigh audibly before she skipped off the porch, darted into her car and drove away.

"She thinks you're gorgeous, but she's spoken for." Jillian couldn't squelch her natural instinct to derail whatever jolt to his pride Elisa had just inspired, even if she did sound slightly jealous—which she wasn't. He was just a man, after all. A man she wanted to make love with at the first opportunity if he proved half as sensual as her secret surveillance led her to believe.

He shook his head and blushed deeper. The heat seemed to transfer from his body to hers within the sound of a silent sigh. "Thanks for telling me, but I wasn't wondering about her."

"You weren't?"

For the first time, Jillian watched his grin completely leave his face. A spark of something more intimate than a smile lit his green irises—irises that conducted a sweeping, all-inclusive study of her, starting low at her ankles then upward, lingering where men's eyes tended to linger, then meeting her gaze straight on.

"You are another story altogether."

She considered feigning insult at his brazen scrutiny, but the only emotion she could manage was satisfaction. Besides, acting flustered or huffy would be expected—and Jillian made it her mission to react in un-expected ways.

"Is that so?"

"If my being honest doesn't offend you."

Jillian gulped. Ordinarily, she valued honesty, es-pecially when she was practicing full disclosure and truthfulness herself. But she had a roomful of electronic looking and listening devices in her bedroom upstairs that wouldn't exactly endear her to a man who appar-ently formed his come-ons with a clear conscience.

"Honest is good," she answered, though at that mo-ment, Jillian felt very, very bad.

NOT THE SMOOTHEST nor the subtlest attempt he'd ever made to check out a woman, but she didn't seem to mind. The honesty thing probably threw her off-guard. Women loved that crap. And though Cade really wasn't the type to tell a woman what she wanted to hear just to get her into his bed, he was adept at bending the truth to his advantage. He was an undercover cop. Ly-ing was second nature.

And yet, he'd given her his real name, without think-ing. He'd simply let the truth spill from his lips freely, and he couldn't remember the last time he'd done that. He'd had so many aliases over the years, carefully hid-den beneath fake IDs and fictional backgrounds, he was sometimes only a few seconds away from calling his father to verify his true identity.

But his instinct with his neighbor had been honesty. Amazing.

Still, lying from this point forward might be wiser. If he told her what he was *really* thinking or shared the sexy fantasies he'd been conjuring since first catching sight of her yesterday, she'd be running for the phone to call his colleagues at the precinct to report a certifiable pervert living across the street.

Instead, she folded her arms across her chest, emphasizing the round lusciousness of her breasts and tightening his groin. He didn't know if her pose was accidental or by design, but the result spurred his blood to rage in his veins.

"I'm being rude," he said. "I should probably get the hell out of here and come back when I can act like a gentleman."

Jillian nodded, but her smile made him wonder if she really agreed.

"Being a gentleman is a good thing, like honesty." She licked her lips. Lips naturally pink and curved just right. Lips he'd be kissing right now if his gentlemanly tendencies hadn't been ingrained by his military father since birth.

"Most of the time, anyway," she added.

She let that possibility linger in the air while she turned to retrieve her coffee cup. "Sure you wouldn't like to come in? Have some more coffee?"

More coffee? His natural inclination toward suspicion in everyone he met sent a shiver along the back of his neck. He ran his hand over the tingle. It was after nine o'clock. She'd made a safe assumption that he'd already had at least one cup by now.

"*More* coffee?" he asked. He'd probably been doing surveillance for too long. He was incredibly careful when talking to his marks, like Stanley, to make sure he never slipped and revealed the facts he learned by spying. Though on second thought, the possibility that redheaded Jillian Hennessy might be spying on *him* raised his temperature another degree.

"If you haven't had any coffee yet this morning,"

she said, turning her back to him while she refilled her mug, "I applaud you. I'm on my second pot."

She blew a controlled breath across the dark brown liquid, drawing Cade's attention back to her incredible mouth. Set against pale skin dotted with a sprinkling of freckles that dusted her nose and the top of her cheeks, her lips rounded in a sweet little O, then opened to drink. Awareness shot through him with a scalding heat, hotter than any coffee.

"All that caffeine isn't good for you," he said, hoping a conversation would thwart his burgeoning fascination. Coming here, wrong delivery or not, was a bad, bad idea.

"At the moment, caffeine is my favorite vice."

She leaned her elbows on the countertop, balancing her cup just below her mouth in a position that was both casual and seductive. And incredibly effective.

Women were his favorite vice. Always had been, always would be. Unfortunately, his undercover work kept him from indulging very often, other than some flirting here and there to get information he needed. Though Cade was unofficially on assignment, Jillian had nothing to do with his obligation to prove Stanley was a fake. She didn't even know Stanley—hadn't even met him so far as Cade knew. She couldn't facilitate his investigation, buy him credibility or cement his position in the neighborhood. Knowing her was just for him. No cops, no bad guys, no ulterior motives. When was the last time he'd pursued a woman simply because she turned him on?

"You're hooked on caffeine? Not getting enough sleep?" he asked, his lust spiking as he referred to her bedtime habits.

Her lashes fluttered around eyes the color of indigo.

The unusual combination of Irish red hair and freckled skin paired with exotic eyes a color he'd never seen, spurred him to step inside and close the door behind him. She'd invited him in, after all. Stanley would sleep in. He never rolled out of bed before ten. And though he was quite certain his racing heart didn't need another jolt of caffeine, Cade accepted the empty mug she slid from the countertop into his palm.

She laughed and shook her head while she poured. A citrus scent wafted from the thick strands of her hair, teasing his nostrils with a sweetness that offset the bitter aroma of the coffee. He took a deep breath, but it wasn't enough. The image of him burying his face in her hair flashed in his mind, causing his gut to clench with need.

He took a sip and gazed straight into her dark blue eyes. Close up, he observed the glinting sapphire flecks in her irises that captured the sunlight when she smiled.

"Is there really such a thing as enough sleep?" she answered. "That's another vice, I suppose."

"I guess vices aren't always bad for you."

Her grin slanted into a smirk and she slowly backed away, as if embarrassed by his comment, though no blush pinkened her skin. Her fingers toyed with her empty belt loops and she shifted her weight slightly from one foot to the other while she thought about what he'd said.

"No, I can think of a certain vice that's actually quite wonderful, if done right," she said.

Cade nearly blinked. His mouth nearly fell open. Nearly. He was too trained and too adept at playing it cool to let one sensually charged redhead shatter his controlled veneer.

"And what vice is that?"

She grinned and crooked her finger, inviting him to follow her out of the kitchen. To her bedroom, perhaps?

"It's more fun if I show you..."

4

JILLIAN CLOSED HER eyes as she walked, blocking out her apprehension. She habitually screwed up spontaneous moments because she'd second-guess her judgment, particularly when a man was involved.

Go with the flow, Jillian. You said you were going to have an affair with the man. You can't very well do that without a little high-powered flirtation.

Thankfully, she'd already learned her new house well enough to make it from the kitchen to the living room without tripping over a credenza or bumping her knee on a coffee table.

She couldn't believe she was doing this—leading him inside, baiting him with a promise of something much more decadent than reality would prove. For now. But she was both shocked and grateful that her ability to think with some degree of clarity hadn't ceased simply because she was luring the sexiest man she'd met in years past her stairwell and into her private den.

When Cade's footfalls paused behind her—at the foot of the polished oak banister's curled edge—she stumbled on nothing but thin air. If he dashed upstairs for some reason, on some whim, he'd discover her cameras—a vice she'd developed in one day, thanks to him. And *not* the one she planned to show him.

Her heart slammed against her rib cage. What if he

knew? What if he'd flirted with her just to get inside, to verify his suspicion that she'd watched him all night long?

Though she'd turned off the monitors before she came downstairs, she knew that one quick, rambunctious detour and her secret would be found out. And since Cade seemed to have struck up a friendship with Stanley, the man she was *supposed* to be watching, she'd be facing more than just potential embarrassment—she'd have to deal with a ruined cover, too.

Cade's decelerated pace at the stairs pulled her like a towline to a painful stop.

Her eyes flashed open as she spun to face him.

"We're almost there." She injected her tone with a musical lilt that belied her fear.

"You keep this vice out in the open?" He glanced up the stairwell, sapping Jillian's breath with one casual sweep of his gaze. "You're a brave woman. Most people I know hide their vices."

She slid her fingers into her belt loops and tilted her balance onto one hip, hoping to look casual and impertinent and not the least bit worried that he might discover her real vice.

He'd used honesty to disarm her just a few minutes ago in the kitchen. She could try the same tactic, to a degree.

"Not all vices belong in a bedroom," she claimed, afraid she was botching this seduction in only the first phase of execution. See what happened when she didn't plan things out? How can a woman seduce a man who isn't allowed in her bedroom?

Duh.

"True," he agreed. "I myself prefer the kitchen."

Her eyebrows popped up before she could cap the

reaction. "Your weakness is your palate?" Which she happened to know consisted of a serious sweet tooth.

"My weakness is my appetite." He patted his stomach, flat beneath the T-shirt he'd tucked snugly into his jeans. She wasn't *supposed* to know that he devoured entire boxes of chocolate doughnuts for breakfast. She wasn't *supposed* to know that he used vigorous workouts to beat the calories off his body.

She wasn't *supposed* to know that he slept in the nude.

She clucked her tongue in disbelief, trusting her instincts, trusting her training as a private investigator to get this conversation back on track. Her field experience was on the light side, but she'd learned from watching Mick that pushing the conversation into forbidden territory could sometimes distract the intended mark. Hell, her ex-husband had used the tactic on her with winning results until she learned to decipher his system.

She took the time to peruse Cade from his running shoes to his midnight black hair, hiding none of her appreciation. Why hide? What better way to show her interest? "You don't look like a man who can't control his appetites."

Cade folded his lips inward and Jillian guessed he was having a damned hard time keeping their conversation friendly and innocent when so much of what they'd said this morning simmered with a charged innuendo. They'd literally known each other for no more than ten minutes, but she had no doubt they shared a mutual attraction—one both of them toyed with pursuing.

"I find ways to keep my appetites from getting the best of me," he answered.

She shrugged nonchalantly. She too found the means to keep her hungers under control, but if things worked out as she'd decided this morning, she'd need no more solo runs in the sexual satisfaction department, at least for a while.

"Don't we all. Unfortunately," she admitted as she turned and flipped on the light in the den, "this is one appetite I haven't been able to sate. And it's costing me a small fortune."

She walked through the archway and waited for him to follow. When he did, his eyes ignited at the sight of the big-screen television that dominated the opposite wall—a present from her uncle to celebrate her first field assignment. The sleek, thin state-of-the-art screen dominated nearly an entire wall. Only Uncle Mick, her father's brother, truly appreciated Jillian's inherited collection. Her one vice. Okay, the one vice she could share with a man she'd known for less than a quarter hour.

Videos. Rows and rows of bookshelves filled with videos from the classic to the bootlegged to the taped from television with the commercials haphazardly fast-forwarded through. She hadn't known that Mick had transported her babies from where she kept them in her climate-controlled, fire-safe office until she'd gone into the den this morning searching for the phone number of the mechanic working on her car. This room contained the only other window-cooling unit in the house, besides the one upstairs. This study would be her haven—her escape from work and responsibility. Only Mick would consider such luxury at a stakeout to be a necessity.

"You really like movies." Cade crossed the room and perused a shelf of Alfred Hitchcock classics.

"I told you, it's a vice."

"Have you watched them all?"

Jillian's smile was bittersweet and she was glad he still had his back to her and couldn't see. "No. I haven't actually taken one out of the case in, gosh, more than a year."

He picked up a recent title from her shelf of sci-fi releases, still shrink-wrapped in clear plastic. "But you keep buying them."

Jillian crossed the room and plucked the film case from his hand. "Yes, I do. I can't stop myself. I have no idea how I'm going to survive the conversion from video to DVD. I've already started, see?" She pointed to a row of thin, short cases lined meticulously on a shelf over the top of the television screen.

"If you don't watch them, why do you collect?"

Jillian paused before answering. The truth wasn't a big secret or anything particularly shocking, but it did reveal something about herself that she didn't share with strangers, particularly strangers she had a strong interest in seducing. She counted on Cade to provide a whirlwind, essentially meaningless, affair centered on sex and pleasure and no deep involvement. If she told him, she'd be opening a chamber of her heart she fought every day to keep closed. Because when closed, her sorrow couldn't leak out.

"Habit," she answered, but knew it wasn't enough. "My father started the collection years ago. When he died, I inherited it and pretty much keep it going in his memory."

Cade's gaze wandered to a shelf in a corner case, giving her a moment to regroup. Her father had been a film buff of epic proportions. Miles Hennessy's tastes ran from the artsy to the forbidden, and even Jillian had blushed dark scarlet when she discovered his extensive collection of erotica—a collection she'd personally more than doubled in the last year alone.

Those, she'd watched.

When Jillian finally got up the nerve to ask her mother about her father's "eclectic" tastes, Margaret Hennessy had done nothing more than grin with a distant yet distinct look of satisfaction in her smiling Irish eyes. That had been more than enough to immediately cut off Jillian's questions. She preferred to just be thankful that her mother had obviously wonderful memories of her husband, a man whose death came too early and too fast.

Not one of her three brothers or her sister complained when Jillian received the legacy of the films. Patrick now had the revolver, used during Miles Hennessy's stint in the National Guard. Sean had Da's leather bomber jacket and the classic Harley-Davidson motorcycle that their father had tinkered with for twenty-something years. Ian owned his complete collection of baseball memorabilia, including the torn ticket stub from Miles's first visit to Camden Yard. And Meghan, the baby of the family, had the doll-sized pink tutu—the one with the silver sparkles that her daddy had bought her after her first year of dance lessons. She'd given it back to him for safekeeping when she went away to Julliard to study with the pros. And in his will, he'd returned the cherished costume.

And Jillian had the movies, even the films he'd transferred from 8mm onto videotape of family outings and special events.

Of all his five children, only Jillian truly shared her father's love of film, a love he'd transferred into a career writing reviews for several news services before his leukemia, the disease he'd battled three times in his life, finally claimed the energy he needed to sit at the computer. With no interest in dictating, he spent his last months surrounded by the things he loved most— his family and his films. Now Jillian had his legacy...and she was using it to flirt.

She groaned inwardly. Wouldn't Da be proud?

She hadn't noticed that Cade had taken down her copy of *9 1/2 Weeks*—the uncensored director's cut— while she had been thinking of things she tried never, ever to think about.

"You may find this hard to believe," Cade said, "but I've never seen this."

She should invite him over. She should volunteer to pop some popcorn, dim the lights and see where the provocative film led them. Instead, she wavered. "You can borrow it anytime. I know I'll get it back—I know where you live." She ended with a joke, and Cade thankfully had the decency to look disappointed.

"I don't think this is the type of movie a man should watch alone." He slid the encased video back into place and slowly slid his hands into his pockets.

"Probably not," she agreed.

After he replaced the video, silence ensued—a woolen silence, thick and warm and just a tad itchy.

"I guess I should get out of your way. You probably still have some unpacking to do."

She nodded, despite that she was entirely unpacked, moved in and, apparently, ready to do nothing but watch Cade from afar. Oh, and Stanley, too.

"Never seems to end," she said, feeling like a coward.

Cade took one step toward the door, then stopped. Jillian blocked his path just enough that passing her would require touching. He swallowed deeply, drawing her attention to dark stubble on his rugged square chin.

Jillian moistened her lips and slowly leaned out of his way.

When he crossed through the threshold and unlocked her front door, he turned and smiled. Humor lit his eyes like emeralds and when he smoothed a wavy lock of raven hair from his forehead, Jillian fought a wave of sensual dizziness.

"I work out of my home," he told her. "Let me know if you need any help with anything...like sharing another vice."

His teasing eyes and tone spurred her to push herself out of her comfort zone, out of the safe little world she'd created over the past few years with videotapes she didn't watch and fantasies she hadn't acknowledged since she caught her husband with his mistress-of-the-month.

"Oh, no. It'll be your turn to share a vice."

Cade's nod was self-satisfied and accompanied by a devastatingly devilish smile. "Sounds like a plan. But you should be careful, Jillian Hennessy. I have a pretty full collection of vices."

He left, but as the door clicked quietly shut, Jillian couldn't contain her response. "Oh, yeah, I'll just bet you do."

NO RECORD. NOT EVEN A parking ticket. Not that he was surprised. Jillian Hennessy didn't strike him as a wrong-side-of-the-law type. Cade pressed the end button on his cell phone, feeling only slightly guilty for calling in a favor and checking out his sexy new neighbor. He knew he had several more avenues he could pursue to find out more about her, but he kept his search to the Division of Motor Vehicles and the court system. He now knew her birthday, her former address, her exact height, and could admire that she had signed on as an organ donor. She wasn't registered as owning a car, which surprised Cade since Tampa wasn't a public-transportation type of city. She must have company wheels, though the vehicle had yet to show up in her driveway.

Local court records had her listed as a witness in a domestic case from over two years ago and, just before that, as a plaintiff in her own divorce.

So his search hadn't been a total washout.

He stood on his back porch, his cell phone clutched in his hand while Crash, the cat he'd inherited along with the house, pawed at the laces of his athletic shoes. Cade moved his foot a few times, drawing the strings a few inches away, then closer, increasing the cat's pleasure, yet knowing the feline's play wouldn't last long. The overfed tabby teased Cade with hints of energy, but whenever Cade pulled out a catnip ball or a tangle of yarn, the cat rolled over and went to sleep.

When he'd first moved in, he'd thought the cat would provide some distraction for the long stretches when Stanley took off and Cade couldn't watch him. For a man with a supposedly debilitating injury, Stanley Davison was gone more often than he was home. Cade and his partner, Jake Tanner, had already decided that following Stanley on his jaunts around town in his lawsuit-paid-for Mercedes was risky, so Cade limited his reconnaissance to once or twice a week. Jake picked up some slack on his off-hours.

So far, Stan's outside activities included long lunches at the Blue Star Diner, extended excursions to a local plant nursery, an occasional trip to the library and his physical therapy sessions—all financed by the city. Cade also knew that the chance that Stanley would slip and reveal his fake injuries decreased when he was in public. Insurance fraud scammers usually screwed up at home or on vacation—private moments Cade was supposed to capture on film.

Too bad the only private moments Cade wanted to capture were with his sexy neighbor across the street.

Cade closed his eyes, forcing his feet to remain rooted on the back porch. If he gave in to temptation and sauntered around to the front again, he'd only make matters worse. After he left her house, she'd opened all the blinds, bathing the interior of her house in bright, summer sunlight and allowing Cade to watch her movements throughout the lower floor of the two-story cottage. She spent a great deal of time on the phone, and he suddenly wondered what she did for a living, if she had family in the area, if she was still unattached since her divorce...if she'd deflected his suggestion to watch the erotic movie with him because she was way too turned on. Like he was.

"Gonna prune your roses again?"

Cade slipped from man to cop to cover in the instant it took him to turn toward Stanley, who'd finally emerged from his house. Stan usually slept in, but this late? Cade slipped his cell phone into his back pocket, covertly glancing at his watch while he grabbed the soda he'd perched on the porch rail. Nearly eleven o'clock.

"No way. I don't have to work on these things every day, do I? I'll dig them up and replant them at Mom's myself if that's the case."

Stan shook his head and laughed. A genuine laugh. An authentic indication that after two weeks, Cade was finally making some headway. He'd thought the roses would be the key, but the connection with Stanley actually came by commiserating about a grown man's trouble with his mother. In Cade's case, a fictional mother, since Sherry Lawrence had died in a car wreck when he was only two years old. Stan's mother, however, was very real and lived several hundred miles away in New York. According to the depositions, she had nothing ill to say of her son. And thanks to his newfound, lawsuit-supplied wealth, Stan rewarded her loyalty with a deluxe suite in an extremely posh retirement home on Long Island and vacations to Boca Raton.

But Stan still complained and Cade used his bemoaning as an "in." And it had worked. Just like the misdelivered lemonade basket had worked with Jillian, dumb luck or not.

"Once a week is plenty of attention for roses," Stan said, looking out over his garden, which was starting to show some signs of neglect. "Guess I better get myself in gear and do some pruning of my own. This place is starting to look like a jungle."

"Need some help? I don't have any prospects this week that need scouting. I'm starting to get stir crazy."

Cade had come up with the cover of being a major league baseball scout for several reasons. Not only had it provided another connection with Stanley, a sports fan, but it gave Cade an excuse to work out of his home and own all manner of surveillance equipment like binoculars and zoom-lens cameras. Besides, Cade loved the game and had an extensive knowledge of the workings of the sport and the business that drove it. The opportunity to be someone else had lured him to undercover work in the first place.

Yet ever since he'd made the move into undercover

police work, he'd never had a chance to live out any personal fantasies. Back-alley bars and low-rent dives never quite set the scene. But a charming neighborhood on the south side? With a gorgeous woman and hours of free time?

His gaze wandered to his kitchen window. With a straight shot to the windows at the front of the house, he could see Jillian's place across the street. He couldn't see her, but the idea of living a fantasy brought her image right back into his mind with a thud, not unlike the smacking sound a fastball made when it hit a catcher's mitt.

It even stung a little.

He was in deep.

"No gardening, today," Stan said. "I have another, finer flower to groom this afternoon." He grinned from ear to blushing ear, looking like a teenage computer geek who'd just scored a date with the prom queen.

Cade exaggerated his impressed expression. "Stan, the man! Who is she?"

Stan shrugged, feigning a nonchalance Cade immediately recognized as fake. He must be using up all his lying skills with the physical injury. When he left his porch to join Cade at the fence, he walked with all the stiffness of a man who had indeed sustained soft-tissue injuries, the hardest type to prove. The city's doctor had said he was fit as a fiddle, but his personal doctor claimed otherwise. It had all come down to who was more credible on the witness stand, and Stan's doctor had won.

"Don't want to say just yet," Stan answered. "Don't want to jinx it. I'm meeting her for lunch."

"Taking her someplace nice?"

Stan snorted. "I said I was *meeting* her, not taking her. Very casual. Don't want to overwhelm the lady."

Cade nodded and took a long sip of soda. "Good plan."

"What about you? Maybe what you need to stave off your boredom is a little romantic dalliance."

Fighting the urge to slam the soda down, he took a loud swig. The last thing he wanted to discuss with this cheat was his nonexistent love life, but Cade knew better than to cut short any route to an increased rapport with Stanley. "I'm between women right now."

Stan shoved his hands in his pockets. "Been there. Have you seen our new neighbor yet? Caught a glimpse this morning when she went out to turn off the sprinklers. She's not bad."

Cade sipped this time, his grin muted. *Not bad at all.* But he kept his thoughts to himself.

"She had some friend over at her place this morning. Much more my type. Curvier. With an attitude. Some hot stuff. I wonder if I should bring some flowers to our new neighbor and try to finagle an introduction."

Even though Stan was talking about Elisa, Cade didn't like the idea of the lying SOB getting anywhere near Jillian, particularly with flowers.

"I met the friend this morning. She's involved."

Stan frowned, then blew the information off with a whistle. "Too bad. Well, if all goes right with me, I'll be involved myself."

Turning with a wave, Stan limped back to his porch and worked his way up the newly installed ramp. Though he was suddenly glad that Stan was leaving, Cade realized that his new, chatty relationship with Stanley shouldn't be dismissed so readily. Cade only had a few weeks left. He had to speed things along.

"Hey, I'm going to watch the Chicago game this afternoon," Cade shouted from porch to porch. "Want to come on over and pop some brews?"

Stan shook his head. "Love to, neighbor, but after lunch I'm heading for the library and then I have therapy and dinner with a pal of mine over at the beach. I won't be back until late. Thanks for the invite. Another time?"

Cade nodded and watched Stan disappear into his house, then did the same himself. Another time. What the hell was he going to do with the rest of his afternoon now?

He jabbed Jake's number into his cell phone.

"Stan's got a date. Think you should swing by the Blue Star and check out his action?"

"Yeah. Just what I want to do," Jake groused. "Check out that pinhead's love life."

"Probably more exciting than our love lives," Cade said, following a nearly worn path to his front window.

"Speak for yourself."

Cade stopped before he tweaked an opening in the blinds. Nearly the same age, Jake and Cade had more in common than most partners on the force. Both had military backgrounds and went straight from the service to the force. Both were currently unattached bachelors with reputations as lady-killers that outshone their realities by leaps and bounds.

Both men preferred the pursuit of difficult cases and hard-to-catch perps over difficult relationships and hard-to-get women. But Jake had been showing the signs of restlessness lately that Cade attributed to too little sex over too much time—the same signs Cade was showing right now. In Jake's case, the situation was exacerbated by the presence of an alluringly mysterious mystery writer in a community police academy class Jake taught every Saturday afternoon.

And now Cade had Jillian.

"Whoa. Did you finally have the nerve to hit on shy and unassuming Devon Michaels?"

Jake cleared his throat. Twice. And didn't say a word.

"You did more than hit on her," Cade guessed. "You asked her out."

"Not exactly."

"Then what, exactly?" Cade tore away from the window and threw himself onto the cheap but newly recovered couch. "You're killin' me here. I'm bored out of my mind, Tanner. Throw me a bone or I'm going to start watching soap operas every day. Did you know Tad the Cad is up to his old tricks again? Well, he is. And this Chandler dude, there's actually two of them. Twins. I shouldn't know this shit, man."

Only one episode of *All My Children* and Cade was already starting to watch the time for the one o'clock hour. He really had to either crack this case very soon, or find another means to entice Jillian Hennessy into sharing a little afternoon delight.

"You're scaring me, Cade."

"Tell me about it."

"Maybe you're the one who needs a woman."

Cade let his eyelids drift closed and, suddenly, the tangy scent of lemons filled his senses. "You know what, partner, maybe I am."

5

SHE COULDN'T TAKE IT anymore. Though she'd only been away from the office for a little over twenty-four hours, the old Jillian Hennessy—the one who could concentrate on ledgers and spreadsheets for hours at a time, the one who could stare at inter-office requisition forms or pages and pages of surveillance reports without so much as getting up for a fresh cup of coffee—now had a serious case of ants in her pants.

Courtesy of Cade.

Hearing Elisa recount her makeout session with Ted over the phone hadn't helped. Her friend had spared her the most intimate details, of course, but not the conclusion that Jillian had been a first-rate coward to back off from Cade when she'd had the opportunity to arrange, at the very least, a sexy movie date. How often, at her age, did she get a chance to experience something as invigorating, forbidden and insane as sitting on a couch in a darkened living room while erotic images and acts played before her like an instruction manual?

So why was she now suddenly reluctant to go upstairs and find out exactly what Cade was doing right at this very moment? From what she could tell with her binoculars, Stanley Davison had just left his house—and with what looked like an overnight bag. She'd called in her backup investigators to tail him and alerted Ted that the house was empty and could be rewired without detection.

Officially, she had nothing left to watch.

But, oh, what she could do with a little spare time and some incorrectly installed equipment.

Lingering at the bottom of the stairs, Jillian imagined a portal through her front door—a tunnel of vision from her house to his. Only she didn't have to imagine. Her equipment gave her the opportunity to do more than conjure up images in her mind. Essentially, she had two choices to offset her newly discovered obsession. She could go next door and see what he was doing in person, or she could give in to temptation and check out his movements with her cameras and computers.

Jillian jogged up the stairs with a sigh of surrender. Maybe if she knew just a little more about him, she'd muster the gumption to go through with her planned seduction. Her instincts told her Cade Lawrence was a good guy, and with the exception of her ex-husband, her instincts were usually right on the money.

Maybe if she'd had a chance to watch Neal for a few days in his natural habitat, she might have figured out he was a two-timing Lothario before she married him. Her mother's favorite mantra, "Live and learn," rang in her ears.

Jillian grinned, sat down and typed in her access codes. *Not bad.* She'd just succeeded in rationalizing her voyeurism as being sanctioned by her mother. *Not bad at all.*

If she could watch Cade just one more time, learn maybe one more private thing about him, she could work past the reluctance that had suddenly attacked her when he'd examined her video collection with clear fascination. She'd piqued his interest and he'd done a major number on hers, yet she'd backed away.

She clicked on the extra monitors, and knowing the tech team would soon rewire her equipment to default to Stanley's house, she worked a little computer magic to ensure that the new codes didn't interfere with her burgeoning career as a Peeping Tom. She saved the commands that controlled the cameras and listening devices in Cade's house to a personal file, entitling it "Watch Me."

Then, she flipped from room to room, searching for her quarry. A half hour ago, she'd glanced out her front window to catch him talking to Stanley again, though their angle had kept her from lipreading their conversation. But the back porch and yard were now empty except for Cade's cat snoozing on the swing.

No movement in the kitchen, living room or bedroom, though she did note that the television was tuned to a soap opera. She checked the attic—no sign there. She wondered how a room that had looked so romantic and forbidden the night before now looked quiet and dusty and dark.

Finally, she checked the garage. After a moment, a flash of light startled her. The side door, leading from the detached garage to the house, flung open. Cade walked in, shoved his hands on his hips and looked around. He pushed aside some tools on the workbench, opened a few creaky drawers in an old wooden chest and slammed them shut. He wasn't looking for anything in particular, it seemed. His movements then quickened. Annoyance turned to frustration, like a man who wanted something he couldn't find. Or worse, couldn't have.

Fascinated, Jillian wiped dust off the monitor with

her palm, imagining she could feel Cade's borderline rage through the screen. He shoved a metal bucket out of his way with his foot, nearly kicking it. But if Jillian had learned one thing about Cade last night, he was a man who could control his movements, perhaps even his emotions, simply because he wished to.

Still, he moved with the fervor of a caged animal. Not wounded, just trapped—desperate to tear free from some invisible shackle. Her fingers trembled when she watched him poke his head out of the door toward her house as if he sought something in that direction.

But he returned, shaking his head. Bending at the waist, he braced his hands on his knees and started... chuckling? By the time he lunged into a hamstring stretch, he was laughing out loud, his momentary lapse into anxiety effectively humored away.

Amazing. Anyone, much less a man, who could manage to laugh at himself so quickly and easily rose considerably in her estimation. He allowed his emotions to surface and didn't take himself too seriously— solidifying Jillian's guess that Cade Lawrence would be the perfect temporary lover.

His warmup was minimal and, before Jillian could blink, he dashed out the door.

Straight toward her house.

"DO YOU RUN?"

"Excuse me?"

Jillian leaned against the barely opened front door, her voice ragged with exertion as if she'd run to answer his knock or was doing something physical just before he spontaneously decided to invite her on his run. She wiped a thin sheen of perspiration off her forehead and temple, spurring Cade to seek out signs of moisture that might have formed elsewhere on her body.

Like just above her curved upper lip. Across her bare shoulders. Between her breasts—just enough to form a curved shadow on the light-blue cotton of her tank top.

"I'm going for a run," he said. "Thought you might join me."

"It's after one o'clock! No one in Florida runs at this time of day, unless you have a thing for heat-stroke."

Cade laughed as he twisted a kink out of his lower back. "This neighborhood is shaded. It's not so bad."

Her lifted eyebrows told him she didn't buy his claim one bit. Okay, so he was stretching the truth a little. Even with century-old oak trees sheltering the streets from the full anger of the sun, a run at this time of day would be a sweltering endeavor. But Cade had no other choice. He had to get out of the house for a while. He knew the price of his restlessness too well to ignore it. Ordinarily, he'd pack up his pickup and head to the beach for a few hours. Maybe go canoeing up the Hillsborough River or just get on Interstate 75 and drive until the stir-craziness subsided.

Cade couldn't remember a time when he didn't have to deal with the curse his father called "perpetual mo-tion disease" only half-jokingly. Cade needed to move. Cade needed to go. Cade needed to be doing something or he became irritable, destructive and, sometimes, downright mean. In his childhood, his personality caused him to spend a lot of time with the principal or headmaster of whatever military academy he happened to be attending at the time.

In adulthood, he'd become better at making sure he was only mildly annoying to those around him. His best course became striking at his boredom before it became a problem. Normally, he only had serious lapses when he was on a forced leave—like he was now. Recently, though, he'd found himself questioning his choice to pull and fire his weapon on his last collar—wondering if he could have handled the situation in another way. This was not good. Cade relied on his instincts to stay alive in life and death situations.

Questioning after the fact was normal enough he supposed, so long as it didn't lead to doubts during a tense situation. So he latched onto the one area where he had no doubts—his attraction to Jillian Hennessy.

Jillian, who most definitely was the real reason for his sudden and irrational urge to pound the pavement in the noonday heat.

He'd *never* had such a serious case of frustration on account of a woman he hadn't even kissed yet—a situation he would rectify damned soon if Jillian didn't stop licking those rosy pink lips of hers while she pretended to consider his offer.

"Sorry, Cade. I don't even run on cool days."

He swept her body with an appreciative glance. There was no way she maintained such a compact, sleek figure without sweating a little.

He raised his eyebrows. "Really? Then what do you do for exercise?"

She grinned, obviously aware of the underlying implication beneath his question. She'd need to do an awful lot of gymnastic lovemaking to hone a body like hers. "Wouldn't you like to know?"

"As a matter of fact, I would. Very much."

Jillian's eyes narrowed, but didn't lessen the wicked twinkle in her dark blue eyes. She not only didn't mind his innuendos, she obviously enjoyed them. Could dish a few of her own without a moment's hesitation. The woman was a first-class, Olympic gold medal tease. He loved it.

With unguarded appreciation, she watched him stretch his quadriceps. She even checked out his ass, which pleased him even more. His decision to go running despite the ninety-degree weather could possibly pay off big.

She finally spoke. "Why don't you go run, get all hot and sweaty, and if you don't pass out or require hospitalization, I'll show you."

JILLIAN SWAM THE LENGTH of the pool for the twentieth time, reversing her direction with an underwater flip and push off the side. The water, slick and cool beneath the surface of a relentless sun, sluiced around her body as she kicked and stroked. Her lungs, tight with held air, started to burn. She turned her head to the side and snatched a breath, but kept swimming, never breaking her stride.

Her muscles protested, but she pushed on, determined to finish at least a quarter mile. She hadn't gotten into a pool for nearly two weeks, until Cade's suggestion about exercise sent her scrambling for her swimsuit. The presence of a pool with the house, long but narrow and perfect for exercise, made up for the unreliable air conditioner.

She was out of practice and, as she battled to complete one last lap, she wondered if she shouldn't have eased herself back into a rhythm rather than diving in and pushing hard. But try as she might to take a more reasoned course, Jillian wasn't the type of person to ease into anything. What she wanted, she pursued single-mindedly. This wasn't always the wisest course of action, but Jillian could no more fight her basic nature than she could fight her attraction to her neighbor across the street.

She was just coming up for air when the current in the pool changed. She heard a splash, felt a rush of water that pushed her toward the surface…then two strong, male hands locked onto her waist. He gave her a split second to fill her lungs, then pulled her back under the water.

Jillian knew without looking that the hands on her were Cade's.

He didn't keep her under for long, releasing her to pop back up and take a deeper lungful of air. He then continued to swim the length of the pool, leaving Jillian breathless as she watched him slice through the water with powerful grace. And this after an hour-long run in the unforgiving Florida summer heat? The man's stamina rocked Jillian to the core.

She splashed over to the edge near the house just as he emerged on the opposite side. He shook his head, whipping his hair free of excess water, then slicked the dark strands back with his hands. His skin, flushed from the sun, beaded and glistened as if he were some Mediterranean god of the sea.

"Whew! Now this is the way to finish a run!"

He kicked off and backstroked over to her, giving her a breath-stealing view of his broad, bare chest and thick, powerful arms. Oh, and those heavenly shoulders.

"Wouldn't you rather swim than run?" she asked.

He let his momentum push him the last few feet until his face was just inches from hers. "I don't know. Swimming seems so recreational. With running, you can feel your muscles working. No pain, no gain. But being in the water, with you, I feel all energetic again.''

''Do you now?''

Jillian heard the slam of a car door and the retreat of an engine. Good. Ted and his team were done and gone. They'd moved in with their signature swiftness, bugging Stanley's house and updating her computer in less than an hour. She was now good to go on her official assignment, which she would do tomorrow, or whenever Stanley got home.

But for now, she had Cade nearly naked in her backyard pool, looking as cool and inviting as the water had been from the moment she jumped in.

''Who was that?'' Cade asked. His expression was the picture of innocent curiosity, but Jillian's heart still jumped a beat. This man didn't miss much.

''Who?''

''The truck out front. AAA-Team Electronics. I've never heard of them.''

''Really? They came highly recommended. I was having trouble with some wiring. They fixed it right up.''

''They weren't here long.''

''I know. They were in and out, just finishing up paperwork in the truck, I guess. I would have hated if their work interfered with my swim. I did promise to show you that I do know how to exercise.''

She winked and splashed him lightly, both proud and dismayed that the misrepresentation of the truth rolled off her tongue so easily. A cherished talent for a private investigator. A not-so-good practice for a potential lover.

''I made some lemonade.'' She gestured toward the

icy carafe sweating beneath the umbrella on her patio table. "Want some?"

He licked his lips, but shook his head. "Not right this minute. You were doing your laps. I shouldn't have interrupted."

"Were you watching me before you dove in?"

"You're very graceful."

Jillian slipped under and emerged face up, pushing her hair completely off her face and blinking droplets from her lashes. Though her unheated pool was only about seventy-six degrees, a distinct warmth swirled around her, perhaps inside her—she couldn't tell which.

"I love swimming. It's really the only way I'll exercise regularly."

"The only way?"

He raised his eyebrows in that certain style Jillian recognized as an invitation to find a naughty meaning in what he suggested. In less than a day, she was already learning how to read the man.

"You have a wicked mind," she chastised.

"Some women say I have a dirty mind."

"I don't think sex is dirty. Do you?"

"Not if done right."

She pursed her lips, keeping her next supposition to herself. She had no doubt that her neighbor knew precisely how to do sex right. The question was, did she have the nerve to find out just how right it could be?

With hardly a splash, she kicked back toward the stairs, settling on the third step so that she was still underwater from the shoulders down.

"You know, I don't know much about you. Maybe we shouldn't talk about sex until we pin down some

of the basics. Like what do you do for a living...or are
you just independently wealthy?"

He stood in the shallow end, forcing her to watch
the water slide down his rock-hard body in rushing
rivulets. He held out his hand as he approached. "Cade
Lawrence, currently a scout for the Yankees. Pitchers
are my specialty. I'm single and have never been married. I have one pet that came with the house. I'm a
Scorpio. My favorite color is red." He reached out with
the hand she hadn't yet taken and briefly stroked a wet
strand of her hair that curved along her shoulder.

Their eyes met and Jillian decided that her favorite
color was now green. Emerald green, centered with
black and glistening with flecks of amber. But she
didn't want to interrupt his string of personal information, so she kept her confession to herself.

He let his hand slip down until it disappeared in the
cool blue water. "Yes, I like red a lot." His voice grew
husky, hot—like the air around them. He stepped back
an inch or two, lightening both the mood and his tone.
"Except in relation to my bank account, which is currently in the black. I love Japanese food, can't get into
sushi though, but dig caviar. I prefer my vodka *very*
cold and I have an incredible weakness for women who
can make a one-piece bathing suit look more sexy than
a bikini."

Jillian glanced down at the suit she'd chosen, one
she'd considered modest until she watched Cade's eyes
darken with obvious desire. She had briefly toyed with
donning her one bikini, a string contraption she'd
bought on a whim and had yet to wear. She was very,
very glad she'd changed her mind. Even with her neck
and breasts completely covered with Lycra, the bare

skin on her shoulders, arms and back tingled as Cade's gaze swept over her.

"That's a lot of information," she concluded.

"Anything that makes you regret inviting me back after my run?"

She shook her head. Good thing he had no way of guessing that she also knew about his sweet tooth, his skill for tae kwon do and his addiction to soap operas. Dishonesty didn't sit well with Jillian, but she sure as hell didn't know how to come clean on this one. Maybe she didn't have to. Maybe she could figure out a way to be honest with him from now on. Well, not about Stanley. She couldn't blow her case just to satisfy some antiquarian ideal about being up-front and open with a potential lover.

Aha! Now there was something she *could* be completely and totally honest about. Her interest in Cade. Her instantaneous case of lust. No downside to spilling the beans on that.

She nearly had the words formed when he slowly walked up the stairs and out of the pool, a river of water pouring down his powerful legs and tight butt.

"Why don't I pour us both a lemonade while you finish your swim?" he asked.

"I'm finished."

He grabbed a towel and patted his face, his smile lopsided with disappointment. "You said I could watch."

"You watched me before you dived in," she reasoned, suddenly aware of the subtle change in the shape of his eyes, in the intensity of his gaze.

"But you didn't know I was watching," Cade reminded her. His voice dropped again to that seductive, throaty whisper, the kind a man used just before he slipped inside a woman and filled her deeply with all he had. He leaned back into the lounge chair and took a sip of lemonade.

"Knowing someone's watching changes the whole dynamic, don't you think?"

6

CADE SLOWLY BRUSHED THE towel over his thick arms and hard chest, then settled in a chair with his glass, crossed his legs at the ankles and took a long swig of lemonade. His grin was pure challenge; his stare utter impudence. If Jillian wasn't one-hundred-percent confident that Ted and his tech team had installed completely undetectable equipment, she might have suspected from his comment and arch expression that he knew all about her clandestine activities. Watching him. Wanting him.

But Ted was an expert and Cade was just being sexy. Damned sexy. She couldn't be any more certain unless she could read his mind. Her instincts told her—the intuitive, feminine part of her she rarely used anymore, preferring to believe only what she saw, only what was typed up in some surveillance report. Facts and figures didn't dash your hopes or break your heart.

But with Cade, Jillian relished trusting her ability to see the truth by watching his body language, listening to his words. Cade's unabashed interest acted like gunpowder sprinkled liberally on a dying flame.

Flash. Spark. Pow!

Besides, she deserved to be watched by him. Served her right for sneaking peeks with her camera, manipulating the truth to justify her voyeurism.

And perhaps his watching her could also serve her goal of seduction.

She swam leisurely, choosing a backstroke for the long, languorous rhythm, just as Cade had moments before. The water rolled over her body, acting like a clear blue curtain that revealed and then shrouded her every movement, every inch of skin. All the way to the other end of the pool, she kept her gaze locked with his, daring him to look away, knowing he wouldn't, wanting him to memorize how taut her breasts were, how smooth and sleek her arms and legs were.

She reached the end and flipped beneath the water, then continued slowly, but purposefully, choosing a breaststroke next. She continued for three more laps, each movement causing her suit to constrict around a body primed for sex. She wanted him. In the water. Beside her. Beneath her. Naked. Free.

As if he'd plugged directly into her fantasy, he dived in beside her and matched her stroke for stroke. They swam together, synchronized, despite Cade's longer reach. He pulled back just enough, contained his overwhelming strength so they could remain equal, side by side, in sync. They did two laps. Three. His energy vibrated through the water like sonar until Jillian broke stride midway to the other side. She stopped, treading water. Aching for the forbidden. For him.

Cade instantly sensed her retreat and swung back. Their feet and hands brushed as they stirred the water to stay afloat.

"Tired?" he asked.

She shook her head. Yes, her muscles ached. Yes, her lungs burned. Yes, she felt as if she wore a diver's weight belt, despite her buoyancy. The heaviness, the breathless tension, were all on account of Cade.

"Why'd you stop then?"

"I don't want to swim anymore. I want to kiss you."

Jillian refused to regret her honest, spontaneous admission, especially when Cade's eyes darkened with interest rather than surprise.

"I've been wanting to kiss you since I first saw you yesterday," he told her. "Before we even met, I had this overwhelming urge to find out what you tasted like."

The man-made currents pushed them closer and Jillian slipped her arms around his neck while their legs entwined and thrashed to keep them above water.

"Hard to fight that initial attraction, isn't it?" she asked.

"Impossible."

Their lips met and, for an instant, neither of them moved. Jillian focused on the sweet pressure of his mouth on hers, the tart taste of the lemonade, his hard chest and legs pressed against her soft breasts and belly. Cool wetness surrounded them and liquid heat flowed inside her.

Cade held her close, and as their mouths opened to share a breath, they slipped beneath the surface into a glittering, intoxicating dream. Tongues. Warmth. Knowledge.

The fantasy flooded when water rushed into their mouths. Cade pulled Jillian to the surface and swam them both to the side, sputtering and coughing and laughing.

"I'm a big advocate of wet kisses," he said, "but maybe we're tempting fate a little." He kept one hand pressed possessively against the small of her back. His hot palm contrasted with the cool swirl and splash of the water, inspiring Jillian to push past the last vestiges of her inhibitions.

She had nothing to lose with Cade. Her instincts told her he was honorable, trustworthy. And if he wasn't, she had no illusions for him to destroy. She wanted a brief affair. An invigorating, memories-for-a-lifetime encounter. No regrets—and that included the grief she'd suffer if she didn't grab hold of him and life and love and see where it took her. Right here. Right now.

"We're safe in the shallow end," she said. "Why don't you show me a little more of those wet kisses? Being that you're a 'big advocate' and all."

"Did I say 'advocate'? I meant to say expert."

"Oh, now you're getting cocky. I like that. You're not only tempting fate, Cade Lawrence, you're tempting me. I don't usually kiss men I've just met."

He swiped a soft kiss across her cheek and pulled her flush against him. Water or no water, there was no mistaking the distinct, lengthy shape of his desire pressed against her stomach. "You have no idea how pleased that makes me."

Actually, she did. "Then show me."

He obliged...until she couldn't breathe. Until she couldn't tell where his mouth ended and hers started. Until the water on them seemed to evaporate with the heat of tongues and lips and hands and until she learned his mouth as if they'd been kissing like this for years. He skimmed his fingers up her back. She plunged hers into his hair.

Her nipples pebbled beneath her swimsuit, brushing hard against his chest. Her heartbeat raged. She took quick, shallow gasps for air, but still she wanted more. She kissed a seductive trail from his mouth and chin to his ear. "Touch me, Cade. I won't bite. Well, maybe I'll bite. But I won't bite hard."

He chuckled and with painful slowness traced his hands down her sides, over her waist and hips to her derriere. "I think you're the one with the wicked mind."

She shook her head, cooing as his large palms and fingers splayed over her flesh, then clutched tight with a possessiveness that spoke of pure, animal desire. Yes. Her mind was wicked. Her body was wicked. And the decadence brought her spirit to life like gasoline on a fire.

So basic—to be touched, desired, needed for no other reason than because she was a woman. A sexy, sensual woman who could tempt a desirable man like Cade simply by being who she was.

His touch was slow, thorough. He learned her curves as he enticed her closer, rewarding her with hard kisses when she slid her hands down his back and began an exploration of her own. She stopped only when his fingers brushed the sides of her breasts, so quickly, she wondered if she'd confused the lap of the water with pressure from his thumbs. Instantaneous need overwhelmed her. Her blood raged and pumped and made her dizzy.

Cade absorbed her shiver, instantly recognizing the power of their attraction. He'd never experienced something so intense or so real. Not this quickly. With Jillian, he wasn't playing a role or squeezing in a lover in between assignments. Here, with barely a yard of fabric between them and the warm waves licking at their skin like a thousand tongues, he wanted nothing, needed nothing, but her honest, uninhibited response to his touch.

She'd give him that, he knew. The same way he knew he was asking too much, too soon. His instincts shouted that Jillian Hennessy wasn't a woman to be loved and left.

He kissed her temple and gently created a distance between them, though he couldn't manage to let her go.

"What are we doing here, Jillian?"

She immediately leaned against him, denying him the safety of space. A bemused grin tilted the corners of her luscious mouth, making him wonder what exactly was stopping him.

"Well, I live here, remember? Just moved in yesterday."

"No. I mean, you're complicating my very simple lifestyle. It's not so bad, mind you. Just not what I expected. Definitely not what I planned."

She laughed, kissed his nose and swam over to the stairs, this time stepping out of the water, with measured steps and a gentle rock to her hips. He endured each and every drip and dribble of water flowing off her body. Sweet torture.

"I'm sorry to hear that, Cade." She snatched the towel he'd used earlier from off the back of a chair. She lifted the white cloth to her face, dabbed away the moisture and then blatantly inhaled his scent. "Mmm. No, I take that back. I'm not the least bit sorry. You haven't exactly fit into my plans perfectly, either. I was supposed to move in, settle down and get to work on a project my company really needs to have succeed. Now, all I want to do is seduce you."

"What's stopping you?"

She swiped moisture off her arms and legs, then twirled the towel around her hips and secured it at the waist. "I could ask you the same question, but I think I know. You want me to make the rules. Set the pace. How gentlemanly."

Jillian grinned. Her sharp wit and self-awareness made her hard to fool, so when it came to their personal interactions, Cade decided not to even try. Despite his undercover status, he could keep this part of his life honest, at least to a degree. Just like when he told her his real name. If he was careful, he could make sure his lies about his job didn't demean anything they shared in her pool or, hopefully, in her bed. Or his.

But if she thought he was practicing any form of gentlemanly restraint by delaying their attraction right now, she was mistaken. He was simply covering his ass—making sure she understood the situation and didn't get any wrong ideas of what he wanted or for how long. The one time in the past when he hadn't been clear on that point, he'd not only lost his lover after a cruel shouting match, he'd blown his cover and nearly gotten himself killed.

"I'm no gentleman, Miss Hennessy, or I wouldn't be thinking what I'm thinking right now."

"Which is?"

"Sure you want to know?"

She knelt down at the edge of the pool and drew her face close to his. "Does skinny-dipping play any part in it?"

He swallowed. "Skinny-dipping is good."

She bit her lip and glanced around, apparently considering the possibility with seriousness. Her backyard was relatively private with a tall fence and thick hedges, but the houses on either side had second-story windows with open blinds. Did she have the nerve? Who was this Jillian Hennessy? Except for the part about being a baseball scout, everything Cade had told Jillian about himself was the honest-to-God truth. Yet, he knew very little about her...and really only what he'd learned by calling in some favors. Could he be inviting trouble yet again?

"I like the way you think," she said, "but aroused as I am, I'm no pushover. You're gonna have to work a bit harder than one incredible kiss to get me naked."

She stood, sauntered to the table and finished what was left of his lemonade. Cade remained in the water, stunned and impressed and willing to do whatever it took to have Jillian Hennessy. Naked. And soon. He braced himself on the edge and then pushed out of the pool.

"You're talking dinner? A movie?"

"That's a start," she said.

Stanley was going to be gone until late, possibly all night. Tomorrow, Cade would find a way to turn up the heat on that end of his assignment. For now, he had a much more interesting task to work on.

"I'll pick the restaurant, you pick the flick," he said. "We'll deal with the possibility of skinny-dipping together. How's that sound?"

Jillian nodded, then gasped when Cade swiped her towel. It was thoroughly wet, but there was no way he was walking home in saturated jogging shorts after this encounter. He wrapped the towel around himself and grabbed his shoes and shirt from where he'd tossed them on her patio.

"Seven o'clock. And if you must wear clothes, dress casually."

SHE DIDN'T KNOW WHICH movie to choose, so before she shut off the lights and locked the front door, Jillian took out a volume of the *Red Shoe Diaries* and placed it on the coffee table in front of her big-screen television. The first vignette in the collection of sensuous short films was called "Swimming Naked." Cade would either laugh at her little joke or take the hint seriously.

Either way, Jillian couldn't lose.

She checked her watch, jumping when the phone trilled in the kitchen. At five until seven, Jillian swore. For the first time in a long, long while, she prayed someone from the office wasn't calling, though she couldn't imagine who else had the number. She'd already spoken to Cade twenty minutes ago when he'd called to make sure she wasn't backing out of their date. Was the man nuts? Tonight, she wanted to enjoy herself. Really enjoy herself. Selfishly and wholeheartedly, for the first time in years.

"Hello?"

"Hey, Jillie."

She groaned inwardly. Her brother. "Patrick."

"Don't sound so thrilled to hear from me. You might hurt my feelings."

Jillian bit her lip, hating what her uncle's indecisiveness over the future of the Hennessy Group had done to her relationship with her eldest brother. She loved Patrick and had worshiped and admired him from childhood into adulthood without ever being disappointed by her handsome, overprotective sibling. He'd been the rock she'd leaned on when their father died. He'd become a decorated homicide detective in Atlanta, the pride of the family. His visits home spurred great celebrations, complete with their mother's infamous corned beef and a keg or two of Uncle Mick's home-brewed ale. His last visit home had been a record breaker in terms of fun...until he announced that he'd retired from the force and planned to stay in Florida.

Her mother had cried with happiness for nearly two days. And Uncle Mick? You would have thought the man had won the lottery. He immediately moved offices around so Patrick could have the one next to hers. He'd instructed his niece to bring her brother up to speed on all their cases. "Patrick needs to know everything you know, Jillian," Mick had insisted. Out of her love for both of them, she'd complied, biting her tongue that Patrick could *never* know everything she knew because he hadn't been working in the office since he was eleven years old.

The Hennessy Group was her legacy, the reward for giving up her grade-school summers to sharpen pencils for the bookkeepers and for using all her breaks from high school to study procedures and pour through case reports. She'd never imagined Mick would leave her out in the cold when he retired—until Patrick came home.

"I'm not hurting your feelings, Patrick, and you know it. What's up? I have plans tonight."

"Cancel them."

"Excuse me?"

"I just spoke with Jase. Stanley's heading home early. Something happened and Jase says Stanley's looking pretty riled. Might be a great chance to see him lose it and tip his hand. I want your eyes and ears peeled."

Jillian pressed the phone to her chest and took a long, deep breath to avert a growl. She couldn't believe this was happening. The fact that Cade Lawrence was about to stroll up her driveway and knock on her kitchen door as planned so they could go out on a long casual date that would hopefully end in some incredibly erotic sex, preferably in her swimming pool or on the chaise lounge she'd set seductively among a rather thick, tall collection of hibiscus and azaleas in her backyard. Well, it wasn't the whole problem. Patrick was the problem. Patrick and his authoritative tone.

"Why did Jase call you?" she asked.

"He was checking in. Don't get your skirt in a bunch, sis. I'm covering the desk while Uncle Mick has dinner with the CEO of that insurance company we're trying so damned hard to impress."

"Covering the desk does not give you authority over me, Patrick. I'm the lead investigator. This whole operation was my idea in the first place. How dare you come in here and start bossing me around!"

Perfectly on schedule, a knock sounded from the side door. Jillian took another deep breath. "Hold on, dammit," she snapped. She slid the phone onto the counter to keep from throwing the handset down too hard. With a pasted-on smile, she peeked through the lacy window on the upper half of her door. Cade grinned from the other side, and Jillian's ire and indignation eased. God, he was gorgeous. Gorgeous and sexy and waiting for her to open up and let him in.

"Hey," she said, gesturing for him to come inside.

"Wow. You look lovely."

She twirled around so her short sundress whirled around her thighs. "Thanks, you clean up nice yourself. Look, I'm really sorry, but I have to finish this phone call. Work," she said with a grimace, glad she'd already thought up an explanation about what she did for a living since she was certain he'd ask her about her job sometime tonight. Sooner than she expected, thanks to Patrick's bad timing.

"Go ahead. I'll wait here."

"Grab a drink if you'd like. I won't be a minute."

She scooped up the phone and padded casually to the study where she could close the door behind her.

"A date? You frickin' have a date?" Patrick groused immediately after she'd told him she was back. "You're supposed to be on the job, Jillie, not out having fun."

Jillian counted backwards. Ten to one. Slowly.

"Patrick," she asked, her voice a symphony of utter calm even though her fingers gripped the portable phone with enough power to crack the casing, "you're treading in some very dangerous water here. When we're on the job, when we're in the office, I am not your little sister who you can intimidate. Like it or not, I'm leading this investigation. I call the shots. And if I want to change my plans tonight, that's up to me. *Me.* Not you. And if Jase or Tim or any other of our people call in about this case, I expect you to refer them to me. And if you don't like it, we'll take it up with Uncle Mick tomorrow. Because tonight, I...have...plans."

Her words were firm, staccato, final. She waited for Patrick's response, wondering if he was even slightly prepared to hear her take a stand. Since his return, Jillian had been quiet about her opposition to his joining the Hennessy Group. She'd respected his position as her oldest brother and his experience as a former cop. Up until tonight, he'd mostly remained out of her way, learning the ropes, schmoozing with clients and Uncle Mick while she worked her fingers to the bone checking and rechecking Mick's work to ensure that the company's fine reputation remained intact.

Well, enough was enough. She'd intended to lay her cards on the table with her brother at some point, but while she certainly hadn't intended to do so until this case was over, he hadn't left her any choice.

She heard no reaction from Patrick on the other end of the line and she wondered if they'd been disconnected. Then, he whistled—a disbelieving sound that made her wince.

"Yowza, sis. Got a little pent-up rage going? I'm just trying to help."

"Patrick, you're trying to take over."

Silence. No denial. No accusation that she was overreacting or being paranoid. Just silence, which drove her point home.

"I guess we should talk about this tomorrow," he said.

"I'll be in around noon unless Stanley changes his routine and decides to go run a marathon instead of having lunch at the Blue Star. Make sure Mick is there, okay?"

Patrick agreed, then hung up. Jillian noted that he hesitated for a moment as if he'd left something unsaid. She pressed the off button on her handset, fighting the urge to try and figure out what her brother had wanted to say. Patrick Hennessy wasn't one to hold back his opinions, but he also didn't speak off the top of his head. Whatever he'd considered saying, he'd thought better of.

Good. For both of them. Because whatever he said, at this point, Jillian figured she wouldn't like. And she certainly didn't want her evening ruined any more than it already was.

Jillian glanced down at the coffee table, at the sexy video and the multiple remotes she'd stacked in a neat line and tried to compartmentalize her conversation with her brother so she could set it aside to be dealt with tomorrow. Once she stored away all the anger and resentment, one fact remained out in the open.

Stanley was on his way home. Something had happened to upset him. Damn, damn, damn. Patrick was right. This was a perfect opportunity for Stanley to make a wrong move.

A wrong move that her video equipment would catch, whether she was upstairs watching or not.

A soft knock on the study door made her jump.

"Jillian, you okay? I saw the light go off on your phone…"

Jillian glanced down at the handset. The base unit in the kitchen would show that she'd disconnected the line and had ended her call. The man was incredibly observant, causing yet another chill to slither down her spine.

She slid the pocket door open and came out, closing it behind her. She didn't want to tip her hand about the movie just yet.

"Yeah, sorry. Call's over. Crisis handled."

She made a beeline to the kitchen and Cade paused, but then followed. "Glad to hear it. What exactly do you do anyway?"

Jillian swallowed deeply as she balanced the phone back on the base unit. She hated lying to Cade—she hated lying to anyone—but she certainly couldn't tell him she was the lead detective on a not-so-legal surveillance operation. Not that her cause wasn't a good one. Insurance fraud cost the general public millions of dollars in raised premiums. In all the cases where the Hennessy Group skirted Florida's strict wiretap laws, they did so only until they figured out a way to catch someone legally. And they did so only when they were relatively certain they were on the right side morally, working for the cheated-on spouses or the small-business owners trying to stop employee theft.

They had been fooled only a handful of times, thanks to Mick's inherent ability to see through crap. The man wasn't good with details, but he could smell a lie like a bloodhound smelled meat.

Hopefully, Cade didn't have the same talent, but she wondered. Really wondered.

"I'm an independent researcher."

"That's vague. Who do you work for?"

"At the moment, a detective agency. I do background checks, Internet sweeps, credit reports. Boring stuff. At the computer, which allows me to work from home. Can't complain there."

"Which agency?" he asked casually. "I know some private investigators in the area."

And why would a baseball scout know private investigators?

She shook her head and smiled casually, hoping she hadn't somehow blown her chance to make her job a nonissue between them. She hadn't lied to him about her last name, and while the Hennessy Group had no need to advertise and kept a very low profile except in the circles that mattered, someone who knew private investigators might know about the family business.

"I can't say," she said with a little whine she hoped came off as sweet rather than annoying. "I'm sorry. But I signed an agreement with this firm that keeps me from discussing any aspect of my work. You understand, don't you?"

None of that was a lie. In fact, all things considered, very little of what she'd said had been a mistruth. She did have a confidentiality clause in her contract. It was standard for all employees, including the owners.

She turned away and grabbed her purse from atop the refrigerator. Screw Stanley. She'd rely on the expensive equipment in her bedroom to capture any misstep he might make tonight. She promised herself she'd review the tapes first thing, before her meeting with Mick and Patrick. The theory that Stanley's mysterious frustration might cause him to reveal that his injuries were overstated or downright fake was a good one, but there was no guarantee. And his frustration would be nothing compared to hers if she cancelled on Cade and ended up watching Stanley channel surf all night.

"So we can't talk about work," Cade concluded. "That's cool. I'm sure we can come up with some secrets we are at liberty to share."

The prospect sent Jillian's heartbeat into overdrive. Oh, she had lots of secrets she'd share with Cade now that she had the chance. Things she'd never told anyone, not even Neal or Elisa. Her goals and dreams. Her fantasies.

Something about Cade invited trust, particularly since he seemed satisfied to know only what she told him, only what she wanted him to know. Even his manner of dress was casual and unpretentious—very much *take me as I am*. In khaki shorts, a well-worn polo shirt just a shade more olive than his jade-green eyes, thick-strapped leather sandals, hand-combed black hair and an easy grin, Cade evoked a laid-back image that perfectly fit his lifestyle.

And for tonight, her lifestyle, too.

Cade opened the door for her as he pulled his keys out of his pocket. She crossed the threshold, determined to take this opportunity for all it was—a chance to have a relationship with no expectations, no consequences. She reached back at the same time he did to grab the doorknob and their hands touched, but neither pulled away.

With a laugh, they wordlessly worked together. She turned the lock and he closed the door. She handed him her key and he turned the dead bolt.

Easy cooperation, as if they'd performed this ritual a thousand times.

And Jillian was way too Irish not to believe in signs.

7

THEY DINED ON FRIED clams and French fries at a ramshackle fish house on Old Tampa Bay. Peanut shells carpeted the creaky wood floor and the tables needed refinishing, but the beer was cold, the dessert decadent and the company intriguing. Cade couldn't remember the last time he'd had so much fun discussing a recipe for good tartar sauce or arguing over exactly what shade of yellow a real key lime pie should be.

Jillian Hennessy loved food, knew her beer like any good Irishwoman should and had the most impossibly expressive sapphire eyes. Her irises alternated between a mischievous, twinkling blue to a seductive, dark indigo, depending on their topic of conversation, which had ranged from the innocuous discussion of favorite restaurants to a teasing, unbelievably frank reminiscence of lovers past. Once he'd paid the check and driven them home, he couldn't wait to see what more he could learn about a woman who admitted without reservation that she'd saved her virginity for marriage only to have her husband throw her gift away.

Cade wouldn't be so stupid. When he and Jillian inevitably parted, he'd say goodbye with a hell of a lot more style. He was, after all, a master of farewells and, aside from the one bad experience, he didn't have one scorned woman among the many he'd left. Of course, he'd always been careful to choose strong, independent women who could take his leaving in stride. The fact that few of them knew his real name had helped, too.

Cade had even been dumped a time or two, which proved healthy for his ego. Cockiness was a natural by-product of his job. Every day that he survived, particularly when he was infiltrating a drug gang or setting up a sting to catch a notorious hit man, made him feel invincible.

But Jillian? She just made him feel alive. Simply, wonderfully, breathing in the air that was scented with her unique blend of sweet citrus and seductive woman.

She also distracted the hell out of him. He'd driven all the way up her driveway, even parked near her door, because he intended to stay a good long while, when he noticed two things in his rearview mirror that a focused cop would have seen immediately after they turned the corner onto their block.

First, Stanley's lights were on in his house, indicating that he was home way earlier than he had originally planned. And second, Jake Tanner's unmarked, untraceable car was parked at his house across the street.

"Oh, someone's at your house," Jillian said, looking over her shoulder as he killed the engine, once again bemoaning Jillian's ability to notice things he didn't necessarily want her to. "Were you expecting anyone?"

Cade chuckled and opened his door. He'd known Jake wanted him to call in. He'd been ignoring his beeper all night and hadn't even brought his cell phone with him. But whatever was up had to be damned important to have Jake hightailing it to Cade's house and risking his cover. "Definitely not expecting anyone, no. Go ahead and warm up the television. I'll be right back."

Jillian paused long enough for Cade to jog around and open her door. Her perfume, the fruity aphrodisiac that had haunted him all night, seemed to sizzle off her skin the minute she stepped into the warm night air. He'd be right back, all right. In a flash.

She swung one slim leg out, then the other, her skin pale, smooth and inviting in the pink light from her porch. Cade fisted his hands, resisting the urge to experience the contrast between her alabaster skin and his tan fingers, her soft suppleness and his rough hardness.

Hardness. Yeah. And not just on his hands.

"Who is it?" she asked, tilting her head toward Jake's car.

"An old friend who always seems to have a crisis at the worst possible time. I won't be ten minutes."

She shrugged and shook her head. "If you have to go, I'll take a rain check."

"There's not a cloud in the sky, Jillian. Let's save the rain checks for when they're really needed. Trust me. I'll be back in ten minutes."

She met his gaze, licking her lips in the way she did when she was thinking. At dinner, he'd been tempted to hit her with some deep, ponderous question just so he could watch her nibble away her frosty lipstick, leaving nothing but a deep, natural pink behind for him to taste.

"Ten minutes. At eleven, I'll come looking."

She turned on the heel of her strappy sandals, giving her skirt a flirty whirl. His mouth dried at the glimpse of pale pink panty she'd oh-so-subtly revealed. He dashed across the street and used the door beside the garage to enter the house. He knew where he'd find his partner—at the window that faced Stan's house, using his binoculars through the blinds.

"Now you're breaking and entering? Such an up-standing citizen to suddenly turn to a life of crime," Cade teased, tossing his keys on the table.

"Where the heck have you been? You turned your beeper off."

"No, I had it on silent mode," Cade answered. "You didn't plug in 911, so I figured it could wait."

Jake cursed. "911? Since when have we relied on that?"

"Since I got a life and a date for the first time in way too long." He checked his watch. "I also have exactly nine more minutes to hear what you have to say before I return to said date."

Jake grimaced, grumbling the objections he undoubt-edly had about Cade's favoring a night with a woman over the situation with Stanley. Only this morning, Jake had encouraged Cade to find himself a woman. He had too good a memory to contradict himself, but that usu-ally didn't stop him from grousing. Yet Jake returned to his spying, leaving Cade to wonder just when his partner learned to back down. And why. Did Jake "The Case Is My Life" Tanner suddenly understand that a woman could be more invigorating, more crucial than busting a perp? Cade filed that burning question for later. He was at eight minutes and counting.

"I followed Stan this afternoon, like you begged me to," Jake said, injecting just enough grouchiness into his tone to make Cade shake his head. "He went to the Blue Star and had what seemed to be a casual, long lunch with a very attractive brunette who arrived in a lacy librarian dress riding on a Harley."

They exchanged impressed glances. Stan the Man, indeed.

"Everything seemed hunky-dory," Jake continued,

"until he went to his therapy session. Whatever happened there wasn't good. He cursed all the way through the parking lot, beat up his steering wheel for a good five minutes before he tore off and nearly took out a stop sign on the way home."

Cade snickered, hiding his surprise. So far as he'd observed, Stanley Davison was cooler than the bottle of vodka Cade kept in his freezer. He'd never witnessed one indication of a temper or emotional weakness, which made Stan a hard con to catch. "You didn't pull him over for a ticket?"

Jake told Cade exactly where he could put his attempt at levity. "I'm wasn't going to blow my tail over a forty-dollar fine for reckless driving. The chief would just love us both if Stanley's lawyer slapped us with a harassment suit. Fact is, something pissed the man off. Royally. You need to find out what gives. Could blow this investigation wide open."

"Or he could have just found out his high tech stock took a hit. Come on, Jake. I'm not exactly his best pal, yet. You don't think it'd be suspicious that I just show up at his place at nine o'clock at night for no reason?"

"Come up with a reason. Can't you be out of milk or something?"

Cade checked his watch again. Seven minutes left.

"What's he been doing since you got here?" Cade asked.

"Watching television."

"Made any phone calls?"

"Nope."

"Logged on to his computer?"

"Nu-uh."

"Any more fits of temper?"

Jake shook his head.

"Well, whatever happened wasn't too traumatic or he'd be doing something other than watching *ER* reruns on Lifetime and drinking protein milkshakes."

Jake used his binoculars again, glanced at Cade with annoyance, checked one more time, then tossed the equipment on the counter and grabbed the beer he'd stolen from Cade's kitchen.

Cade's guess at Stanley's activities obviously proved accurate. It should. He'd been watching the guy for nearly two weeks. Stan Davison was a creature of habit and Cade Lawrence, the cop, ate creatures of habit for breakfast. He knew the man's routine without consulting his notes. Yeah, if he'd been home when Stanley returned all out of whack, he might have been able to work the situation to his advantage. But the opportunity was already missed. He couldn't fix that now.

Not when Jillian Hennessy gave him a deadline only five minutes away—a deadline that could arrive with her pink panties soon falling into his possession.

Jake plopped onto the couch beside Cade and chugged the rest of his brew. "I.A. cleared you in that shooting today. You're free to return to duty. Mendez says you can drop this case and they'll assign someone else."

As if.

"Tell her thanks, but no thanks. I'll see this through. I'm getting close."

"Not close enough, partner. This whole setup is making the brass real nervous. An unofficial investigation of a man who cost the department a couple million dollars...and no real evidence that Stanley wasn't injured just as he and his doctor proved he was."

Cade swallowed hard. He wasn't surprised. The plan

had been risky from the start. "The righteous indignation is starting to wear off, huh?"

Jake nodded.

Cade swore. He couldn't give up now. He hated losing. He hated being wrong and his instincts had told him from the beginning that Stanley Davison was not on the up and up.

And he'd most definitely hate not having at least another week or so to find out more about Jillian Hennessy, her video collection, her panty collection and any other groupings she enjoyed.

After the Davison investigation, Cade had already been selected to penetrate an Ecstasy operation running out of Ybor City, one the current detective team had just linked to a major pusher still doing time at Starke. Getting in was always the hardest part of his job and once Cade started, pursuing any relationship with Jillian would be impossible. Some of his assignments weren't as intense and, with a little planning, he could probably manage to see her from time to time, but he didn't know when.

And he had a feeling "from time to time" wouldn't be enough.

In this stakeout, he could keep the fantasy going. For her, for him, for both of them. The minute he stepped back into the real life of Cade Lawrence, undercover detective, he'd have to work that goodbye he'd become so proficient at.

When he stepped back, which wouldn't be tonight.

"Look, suggest to Lieutenant Mendez that they give me at least one more week, two tops. Whatever caused Stan to go off tonight isn't going to disappear just because he's back in control again. I'll find out what happened, but not tonight. I have..."

The doorbell rang before Cade could read his watch again. Jake jumped up, but Cade pushed him back down and handed him his empty beer. "You're such a rookie, sometimes," he grumbled, then casually strutted to the front door, knowing only one person could be on the other side.

"I had three minutes left," Cade said softly.

Jillian licked her lips and presented two videos.

"My clocks must be fast." Her innocent lilt was a poor cover for the anxious look in her eyes, a look Cade undoubtedly mirrored right back at her. "I know your friend is still here…"

This time, Jake did stand up and make his way to the door. "Hey, I'm just leaving. Thanks to my buddy here, I'm all set." He wiped his hand on his jeans, then pushed Cade out of the way so he could offer his big, beefy palm to Jillian.

"Jake Tanner," he said with that friendly, obliviously sexy tone that always posed Cade with some serious competition.

Jillian's mouth opened a little…with shock? With interest?

She slipped her hand in his softly, dashing his hopes that she'd offer him a quick, businesslike, you're-not-as-good-looking-as-your-partner shake. Cade bit his tongue as Jake squeezed Jillian's palm with his large grasp, holding on for a moment as he looked into her eyes. Cade then cleared his throat and bit back a curse. Jake's smooth moves were his own damn fault. He'd been teaching the preacher's son his best tricks since they'd first met.

"Nice to meet you, Mr. Tanner," Jillian's gaze flashed over to Cade, a wicked twinkle in her eye.

"Don't leave on my account. We were just going to watch a movie."

"No, I really need to go." Jake swallowed a chuckle, shaking his head at Cade's murderous expression. "Matter of life and death, I'm pretty sure."

Oh, yeah, Cade agreed silently.

"I'll call you tomorrow, pal."

The minute Jake crossed the threshold, Cade resolved to forget he'd even been there, only he was having a damned hard time with Jillian watching his partner as he walked all the way to his car.

She turned back to him and instead of the dreamy look Cade had both expected and dreaded, her eyes were wide with pure wonder and curiosity. "Lord, I wouldn't want to be trapped with him in a stuck elevator. He's huge! How tall is he?" She stepped by him and proceeded toward his television, unwrapping the cellophane off the videos she'd brought.

"I dunno. Six foot six...seven, maybe." How the hell did Cade know how tall Jake was? He sized up his partner by his ability to cover his ass, not by his shoe size. Or hand size. Or worse. Jillian didn't seem the type for such speculations, but he didn't know her that well, now did he?

"He played ball in college," he said. "Why? Do you have some fetish I should know about?"

Cade didn't realize that he had raised his voice or was standing with his arms akimbo like a petulant child until Jillian looked at him with a pout that managed to be both victorious and sympathetic at the same time.

"Well, if anyone should know about my fetishes, it should be you, shouldn't it? After our swim today..."

Her voice was soft and husky and when she turned to pop the videotape in his VCR, he thought he saw her hands tremble. She pressed the fast-forward button to cut through the advertisements, previews and opening credits, stopping when a man appeared on-screen that Cade recognized as David Duchovny, the actor who made his name on the *X-Files* television show. Jillian stepped over to his lamp and doused the light, plunging the room into relative darkness. The bluish glow from the TV cast a cool gleam over his living room. His secondhand couch and chipped coffee table suddenly looked exotic and plush. At least they did after Jillian slid onto the cushions, removed her sandals, and stretched out with her sassy pink-enameled toenails poised on the corner of the table.

She patted the cushion beside her. "I hope you don't mind me moving the party here without asking first. My air conditioner is acting up again and it's hotter than hell downstairs. I thought we'd be more comfortable here."

Jillian smiled genuinely, glad that she could at least tell the truth about something. Her air conditioner had petered out, apparently not long after Cade had met her for dinner. With the exception of her bedroom and the study, where the separate window units kept her videos, equipment and bed cool, the money pit her uncle had rented her for their stakeout was at least ninety degrees inside and climbing. She took all of five minutes to realize that this technical snafu gave her the perfect reason to go to Cade's house. Which would help her avoid her own bedroom when things got hotter and heavier than the air.

The move also gave her a chance to appease her nosiness about who had come calling at Cade's house without prior warning. Peeking in through her equipment wasn't the same as a genuine introduction, so she'd left her video cameras trained on Stanley, who was watching what seemed to be an *ER* marathon on the Lifetime cable network, grabbed her video and hurried over.

Of course, Cade didn't have a pool. Kind of blew the skinny-dipping scenario. Maybe. Just imagining them sneaking buck naked across their very suburban, very traditional street to leap into her pool inspired a thrill all its own.

But Jillian had had enough imagining and fantasizing about Cade. Not only did she now have the reality of kissing him to draw upon, she had also had the last few hours to talk to him, laugh with him, admit things to him she wouldn't have believed had spilled from her own lips had she not been there to hear the secrets herself and watch his reaction. If Cade had been shocked by anything she said—particularly the confession that she'd saved her virginity for marriage only to have her husband cheat on her every chance he got—he didn't let on. She's known from the moment she saw him on her video screens that Cade Lawrence was in total and complete control of himself physically. Now she knew he could manipulate his emotions as well. He didn't flinch either at the rawness of her confession or at the cruelty of her husband's actions.

But he had let her know that he considered Neal's behavior disgusting. Not through words, but through the look in his jade eyes, the gentle squeeze he gave her hand. The way he didn't just brush her off with a pat, "Men are pigs," that he wouldn't really mean.

Cade Lawrence was definitely one of the good guys.

Which is why she was now here, no longer the least bit apprehensive about seeing this seduction through.

Cade joined her on the couch, sitting near enough

so that his leg brushed hers. They watched in silence while the confessional story unfolded, the tale of a woman who swam naked while waiting for her fantasy lover to appear. Jillian cast a sidelong glance at Cade, wondering why she was watching a movie when she had her own fantasy lover right beside her.

"Mind if I grab us something to drink?" she asked when the fantasy man—a swimmer—finally approached the heroine.

"Let me. Where's the remote?"

While he tossed pillows, she pretended to wander until she found the kitchen. "You watch. I'll be right back."

Moonlight spilled through his curtainless windows, tingeing the stark white cabinets and countertops with a sensual cobalt hue. Glancing over her shoulder to make sure he hadn't followed, she marched straight over to the cabinet where she knew he kept his glasses. She pressed a tumbler against the dispenser in the door, filling it only a quarter full before she took a long sip, wandering back to the doorway as she drank.

He was leaning forward, watching, his shoulders slightly tense.

She wondered what Cade thought about the film and, this time, watching him wasn't going to give that secret away. The story line wasn't anything new or earth-shattering, but with Cade now in her life, it did hit a little too close to home.

First, the woman meets her fantasy lover by chance. Then, she follows him, watches him make love to other women, spurring her own erotic dreams. Then, she attempts to seduce him, but he says no, revealing that to all the other women in his life, he was not a real person, but just a dream lover. Temporary. Unreal. The women he seduced couldn't have cared less about his interests or needs. They only wanted him for sex.

Like Jillian had initially wanted Cade?

This is what she got for being so frickin' clever. *Choose a movie about swimming naked, Jillian. See if Cade gets the joke.* Great idea.

She finished her water and returned to the refrigerator to fill her glass again, not in the least perplexed about why she was suddenly feeling very hot. Blushing did that to her. She now knew that she didn't want Cade for just sex anymore. In one evening, he'd crept under her skin. He was funny, patient and intelligent. He enjoyed many of the same things she did—mystery novels, seafood and cold beer, frank discussions about chancy topics. He fascinated her, intrigued her, and she couldn't help wanting what she knew she couldn't have—limitless time to share with him and get to know him, to make him a friend and a lover.

But with her job demanding her attention twenty-four/seven, she knew she could only ask for tonight.

Cade approached from behind her so silently, she jumped when he touched her shoulder, splashing water down the front of her dress. She scrambled to slide the glass onto the counter, turning with her arms out, her body rippling with goose bumps from the sudden chill of cold.

"Sorry!" He grabbed a towel from the dish drainer.

She shook her head and her hands at the same time. "That's what I get for lurking around in the dark."

He hesitated. "Before I help, I have to know one thing."

Jillian snatched the towel away and dabbed at her chest, now completely doused. She hadn't worn a bra, so her nipples instantly peaked from the frigid cold, hardening further when she saw the hungry look in Cade's eyes.

"No, there was no secret message in that movie, except for the swimming naked part. I was trying to be funny. Remember, we talked about skinny-dipping earlier?"

"Have we ruled that out?"

His humor lightened the moment, but Jillian's hands still shook.

"I'm already partly there, now aren't I? I'm soaked! God, I'm so clumsy sometimes."

She impotently swiped at her dress, glancing up quickly to gauge Cade's reaction and hoping like hell he wasn't staring at her, thinking, *Isn't it cute that you're a klutz.* But the minute she locked with his gaze, she stopped.

His eyes were darker than the night sky; his expression shadowed. The humor that had lit his eyes only a split second ago had fled, leaving nothing tangible for her to recognize beyond a clear and intense desire. The prolonged silence made her squirm and she couldn't stop herself from dashing the moment, whatever it was, to pieces.

"What?" Her skin prickled. Her heart raced. What did he see that held him so enthralled?

"I don't know who you are," he answered. "I don't know what you like, beyond food and drink."

She continued blotting her dress with the towel, realizing he had indeed taken the message in the film to heart, more than she wanted and definitely more than she planned.

"Maybe that's a good thing, Cade. You have to admit, there's something incredibly erotic about the unknown."

He stole the towel and she didn't protest. He wrapped the material around his hand to form a fluffy glove and he touched the cloth to her skin. He stepped closer. Instinctively, she retreated until her backside pressed against the cool metal of the refrigerator.

In the other room, the movie played on, a jumble of whispered words and moody music that became no more than background noise. The hum of the refrigerator, the squeak of a dozen crickets outside barely registered over the sound of his heavy breathing. Or was it hers?

"I don't find the unknown erotic unless there's a chance of discovery." He smoothed the cloth across her shoulders, displacing one thin strap, then continuing down her shoulder.

She swallowed, dizzy from the sensory overload of his spiced cologne, his hot breath, her wet dress and the pressure of the towel against her skin.

Back to her neck. Down the front of her dress. All the way down. Between her breasts. Over her rib cage. To her navel. Below?

Please.

The appeal caught in her throat just as he lifted the towel and dried her other arm.

"I say we make a deal," he said.

"What kind of deal?"

He lifted her right hand and massaged her fingers dry.

"A mutually satisfactory one. Tell me what you want, Jillian."

"And you'll give it to me? Just like that?"

"If I can, yes."

"Why?"

His dark eyes locked with hers even as he softly dried the moisture on her neck.

"Because I want you. I want to know you. More than I've wanted anyone or anything in a very long time."

"Maybe it was just the movie that turned you on."

With a slow grin, he flicked the towel over her nipple. The sensation was rough and soft at the same time. Quick, but powerful. Efficient and effective in flaming a fire she'd barely kept contained since watching him the night before.

"Maybe the movie just gave me some ideas." He leaned forward to whisper into her ear with his deep, throaty voice. "And maybe that's what you intended."

"I told you. I didn't intend anything."

He licked his lips as he manipulated the towel to the other side, this time lingering as he rubbed the cloth over her breast in long, hard strokes that sparked a jolt of awareness so powerful, she pressed back against the refrigerator.

"Don't lie, Jillian. Not about this. Not about what you want from me. Lie about your job, lie about your past, if you have to. But not about this."

Oh, God! What did he know? Or was it what he didn't know, what she'd refused to tell him, that spurred this directive?

It didn't matter. She'd already decided she could be completely and brutally honest about how she wanted him—and about how she wanted him to want her back. She nodded, agreeing to his request for truth, her lips losing moisture as she struggled with the soft, near-whimpering pants his ministrations evoked.

"What *is* this?" she asked, certain they had to agree

on any expectations before they went further. And they would. Tonight.

"A brief, intense affair," he answered. "An interlude with a woman who, until tonight, was slightly more than a stranger. But I'm learning more about you every moment. Like now. Your breasts are very sensitive, aren't they?"

He lowered the other strap and Jillian's breath caught. The only movement in her body was the telltale trickle of moisture between her thighs. With a quick tug, he pulled her dress down to her waist. Then down further, revealing her completely, except for the pale pink panties that covered very, very little.

This was crazy. Unbelievable. Forbidden.

"Yes."

He tossed the towel aside and whipped off his shirt. His muscles shimmered in the soft moonglow. His skin radiated with sun-kissed fire. But she already knew that. He was hard and cut from raw, physical exertion. But she knew that, too. She'd seen him naked on her monitors and half-dressed in person this afternoon.

What she didn't know—what she couldn't learn from watching—was what kind of lover he would be. But her instincts told her she would soon find out.

8

CADE FROZE as Jillian removed a clip and set her red hair free. The auburn mane framed her features like a ring of fire, highlighting the blush of her pale skin and the sapphire depths of her eyes.

God, she was beautiful. And brave. She tossed the clip on the floor and waited, her back arched against the refrigerator in blatant offering. If she possessed any degree of modesty, a quality Cade always believed was incredibly overrated, she displayed none of it now. She kicked her dress away, drawing his attention again to her pretty pink toenails.

Slowly, he allowed his gaze to drink her in, bottom to top. In a swimsuit, she'd been remarkable. Nude, she was breathtaking. Slim legs. Slightly flared hips. Trim waist. Generous breasts. Soft shoulders. Lavish lips. And soulful indigo eyes that searched his with impatience. Desire.

Before he tended the needs flashing in her eyes and pebbling her nipples into delicious, pink points, he wanted to be as exposed to her as she was to him. He tore off his jeans and boxers, revealing his erection, long and hard, which said more about his own needs than he could ever form into words.

In response, she bit her bottom lip.

"You must swim a lot of laps, Jillian."

She smiled, smoothing her hand across her flat belly. "Is that a compliment?"

Cade chuckled. "Not a very good one if you have to ask. But you know," he reached out and touched her shoulder blade, one finger to the cleft between bone and muscle, "swimming doesn't shape breasts like these. That's just good genes."

Her throat bobbed with her deep swallow, her voice slightly unsteady. "You're a tit man, then?"

He'd started to draw his finger downward, but stopped when the raw word rolled off her tongue. His eyebrows shot up, but she didn't seem ashamed when he showed his surprise.

"Tits are what you see at strip clubs," he clarified. "It's a word a guy uses when he's talking about some nameless chick he's picked up in a bar for a quick lay."

His rough tone broke her bravado. She pressed her lips together tightly.

"You don't want that, do you, Jillian? Because I don't. No promises is cool. No commitments, fine with me. But when I suckle your nipples so deeply that you'll come from just a touch..." He smoothed his finger downward to make his point, tracing her areola with his blunt nail, then pressing further to her navel, then below, until he touched the center of her need through the filmy material of her panties, "...it's because we're making love."

She gasped. "Show me."

He should have kissed her first, learned her mouth again, proceeded slowly...but the fire of expectation in her eyes, the pure need for him to live up to his promise, here and now, spurred him to cup her breasts, taking one instantly into his mouth while he readied the other with his calloused thumb. He sucked her long, hard, nipping until she whimpered, then laving the pain away with his tongue until she cooed. She thrust hungry hands into his hair, guiding him to her other breast, demanding what she wanted.

But she didn't have to make demands. Cade intended to give her all she could take—and more.

He slipped her hands away, ignoring the way he instantly missed her touch. There'd be time for that later. Right now, he intended to prove that he could indeed make her come without using more than his hands and mouth.

He grasped her wrists and wrapped the fingers of her left hand around the handle to the freezer. "Hold on."

Her eyes lit with wicked delight. "What shall I do with this one?" She wiggled her fingers then glanced down at his erection.

If she touched him, he could forget about focusing only on her orgasm. With no second handhold to ensure his control, he grabbed the glass she'd spilled earlier, still half filled with ice-cold water. "Think you can hold this without spilling a drop?"

She took the cup and skewered him with more challenge than a woman had a right to serve. "I have a much better idea. Since we aren't going to make it to my pool…"

Jillian tipped the glass over her shoulder, pouring the water down her body and splashing him so he instinctively jumped back. Ice cubes clattered on the floor, shattering around her feet. She yelped and laughed when the iciness met her flesh.

But fascinated as Cade was by the way the droplets sluiced down in a cold rush, glistening in the silver light from the moon, saturating her panties until they were translucent, his mouth dried like a desert lake.

"You're a dangerous woman."

She didn't respond with more than a sigh when he lapped the moisture from her shoulders, taking in the essence of her damp skin. Salty. Sweet. Fragrant. Smooth. Cold and hot—yet neither cold nor hot enough to bring her to the height only he could help her reach.

He fished around on the floor until he found an ice cube, then stood and pressed it to one nipple, swallowing her shocked gasp with a long, languid kiss. She shivered and struggled ever so slightly, but not enough to pull away, as if torn between the pain and pleasure.

"So cold." Her murmur, accompanied by a chatter, vibrated against his lips.

"How cold?"

He held the cube steady and nibbled a light path down her neck.

"Freezing."

"And?"

"It burns a little...but...wow."

"You want wow?"

Her tiny nod directed his mouth down. He removed the cube, and flicked the iced nipple with a rigid tongue.

Jillian told him exactly how thrilling the sensation was, how wet she was, how much she wanted him to swallow her whole. Somewhere in the ether of his pleasured haze, he realized he'd never made love to a woman so vocal about how he pleased her. Her soft whispers and throaty confessions complicated his plan to make love to her with a careful design. He wanted to touch her everywhere all at once, a feat impossible even for him.

But he knew he could simulate the sensation.

He dropped his kisses lower, kneeling and drawing her panties down even as he laved her auburn curls with cool kisses. He glanced up to see her grasp the top of the refrigerator for balance, her eyes closed, her mouth parted, her nipples hard and red from his loving.

With his thumbs, he parted her flesh. Her shivers turned to a gentle quake, his darting tongue spurring a full eruption. He drank her, touched her, loved her until she screamed his name.

And then he suckled her a little more, easing her down from that natural high, loving the taste of her, mourning that very soon he'd have to stop. When he sensed she could take no more, he lifted her in his arms. She curled like a contented cat against his chest and, as he took the stairs two at a time, he wondered how he could feel so satisfied when he was still hard as a rock.

JILLIAN ALLOWED HER eyes to remain closed while Cade dried her with a towel from his bathroom and then lay her beneath his bed's thick comforter. She didn't have to look around, she mused. She knew what his bedroom looked like. It was oh so much more delicious to focus on the sounds and sensations all around her. Inside her. Her slowing heartbeat. Her calming breaths. The echo of her uninhibited orgasm.

She heard the drawer open, then close. The rip of foil. The stretch of latex.

Cade Lawrence was obviously one prepared man. Jillian couldn't have chosen a better lover, though she wondered about fate's hand in all this. Mick's mistake on the surveillance order. Elisa's lemonade basket. The unreliable air conditioner. She had never considered herself so lucky until this very moment.

His cologne tickled her nostrils as he bent over her. "Are you awake?"

Jillian fluttered her eyes open. The room was dark except for light from the moon. A full moon. How appropriate. She felt just as complete, just as luminescent. And if she so desired, she could blame the cosmos for her uncharacteristic behavior.

But she'd rather blame Cade for being sexier than any man had a right to be.

"I'm awake," she murmured. "Sated, but awake."

"I hope you're not completely sated. The night is young."

Jillian laughed, rolled over and grasped his hand. "I couldn't possibly be completely sated until I feel you inside me." She tugged him onto the bed and as much as she wanted to simply snuggle against him and let the warmth of his body chase away the last of the chill from the water and ice, she knew that the night couldn't last forever. She'd just been given the glorious gift of sexual indulgence. She meant to return the favor.

Even as she straddled Cade, his hard length teasing her, Jillian pushed away the thought that she'd known this man for what? A day? Time didn't matter, except that each moment that slipped away was a loss of potential pleasure. With Cade, she feared nothing and enjoyed the bold attitude he inspired—bold enough to cover his erection with her slick feminine folds, leaning down to kiss him as she rocked her hips against his.

He shifted to slip inside her, holding back when her natural tightness caused resistance.

"I don't want to hurt you," he said.

She curled her body to his, wanting him inside her

with a fierceness that belied her lazy laugh. She was wet, slick still from the water, his tongue, her need. She hadn't realized, hadn't considered, that her body would resist him when she so desperately wanted him deep inside.

"You couldn't possibly hurt me. It's just been a long time."

The tautness eased as he slowly, carefully adjusted their bodies. She moaned at the sensation, her pleasure echoed in his rumbling, appreciative groan.

"For both of us," he said.

She sat up, surprised at first by his admission and then by the jolt of electricity of him so rigid and warm within her.

"Oh, wow."

She moved, testing her theory that this position was the most erotic she'd ever experienced.

Oh, yeah.

"Haven't you ever been on top before?" he asked.

She grabbed his waist and moved again, luxuriating in the thick feel of Cade beneath her, inside her, his strong hands grasping her hips, his eyes dark and entirely focused on her.

"I don't remember," she said. With Cade, the past blurred. She focused solely on the here and now—new experiences and anticipation of future pleasures. She wanted only to learn about him. About herself. About the freedom of making love without foolish notions of being in love.

She could be selfish if she wanted, taking what she needed to reach an orgasm yet again. Cade didn't give her the chance, giving before she could take. He locked taut fingers onto her hips and pumped up into her, deceptively languorous and lazy. He sparked an instantaneous fire deep inside which spread over her body like flames on dry tinder. Color exploded behind her eyes—reds and oranges and purples so rich, she imagined she was wrapped in velvet.

But the silken smoothness was Cade's hands—on her hips, across her belly, on her breasts again, now so sensitized to his touch, the madness threatened to erupt again. So soon. She shook her head, trying to fight the fireworks, but when he slid his hand between them and touched her center, Cade destroyed her retreat.

Jillian shouted, screamed, rocked. Cade sat up, captured her mouth and pulled her down as he climaxed, as she felt him pulse inside her. Dizzy, she surrendered completely, allowing him to roll her over, cradle her, their bodies still joined as their bliss slowly receded.

So this is sex with a stranger? She shook her head and bit her lip, knowing she shouldn't consider Cade a stranger anymore. She wondered if he really ever was. Something about him drew her, and that connection between them threatened Jillian with a truth she didn't want to face. About fate and destiny and once-in-a-lifetimes. Not here. Not tonight.

"You're an incredible lover, Cade Lawrence," she said, kissing the tip of his nose to offset the pride that had immediately lit his eyes.

"Takes two to tango, Jillian. You're the most uninhibited woman I've ever met."

"And you've probably met a lot of women." She broke their physical connection, but snuggled around with her back to his chest, enjoying the feel of him, even lax, pressed against her.

"I don't remember." He echoed her earlier claim without a hint of humor, burying his nose in her hair and inhaling.

Jillian allowed the surge of power to fill her. Cade still wanted her. Even now that he'd had her, he relished the smell of her, languished in the feel of her skin as he stroked her arms. He made no move to slide away, shifting the covers to tuck them in as if he meant for her to stay all night.

Memories flashed of her love life with Neal. She'd always carried the illusion that even if she and her ex-husband hadn't shared fidelity, they'd shared a healthy physical relationship.

But Cade had effectively washed all her illusions away. What she'd shared with her husband had been unhealthy because it had been one-sided. She'd done all the giving. All the loving.

With Cade, she'd done the taking, but she had a strong feeling that he wouldn't have had it any other way.

She closed her eyes and listened to the sounds of the night. The drone of the air conditioner. The creak of the old house settling. The steady hum of Cade's breathing, slower, steadier. Was he asleep?

"Cade?"

"Hmm?"

"I'll go home now."

"Why?"

"It's late. You're tired."

"It's not that late and I'll rest." He tightened his hold on her, nuzzled closer. "Don't make me wrestle you down, woman. I'll win, you know."

She laughed at his sleepy, gruff declaration, then surrendered, allowing her own exhaustion to ease her muscles and close her eyes. His warmth surrounded her. His scent, spicy and familiar, cloaked her like a cloud of contentment. She yawned. No wonder Neal rarely stayed in bed with her after they made love. Intimacy hadn't been his thing, and by default, had never been hers, either.

But Jillian didn't regret her loss any longer, nor did she think Cade had any idea of what he'd shared with her beyond some pretty remarkable sex. And that was okay. It would have to be. Intimate strangers existed in midnight fantasies and erotic movies, and sooner rather than later, this fantasy would have to end.

AROUND 4:00 A.M., Jillian finally slipped downstairs, retrieved her dress and scurried home. They'd made love once more after a catnap and Jillian had completely lost all track of time, lost in the tenderness of Cade's touch and the honesty of how he'd searched to find what delighted her and then slowly, skillfully, mastered the technique. She'd managed to coax a few of his own preferences from him, and as she dashed across the street and slipped into her darkened kitchen, she blushed at how willing she'd been to try anything to hear the guttural, animal growl he made when he came.

His honesty and openness finally drove her out of his arms after he'd fallen asleep a second time. He had no idea what a liar she was. What a fake. In his bed, after midnight, she could be the real and true Jillian Hennessy, a woman she was only starting to recognize. But in the morning, she'd have to revert to misrepresenting why she'd moved to the neighborhood, what she did for a living and what she wanted from her future. It didn't matter that he'd given her permission to lie about those insignificant things, she knew better. And while she would find a way to justify her dishonesty—just as she always did, she thought with chagrin—eventually, she'd have to reveal her secrets.

But for now, she had to complete her surveillance work. She had an important meeting to attend and decisions to make about the life she'd never intended to include a man in again, much less a man as charismatic and wonderful as Cade Lawrence.

Exhausted and refusing to allow her confusion to waylay much-needed sleep, Jillian tripped up the stairs, shivering. The air conditioner had kicked back on with a vengeance. She waited until she was in the climate-controlled safety of her bedroom to strip off her damp dress and pull on her FBI T-shirt. She was under the covers when she noticed she hadn't turned off the monitor showing the view of Stanley's living room, the scene barely visible in the early morning darkness.

With a groan, she stumbled over, yawned, stretched and tapped in the exit code. The program, before accepting the end command, split the screen four ways, allowing a view into each of Stanley's main rooms, then popped a rectangular window across the center that asked for a final verification before ending the surveillance.

That's when Jillian noticed that Stanley Davison was still awake.

At 4:00 a.m.?

Stanley, who normally went to bed just after the late shows and didn't drag his body out of bed until just before lunch?

She remembered Patrick's warning about something bothering Stanley, something that happened either during or immediately after his therapy. Though the lights were off in his bedroom, he was stiffly pacing, his hands hooked behind his neck.

Jillian sat down, cancelled the exit mode and expanded the picture of Stanley's bedroom to fill her screen. She upped the volume until she could hear his muttering, but still was unable to make out the words or read his mumbling lips.

She wondered if he knew he was under surveillance. No, she figured if he was onto them, he would have gotten out of the house. She watched him walk back and forth several times before she realized he wasn't limping.

In fact, for two angry passes, he was practically stomping. Like a healthy man...one who hadn't just received a multimillion dollar settlement for permanent, debilitating damage to his spine and neck.

Jillian pulled out his medical records and the transcripts from the trial, certain she had forgotten something. She read over the testimony from Stan's doctor, the head of his therapy clinic. He claimed the soft tissue damage *might* heal with therapy, but such a prognosis was as impossible to guarantee as the diagnosis was to prove. But the doctor, whom Jillian found to have a clean file with the American Medical Association, seemed genuinely convinced.

She double-checked the record button on the VCR, but knew a midnight pacing session wasn't nearly enough evidence to prove anything to anyone. She needed more.

Jillian's eyes felt itchy and dry and her yawns came so frequently, she stopped bothering to cover her mouth. God, she was tired. And Stanley kept pacing. The rage in his step slowly gave way to his usual limping gait. Back and forth he went, like the swinging coin of a hypnotist. Jillian couldn't stand it.

Watching Stanley was nowhere near as thrilling as watching Cade.

She wondered if he'd realized yet that she'd left. If he'd rolled over or gone searching for her. Or if he still slept so soundly, she'd been able to escape without him stirring. Did he still have that sweet little smile on his lips, the one that had almost…almost…tempted her to kiss him before she left, even if it would wake him up and lead to another round of glorious sex?

Even as she cursed her weakness, she typed in the "Watch Me" code and brought Cade's bedroom into view.

He was gone.

Looking for her?

She did a quick sweep, but the house seemed empty. She returned to the bedroom, where she noticed the flutter of a sheer curtain from a corner just outside her view.

She hadn't noticed sheers when she was in his room. No big surprise, there. She'd had other things on her mind than his decor. But she did know that his house had a balcony just above the porch on the sides and back, a feature she'd coveted when she first laid eyes on the house, before she began coveting her neighbor's body instead.

But she had no view of the balcony from her computer, so she grabbed her binoculars and decided to take a look the old-fashioned way.

The minute she opened the door to the hall, a blast of cold air reminded her that the monstrosity that sometimes cooled her house had kicked into polar mode, so she grabbed a robe from the back of her door and shot down the stairs. With all the lights out, she found the unobtrusive opening she'd purposefully bent in the blinds so she'd have a permanent peeking point and scoured the balcony for any sign of Cade.

She found him immediately, setting up his telescope on the south balcony. She glanced at her hall clock. Four-fifteen! She didn't know anything about stargazing, but guessed this to be as good a time as any if he couldn't sleep.

Of course, once the dawn started in less than an hour, even a novice like her knew that nothing would be visible. Maybe astronomy was what he did when he needed to think. Or when he was angry and needed to cool down. Or when he was horny and his lover of the moment slipped away with not so much as a goodbye. Which could also be why he was angry or why he needed to think.

The circular motion of her thoughts nearly made her dizzy until she watched a few moments longer.

Cade's telescope wasn't pointed at the sky.

She scooted across the back of her couch where she'd perched and looked again from a second angle.

Son of a bitch.

Cade was watching Stanley.

Oh, yeah, well, his telescope might *look* as if it were pointed upward at the night sky with fancy gadgetry sticking out from all angles, but Jillian recognized the model as one Ted and her uncle had bought at the trade show. She looked for and found the distinct reflector on the tripod, certain she wasn't wrong. Cade's "telescope" was actually a state-of-the-art spying device...and he was using it to spy on Stanley!

The fact that she was also spying on Stanley didn't lessen her ire one little bit. Okay, maybe a little. Cade was obviously keeping something from her, something along the very same lines as the truth she'd been keeping from him.

She pouted a few minutes, then, satisfied that Cade wouldn't see anything she hadn't already seen with her equipment upstairs, she left. He was probably still setting up the scope and didn't even catch Stanley's brief lapse in limping. She wandered into the kitchen and opened the refrigerator more out of habit than hunger, until she remembered exactly what she'd done the last time she'd been standing so close to this particular appliance.

She slammed the door, grabbed the phone and dashed upstairs. After stripping off her robe, establishing a link to the office main computer and turning off all monitors except the one of Stanley, she'd punched in Elisa's number, pacing all the while.

"—lo?"

"Lise? It's Jillian."

"What's wrong?"

"More than you want to hear about at four-thirty in the morning. Can you pick me up on your way to the office?"

"Can I be late?"

Jillian chuckled, tucking the handset more tightly between her shoulder and chin while she accessed her favorite program for digging up hard-to-find information. She typed in the name "Cade Lawrence."

"Thirty minutes, tops. And call Cynthia and let her know. I don't want to get you in trouble with your boss."

"But you're *her* boss." Elisa's whine sounded much less grating with a yawn attached to it.

"Not the point. Leave her a voice mail and I'll see you at eight-thirty."

She cursed when her first search ended with a glowing blue box insisting, "No Cade Lawrence listed."

"What are you doing up at this hour?" Elisa asked.

"Working."

"I can hear that. What do you type? Two hundred words a minute?"

At the moment, speed didn't matter. Jillian was more interested in accuracy. She directed the computer to establish variations on the name Cade Lawrence and typed in his description. Black hair, green eyes, six feet three inches tall. She also entered the license plate number to his current model Ford truck, which she really hadn't intended to memorize when they went on their date tonight, but it was a hard habit to break. Thankfully, the computer didn't require anything but the facts and a few minutes to process her request.

"Did you get a lead in the case or something?" Elisa asked, yawning one more time, enough to make Jillian incredibly regretful that she'd allowed her sudden burst of angry energy to impose on her friend. She'd buy her a really expensive breakfast tomorrow. Something with steak.

"There was a lead all right, but not in my case. You know what? Tell Cynthia you won't be in until nine-thirty tomorrow and that you'll be with me. And I'm sorry I woke you up. I'll make it up to you."

"Oh, I know you will. I want my pay in details, sister. I know a scorned woman when I hear one."

She wasn't exactly scorned, Jillian decided as she hung up the phone, but she wasn't angry so much either. Not after she had a minute or two to consider all the possibilities concerning why Cade was watching the same man she was watching.

She knew he didn't work for the insurance agency.

They insisted they'd paid the claim and closed the case and Jillian had every reason to believe them. He could work for a rival agency working a similar angle to hers.

But at one time, Stanley had been suspected of running quite a few scams that left a good number of bad people not so happy. Maybe Cade was a mobster. Or a reporter. Or a cop.

A dozen more scenarios played out in her mind, until the computer flashed with a gold box this time. Bingo.

Kincaid Lawrence.
    Born: December 24, 1966, Okinawa Military Base, Japan.
    Parents: James Lawrence, U.S. Army, Colonel, ret. and Sherry Lawrence, deceased.

And that was it.

No school information, no car information, no social security number, no credit report.

So this wasn't going to be easy.

Jillian backed out of the program, wondering why she was more intrigued and curious than angry and betrayed. Probably because Cade hadn't made any promises. Except for the baseball scout thing, a clever lie that could only prove true if Stanley had the potential to hurl for the World Champion Yankees, Cade hadn't told her anything that could be checked out or contradicted. He'd lied to *Stan* about his mother still being alive, but he'd never said a word about his parents to her.

Everything else he'd told her, shown her, had been too personal to be logged in someone's database. His preference for the color red. His iced vodka. The perfect angle he could achieve while inside her to make her come while barely moving.

Whoever he was, he was good...and probably had some agency to wipe out any clues to his identity, since she was relatively certain Cade Lawrence was his real name. Jillian shivered, a thrill shimmying over her skin not unlike the physical stimulation she'd experienced just a few hours ago at Cade's skillful hand. Jillian couldn't deny the allure of a good mystery any more than she could deny the allure she'd already experienced with the mysterious man himself.

There'd be only one real way to find out about Cade Lawrence, she decided as she climbed back beneath the covers and set her alarm clock before dousing the light.

She'd ask.

She grinned and snuggled into the pillows, imagining several interesting ways to pose her question.

9

THE SOUND OF INSISTENT knocking woke Cade from deep, dream-filled sleep. Sluggish and cranky, he grabbed a pillow and stuffed it over his head, hoping whoever it was would go away.

Unless it was Jillian, whose unwelcome disappearance in the middle of the night had been the main cause for his lack of rest. Her escape with no explanation or parting kiss had roused him the minute he'd reached across the mattress and found her gone. Her scent had still lingered on his pillows and he'd dashed down the stairs hoping to find her in the kitchen or in front of the television they'd forgotten to turn off. Instead, he'd watched from his window as she disappeared across the street. He'd considered going after her, and would have if he hadn't returned to the living room to retrieve her forgotten videos and noticed that Stanley was awake next door.

Reasoning that Jillian wouldn't have left if she didn't need some space, and that he'd already missed one opportunity with Stan because of his personal pursuits, Cade figured he should at least try to figure out why Stan was up at 4:00 a.m. when he was usually sound asleep. Stan didn't break his routine often, so whatever the mysterious event was that had occurred this afternoon, it must have been pretty damned significant.

So Cade chose to be a cop for a few hours. That

he'd even considered a choice between duty and a lover left him reeling. He was either showing signs of overwork or was seriously under the spell of his beautiful neighbor across the street.

Cade couldn't deny that he'd learned more about Jillian than just what pleasured her body. She had a sweet sense of humor, was a wicked tease and seemed to revel in the attention he paid her. She was bright, uninhibited and unafraid—the exact type of woman he'd want to have a relationship with if he'd ever make room in his life.

The best he'd done so far was brief flings in between cases and, of course, his one disastrous liaison with Marisel while on the job. That stunning failure convinced him that so long as he remained on undercover assignments, real relationships would have to wait. But for how long? Cade was no expert, but he was fairly certain that women as alluring and clever as Jillian didn't come along every day. Sooner or later, he was going to have to make a change, take a chance.

But he didn't have to decide this morning. The knocking on the door hadn't stopped, so Cade gave up trying to ignore the sound and trudged down the stairs. Before Jillian, no woman could have sneaked out of his bed unnoticed unless he'd only been pretending to sleep. Living undercover, watching his back so he didn't end up with a bullet in it, required him to train his body to wake at the slightest sound, the least movement. He doubted Jillian's clandestine escape had anything to do with superior skill on her part. He'd let down his guard for the first time in years. And he wasn't sure whether or not that bothered him.

He yawned before opening the door, surprised and disappointed to see Stanley on his porch rather than

Jillian. Even if Stan's appearance could be the break he'd been waiting for, Cade decided not to feel guilty about wishing Stan was Jillian coming to explain her disappearance—or better still, wanting to make up for sneaking off.

"Stan. Hey, bud."

"Did I wake you? I'm sorry. You're usually an early riser." Stan shoved his hands into the pockets of his khaki slacks. He was dressed up, relatively speaking, since Stan usually wore jeans and a polo shirt everywhere he went. Today, he was wearing a button-down—designer, right down to the embroidered polo player. No tie, but snazzy nonetheless.

Cade stepped back and motioned for Stan to come inside. He knew his neighbor also hadn't gotten more than the three hours sleep Cad had logged since neither of them had gone to bed until dawn. After accepting that Jillian's departure had possibly meant no more than that she wanted to sleep in her own bed, Cade had pulled his trick telescope out of the corner of his bedroom, set it on his balcony and watched Stan until the sun lit the sky.

He'd made no secret of his astronomy hobby with his neighbor, so if Stan noticed Cade's late-night activity, he'd have no reason to be suspicious. Cade had specifically ordered a model that had two mirrors inside, allowing a watcher to appear to be looking up when he was really watching sideways or behind.

"Were you up late?" Stan asked.

"Bad case of insomnia, man. Tossed and turned," Cade explained, throwing in a yawn that wasn't entirely fake. "Want some coffee? Gotta love these automatic machines."

Stan nodded and entered, glancing around the house

as if this was the first time he'd been inside, which it was, now that Cade thought about it. They walked silently to the kitchen, where Cade pulled down two mugs, filled them, then brought out the sugar bowl and a carton of cream, even though he knew that Stanley drank his black.

"What's got you up so early?" Cade asked.

"Wanted to ask a favor. I've got a delivery coming today. I scheduled for this morning since I'm usually home until lunch, but something came up. I was wondering if you could take the delivery for me?"

Cade took a long sip of coffee. Perfect. A chance to ingratiate himself and peek into his delivery at the same time. "Sure, man. Want me to just keep an eye out?"

"No, I called them. It's a local store, and all I have to do is call them back with your address. I'll be home late this afternoon, so I'll drop by then and pick it up. It's medical equipment, kind of expensive. I didn't want it just sitting around on the porch."

"Medical? You okay?"

Stan shrugged, and his eyes, even hidden behind the horn-rimmed glasses he only wore when his contacts were bothering him, looked pink and itchy. Lack of sleep? Tears? A combination of both?

"Same old, same old," Stan said, following his claim with a long sip of coffee. "I told you about my accident, right?"

Cade shook his head. They'd never discussed his accident in detail, though Stan had mentioned his injury in passing just after he'd moved in when Cade had asked Stan to help him with some boxes. "Just that you got hurt and couldn't work."

Stan nodded and Cade noted the soulful look in

Stan's eyes. He was considering sharing more. *Considering*.

"You're all right, now, though, aren't you?" Cade injected his question with as much concern as he figured Stan would buy. The man was notoriously suspicious, a natural symptom of being a lying, sneaking thief.

Stan laughed, a strained, I'm-a-tough-guy chuckle that washed away the possibility that he'd be sharing any secrets today. "I won't be running any triathlons anytime soon."

"I've done triathlons. They're overrated."

Stan stared into his coffee for a long minute, took one last sip then pushed the cup aside. "Well, thanks for the joe. I've got to get moving. I owe you a six-pack."

Cade didn't rise, wanting Stan to feel comfortable, like he wasn't a guest, but a buddy. A pal. A friend who could come and go. Share his troubles. His secrets.

"You don't owe me squat," Cade answered, "but I never turn down a six-pack." He shouted the last part so Stan heard as he closed the door behind him.

Or the opportunity to pop a few and maybe find out something he could use in his stalled investigation.

Stan was, after all, an expert at convincing judges, juries and well-trained medical professionals that his injuries were real. Why would a cop more versed in hoodlums than hernias have it easy finding the truth in a web of fictions? The man had amassed a small fortune in punitive damages on top of the original judgment. He'd successfully manipulated the compassion of the jury like an Oscar-winning actor, convincing them to award him over a million dollars in lost wages alone. He'd effectively argued that his injuries kept him from pursuing his dream to be a top-notch antique dealer because he couldn't walk long distances to scour estate sales or lift the heavy pieces he kept in his shop—a place barely stocked two months prior to the accident and now permanently closed.

As many times as Cade had reread the trial transcripts, he never once doubted that Stanley's claims of chronic stabbing pains in his back and neck, as well as accounts of his torturous therapy, were carefully scripted and adeptly dramatized. But now that he'd dealt with Stan up close and personal, he could understand how people could be fooled.

The man had puppy eyes.

But puppy eyes or not, Cade had to prove the man a fraud. He had work to do today, work he was certain he wouldn't be able to concentrate on until he found out why Jillian had left.

He stalked to the phone and dialed her number, the one he'd gotten as easily as calling information. The answering machine picked up after four rings. Her recording was brief, matter of fact. "Hi, I'm not here. Leave a message." Businesslike. Emotionless.

Nothing like the responsive, daring woman he'd made love to last night. No hint of her saucy outlook or easy laugh. He hung up. Good. She wasn't home. Very good. No one to distract him. He had to make some headway on his case. If not for Stanley's request that he wait for his package, Cade would have jumped into his truck and practiced some good old-fashioned tailing. Instead, he left Jake a message about Stan's unscheduled morning jaunt and then dashed upstairs to skim over the medical report filed by Stan's doctor. Cade didn't know how long he'd have to inspect the mysterious package, but when he did, he needed more knowledge to decide if the equipment was necessary to Stan's current course of treatment. This was an angle they'd yet to explore and with all other paths leading to dead ends, Cade figured he'd better get creative.

JILLIAN WALKED OUT OF her uncle's office with her fingers pressed to her temples.

Elisa, lingering next to the watercooler, instantly scooped her by the elbow and dragged her into the ladies' room.

"God, you Hennessys don't know when to shut up! I've had to pee for twenty minutes." Elisa disappeared into a stall, her slacks already unzipped.

"You didn't have to wait for me," Jillian reminded her, but was secretly glad she had. The meeting had given her nothing but a pounding headache. And a serious case of heartache, too. She now knew without a doubt that the two men she loved most, her uncle and her brother, were working together to tear her dreams apart. Worst of all, she couldn't find the words to object without sounding like some whiny wimp.

Jillian longed to splash some cold water on her face, wondering how women could always do that in the movies without ruining their makeup. She settled for dampening the thick paper towels her uncle insisted on, a real luxury usually reserved for high-class restaurants and hotels rather than P.I. offices, and pressed it beneath her bangs.

She needed an aspirin.

She needed a drink.

Iced vodka, maybe? Stirred into freshly squeezed lemonade?

God, she missed Cade. A man she didn't even know. A man who was obviously up to something that might destroy their affair, even if they'd made no promises and claimed no claims. But his touch still burned within her and she was going to need a lot more than doomsday suppositions based on his late-night spying to put it out.

"Wow, you look like shit." Elisa stalked out of the stall and washed her hands, her pitying stare snagged on Jillian's wan face.

"Thanks. I believe you told me the same thing this morning over breakfast."

Elisa dried her hands and tossed the wadded towel into the wastebasket from across the room. "No, this morning I said you looked tired. Now you look wiped. What did that mean old hunk of a brother of yours say to you, anyway?"

Jillian glanced around. Though she didn't think her uncle would stoop so low as to bug the ladies' washroom, she could never be certain. She swept her own office for devices every other month. She loved her uncle dearly, but his scruples sometimes weakened when he decided he was working toward a greater good.

"Patrick didn't say much. Mick did most of the talking. Come on, let's go to my office."

They scooted across the hallway and Jillian punched in the access code. With sensitive documents crossing her desk regularly, the door had an automatic lock. She wished her heart came with a similar device. Might keep her from having it trampled on every time she turned around.

Elisa grabbed two diet sodas from the refrigerator behind Jillian's desk, then pulled the aspirin bottle out of her top drawer and shook two caplets into her palm.

Jillian grinned, accepted her friend's ministrations, then joined Elisa on the long leather couch.

"So, what did Mick say?"

"He said Patrick and I needed to learn to work together."

"That's it?"

Jillian shrugged. She'd simplified her uncle's lecture considerably, but the point was, so long as Patrick held to his desire to be part of the family business—a right she could no more deny than their shared heritage—her future with the Hennessy Group would be nothing like she'd planned since somewhere around her twelfth birthday.

"Patrick wants in. He has years of experience to offer and an insider's working knowledge of the justice system and police procedure."

"In Atlanta," Elisa pointed out.

"He has friends across the country from interstate investigations. What he doesn't know, he can learn."

"Hennessy Group isn't exactly known for working *with* law enforcement."

Jillian nodded, wincing at the pain that shot down her neck. In fact, Mick had an unofficial policy forbidding "fraternization" with any officer of the court, a direct result of an FDLE investigation the company had endured when one of Mick's ex-girlfriends, a defense attorney, reported Mick's interest in illegal wiretap devices. "No, we're not. But Mick figures Patrick will still be able to call in favors when necessary. Mick's old contacts are about dried up now."

Elisa slammed back into the cushions with a huff. "So Mick's just going to turn the reins over to Patrick without so much as a 'thank you, lass' for all your years of hard work?"

Jillian laid her hand on Elisa's knee, grateful for her friend's unqualified support, even if she did need to lower her volume by about two notches. "He knows I work hard. He wants us to share."

"Share?"

Elisa was an only child. The concept had always been foreign to her, and while Jillian, a middle child, had bowed to the notion more times than she cared to count, it had never been one of her strongest talents.

Which is why she'd been thrilled that her whole life, she'd been the only child of Miles and Margaret Hennessy to show a real interest in her uncle's firm. While Patrick was out playing football or competing on the shooting squad sponsored by the local police force or taking extra courses in the R.O.T.C., she'd been working with Mick. While Patrick was out on dates or spending weekends at a friend's house so he could make out with the cute older sister in the attic after midnight, Jillian had been reading every mystery novel or Hennessy case report she could get her hands on, hitting pay dirt when true-crime books gained popularity. And when Patrick was out fighting for justice as a member of an elite Atlanta detective squad, she was writing procedure for the Hennessy Group, ensuring smooth operation, checking and repairing Mick's increasingly frequent mistakes.

And now Mick wanted her to share? When she was *this close* to running the show?

It wasn't fair.

It was smart, dammit, but it wasn't fair.

"What exactly does he mean by share, Jillian?"

Jillian waved her hands in front of her, knowing that shaking her head again wasn't wise so long as her head continued to throb. "He thinks Patrick should take the job as lead detective and run all the investigations and that I should concentrate on office operations, since that's what I know way better than Patrick ever will. The worst part is, he's right. And it's my own fault."

"Come on, Jillian. You've worked investigations before."

"Little cases," Jillian reminded her, popping open her soda and taking a long, bubbly sip that burned her esophagus. "Domestic dramas for rich wives and even richer husbands."

"And missing kids. You've organized all our pro bono stuff."

"Key word is organized."

"You found the Marbury kid all by yourself."

Jillian buried her head in her hands, unable to tamp down the rush of satisfaction that case always brought her even if she'd discovered the missing child through computer-based detective work over four years ago.

"I found her through the computer."

"You led the police to the house! After three days of surveillance that you did on your own time because Mick thought the cause was a lost one. Did you remind him of any of that? Jillian, did you?"

"What's the point? One or two cases of mine won't add up to the hundreds Patrick has on his résumé. Mick's right, Elisa. This is best for the company."

"But it's not best for you. It's not what you want."

"No," she said, nodding, glad the combination of painkiller and caffeine was finally dulling the ache in her head, neck and shoulders. Dulling, but not erasing. She needed more than pharmaceuticals to accomplish that. Even if her meeting with her uncle and brother had gone better, she still had the entire Cade issue to deal with. "Looks like I'm going to have to start reevaluating what I want, aren't I?"

Elisa pursed her lips and dug a Blow Pop out of her pocket. "Not necessarily. What about the Davison case? Is Patrick taking over?"

"No way. I'm already in and I'm making progress." She grabbed a printout report from the corner of her desk, the one she'd received from Jase, her backup detective, just before the meeting. "If nothing else, it'll show Patrick and Uncle Mick that I can be effective outside the office."

"Progress? Really?"

Jillian grinned. "Did you know Stan's doctor, the one who testified for him, skipped town two days ago? After paying off all his student loans and his mortgage on the clinic?"

Elisa's face lit like a Roman candle on the Fourth of July. "Where'd he get all that money all of a sudden?"

"Good question. No one seems to know. I sent Jase to the clinic this morning and the place is reeling. The receptionist, the therapist, everyone he spoke to, claimed they were broadsided. Now, they have no doctor on staff and are scrambling to stay open."

"You think Stan paid the guy off for his testimony?"

Jillian shrugged. "That's my best guess. Maybe I'll find out for sure when Stan comes to my house tonight for a barbecue."

Elisa's eyebrows shot up as she unwrapped her candy and took the first lick with an audible smack. "But you haven't even talked to Stan Davison yet."

Jillian waved Elisa's concern away. That she didn't yet know Stan was a minor detail she meant to rectify the minute she got her car out of the shop and returned to her new home. "How hard is it to say, 'Hello. Want to come over to my place for some award-winning Tennessee pulled pork and ribs?'"

"Is that what you said to Cade?"

Elisa wiggled her eyebrows. Jillian had shared a few carefully chosen details about her date with Cade, but she hadn't told her that they'd made love or that she'd caught him spying on Stanley after she'd sneaked out of his bed. So the less she said at this point, the better.

"No, but maybe I will. A casual neighborhood get-together might just be the ticket. Cade and Stanley already have a camaraderie going. Maybe I'll just weasel my way in and see what I can find out."

About both of them. Cade was as much as mystery as Stan. Actually, more so. Cade's identity had been altered, of that she was certain. She knew nothing about him except what he told her and she couldn't trust herself to sort the truth from fiction so long as she wanted little more than to feel him inside her at least one more time.

And that part she definitely would keep to herself. Unlike the other investigations Hennessy Group tackled, the mystery of Cade Lawrence was a case she'd crack all on her own.

Starting the minute she got home.

CADE COULDN'T BELIEVE his luck. Here he was, finally shooting the shit with Stanley in front of the tube, watching the Yankees ream the Braves, popping off the top of what would be Stanley's third beer, and here comes Jillian sashaying up his sidewalk dressed, from what he could see through the slats of his open blinds, in an apron. Only an apron. As she neared, he realized she was also wearing a pale, halter-styled tank top and probably some very short shorts. She knocked, peeked through the blinds and waved.

"Looks like our new neighbor," Stan said, his gaze barely darting from the television. There was a squeeze play under way. A man had to have priorities.

Cade found it surprisingly easy to leave the couch and answer the door.

"Hey," he said, unsure whether or not to invite her in until she turned on that high-voltage smile of hers.

"Hey, yourself. Sorry about my disappearing act this morning," she whispered, eyeing Stan from around Cade's shoulder. "You were sleeping so soundly, I didn't want to wake you."

"Next time, wake me."

"Will there be a next time?"

The whispering came to a halt when Stan pumped his arms and shouted, "He's out!"

Jillian winked at Cade before asking, "Cade, aren't you going to introduce me?"

"Come on in. Jillian, this baseball fanatic is Stanley Davison. He lives next door."

Jillian held out her hand. A straight shot, too, none of that coy bullshit she pulled with Jake. "The gardener! You have a great yard. Jillian Hennessy."

"Hennessy?" Stan's eyes widened for an instant, then he extended his hand, hobbling to his feet. Cade had noticed that Stan's limp had been decidedly more pronounced since he returned from his mysterious errand this morning. And, unfortunately, Cade still had no clue as to either the nature of his emergency or the validity of his injury. The box he'd received from the reputable medical supply company had been nothing but a home blood-testing kit. He couldn't figure out why Stan needed such a device with his type of injuries, but he had a call in to the department doctor to find out.

"Of the New Jersey Hennessys," Jillian quipped.

Stan nodded and seemed to relax. "My mother is from Long Island."

"And you chose Florida like I did. Can't beat the winters, huh?"

Stan dropped back onto the couch. "We're just watching the game. I brought extra," he said, lifting his dark bottle of brew, "if you'd like to join us. It's ice cold."

Jillian glanced sidelong at Cade, who was only now closing the front door. "Yeah, Cade's freezer works exceptionally well, doesn't it?"

Cade rolled his eyes. The woman was shameless. And he loved it.

"Thanks, but I'll wait. I actually came over here to ask both of you if you'd like to come over for a little barbecue. My grill is finally all set up and I've marinated a pork roast and some baby back ribs. I'm actually quite famous for my sauce."

Cade walked past, murmuring quietly, "Mmm. Yes, you are."

She slapped him on the shoulder.

"I'd hate to be a third wheel," Stan said, covering a knowing chuckle with a long swig of beer.

"You wouldn't be a third wheel. Cade is just a big flirt. But if you'd like, you could invite someone. It's still early. Dinner won't be ready until about six, though you could both come over after the game or whenever."

Cade knocked Stan on the arm. "You could ask that

honey you had lunch with yesterday. How'd that go, anyway?"

Stan kept his stare glued to the television. "I could give her a call, I guess."

"Great, but come even if she can't make it, okay?" Jillian instructed. "I'm really excited about moving into the neighborhood and I want to meet people. And I've made more food than even Cade here can devour."

"I'm sure I can find other things to devour," Cade said under his breath, but judging by Stan's stare and Jillian's blush, they'd both heard. He really was losing his ability to blend in and not draw attention to himself. "There will be side dishes, right?"

Jillian laughed. "Yeah, potato salad and beans from the deli. Time was a little limited. I did make a fresh dessert, though. Hope no one's allergic to chocolate."

They both shook their heads.

"Good! So you're both coming?"

Stanley finished off his beer and stood. "I never say no to free food, particularly good barbecue. I'm going to go call Donna right now before she leaves work. Some people actually go to an office every day. Can you imagine?"

Cade shrugged and Stan laughed. They were an odd trio. Three single, childless adults home at four o'clock in the afternoon. Only two of them actually earned legitimate paychecks. The third drew a salary off the taxpayers' dollars, and unlike his cop's pay, the citizens of Tampa, Florida, weren't getting any service out of Stanley Davison.

Still, Cade pushed his righteousness aside, not wanting his thoughts to show on his face. He and Stan had only been bullshitting for about an hour, hardly time to get Stan to open up. He hadn't dropped so much as an accidental hint about what had him so wound up last night.

"Stan, man, you can use my phone," Cade said, gesturing toward the television. "We're tied and Martinez is next in the lineup."

Stanley shook his head as he limped to the front door. "Thanks, bud, but I don't have Donna's number memorized yet and I've got a few things to take care of anyway." He grabbed his package from the credenza near the door. "Nice to meet you, Miss Hennessy."

Jillian waved at him. "Please, call me Jillian. We're neighbors, right, Stan?"

Stan's smile was a little forced, causing Cade's hackles to raise. He knew subtle distrust when he heard it. Something about Jillian made Stanley slightly nervous, and it wasn't her drop-dead good looks. The reaction started the minute he'd heard the name Hennessy, as if he'd had a bad experience with a Hennessy in the past. Or perhaps he had a thing against people with Jillian's Irish ancestry.

Stan left, closing the door behind him. Cade would watch him interact with Jillian tonight, even more carefully than he already intended.

"He's an interesting bird," Jillian commented.

Cade grabbed Stan's empty bottle and turned toward the kitchen. "You don't know the half of it. Actually, I don't know the half of it. Stan and I haven't known each other long."

"How long have you lived here?"

Jillian couldn't believe she hadn't thought to ask that question before now, but Cade seemed the type who instantly felt comfortable in his surroundings, no matter how foreign. He was a socially confident man, one who could inject himself into a room full of strangers, and by the end of the night, be everyone's best friend. She only had to look at the fast-track progression of their interactions as a perfect example. After less than twenty-four hours of being on a first-name basis, they'd become intimate lovers.

"Two weeks," Cade answered, rinsing the bottle in the sink before tossing it in the recycle bin by the door. "But Stan is pretty much a loner. I'm actually surprised he accepted your invitation."

She leaned her shoulder against the doorjamb between the kitchen and the living room, trying not to stare at the fridge and wish they could replay last night's sensual game. "Are you disappointed?"

"Are you?"

Jillian watched as Cade perused her body from her ankles to her eyes. She'd chosen her clothing carefully, knowing that a little sexual attraction could make a man agree to more than he intended. But while Cade might be an expert in hiding his reasons for watching Stanley, he couldn't disguise his genuine desire worth a damn. The pleasure lighting his eyes, the way his breathing deepened, made Jillian feel sexier than she had a right to—more confident than she could afford.

"Oh, I have a few things that belong to you." Cade snatched a white, plastic grocery bag from his table.

Jillian looked inside. Two videos cases, but no sign of her underwear.

"Something's missing," she said.

"Really?"

Either he wasn't trying very hard, or Cade wasn't very good at feigning innocence.

She simply raised her eyebrows.

"Oh, yes. I did find an adorable pair of pink panties on the floor of my kitchen this morning. Or, more specifically, my cat found them. Luckily, he had the good manners to return them unripped."

"How nice of him. I don't suppose I could get them back?"

"Only if I get the opportunity to take them off you again."

"That could be arranged." She held out her hand, palm up. Jillian really could care less about her panties, but she hoped he had them upstairs in his bedroom. She needed an excuse to lure him to his room that didn't include seduction. Yet.

She'd planned to confront Cade about his late-night voyeurism and preferred to use his fake telescope as a visual aid. As attracted as she was to him, as much as her heart fluttered and her skin tingled just because she could smell his distinctive cologne or feel his hungry gaze on her, she had to know why he was watching Stanley Davison. If they were working at cross-purposes—perhaps he was investigating Stan for some rival agency—she'd have to deal with those ramifications before she allowed herself to care for him more than she already did.

Cade gestured toward the staircase, a clear invitation. Jillian dropped the videos on the couch and jogged up the stairs, careful to hide her victorious smile. She made her way to his bedroom, stopping short when she immediately spotted her panties even before she entered the room.

Pale pink, dangling off the lens of his telescope, set up in the dead center of the room.

So she couldn't miss them.

Or his telescope.

As if…*he knew.*

10

JILLIAN SWALLOWED HER surprise and walked straight to the telescope, flicking her panties with her nails, causing the thin material to swing on the hinge he'd hooked them over. She had no idea if he'd hung the panties on the telescope so she would be sure to see them, or if he was forcing them to discuss the fact that she'd caught him watching Stanley.

Only she hadn't said one word about that yet, had she?

"So my suspicions of you are correct," she said, turning and crossing her arms over her chest, but with a jaunty lean on her hip so the accusation lost some of its punch. She didn't know how much he knew. Or how much *she* knew for that matter.

It was his turn to prop his shoulder as casually on the doorjamb as she had in the kitchen, but Jillian was quite certain she didn't fill the narrow opening quite the way he did. God, the man was lethal. The twinkle in those bright green eyes alone caused her lungs to constrict with hot wanting. Add his thick, soft hair, expressive lips and attentive touch and she found herself glancing a little more longingly at the bed than she intended. She wanted to make love to him. Here, with daylight streaming through the sheers on the glass doors, with no darkness to shadow them. With no place to hide.

"You have suspicions about me?" Cade asked, his tone unrevealing. "What a coincidence...I was going to tell you the same thing."

Jillian narrowed her gaze, attempting to read his expression. All she could see was pure male desire. But his words said a hell of a lot more.

"I'm not sure what you mean." Jillian took the offensive, knowing that no matter how much she needed to hear the truth from Cade, she didn't want to push him away in the process. However, after her meeting with her uncle and brother this morning, she'd had more than her fill of men manipulating her into doing what they wanted her to. This time, she had the goods on Cade, or at least more goods than he could possibly have on her. She'd witnessed his spying with her own eyes. And unless he'd sneaked into her house next door, somehow managed to bypass the intricate alarm system Ted had installed before she moved in and found her equipment, his comment was only an attempt to push her buttons or tip her hand.

"I'm the one who saw *you* watching Stanley with this telescope last night."

Cade didn't flinch. "So you were watching me."

She sighed and shifted her weight to her other hip. He had no idea how she'd really been watching him or he'd be looking at her with anger in his eyes rather than slight amusement and blatant lust. "So I glanced out my front window on my way to bed. There's no crime in that, is there? But unless Stanley pitches 100 mph fastballs in the middle of the night from one end of his bedroom to another, you have no excuse for watching him...unless you aren't who you say you are."

There. Full confrontation. Let him try to charm his way out of that direct approach.

"How do you know I wasn't stargazing?"

Well, she couldn't very well admit she recognized spy equipment when she saw it, could she? Or could she?

"I told you, my latest employer is a detective agency. I did research on this model just a few months ago when the purchasing agent needed recommendations."

Again, not a lie. She had indeed done some checking when the invoice for the toy crossed her desk for approval.

Cade shook his head, dislodging a rakish lock of hair across his forehead. Her fingers itched to comb the curl aside, but she formed a fist and fought the natural instinct to touch him. One caress could ambush this entire conversation. Just wanting to touch him didn't help.

His libidinous grin as he brushed his hair aside revealed his unsubtle scheme to distract her. The man didn't play fair.

"I can't discuss this," he said.

"Then you're not a baseball scout."

Cade rubbed his chin, dark and shadowed and she'd bet arousingly scratchy if she kissed him. "No, I'm not."

So he had lied to her before. Well, that she already knew. Confronted, he admitted his mistruth. But her own collection of misleading statements and underhanded actions kept her from taking offense. How hypocritical would that be? Sooner or later, she'd come clean, too. But now was not the time. Not if she wanted more of a confession from him.

"Are you a private investigator?" she asked.

Cade's face skewed in distaste. "No."

"Is your surveillance legal?"

"Yes."

Which left only one last possibility—Cade was a cop. Jillian felt her stomach flip, but hid any reaction. She wouldn't have cared if he were the chief of police, except for Mick's unwritten rule about associating with anyone who could have them charged or arrested.

Jillian had always considered the rule a little paranoid, but she'd understood Mick's desire to keep the company out of trouble. Maybe the time had come for the Hennessy Group to clean up its act and keep all surveillance tactics within the limits of the law. She'd discuss it with Patrick. Soon. With his background, he might just support her.

But that didn't solve her current dilemma. Cade was living in a house bugged with her illegally placed equipment—cameras she'd used to watch him undress, shower, sleep. Cameras that fueled the attraction that led to their lovemaking, which Jillian desperately wanted to repeat.

But she couldn't do that until she understood what was happening.

That Cade was a cop made sense. The TPD had been the ultimate loser in Stanley's case. After the judgment, the department had endured a witch-hunt and unrelenting bad press. Accusations of rogue cops running the force with little concern for citizens' safety, the media rooting out complaints like Stanley's of excessive force and willful disregard, then reporting them with vigor, even when they turned out to be false or exaggerated.

Jillian had not anticipated this turn. The Tampa Police Department running an official investigation of Stanley would not be common procedure. So what was the whole scoop?

She had no ready answers. No plan. Revealing her leap in logic, connecting him to the force, would be neither expected nor wise. But without that course of conversation, she also had no defense against Cade's powerful charisma.

Cade pushed off the doorjamb and stalked slowly across the room. He was every inch the predator, from the flare of his nostrils to the focused, hungry look in his eyes. But being his prey caused her no fear, no dread, nothing but tangible anticipation of his touch.

"I don't want to lie to you again," he said. "Besides, we agreed not to talk about our jobs, remember?"

Jillian took a small step back, unable to permit his lethal grin and snippet of truth to shelve the matter entirely. Not after last night. Not after this morning. Not now that his activities, no matter his motives or official position, could bulldoze her plan for gaining the respect of her brother and uncle, for forcing them to see that relegating her to exclusively administrative duties would be a loss to the company. What if Cade's watching made Stan suspicious? What if he bolted?

Whatever Cade was up to, legal or not, Jillian couldn't allow him to either ruin her case or beat her to the punch, perhaps revealing Stanley's fraud before she had the chance to tip off the insurance agency. If he had information about Stanley that could help, she needed access, soon.

But not so soon as to jeopardize what she and Cade had started last night in the kitchen and ended, temporarily, in the fluffy, inviting bed she now fought so hard not to move toward. Were the sheets cool from the air-conditioning or toasty from the sunlight bouncing off the whiteness? Did his scent still linger on the pillows? Did hers?

What a piece of work she was, thinking about making love with him when all the logic and common sense she possessed told her she shouldn't. Not until she knew precisely what he was up to, and perhaps not even then. But without her wanting him to, without her consent and likely without trying, Cade had slipped inside the part of her she hadn't even thought existed anymore—a part of her she couldn't name—but that made her a living, breathing woman.

He'd touched more than her heart. She had enough love for her family and friends to understand that neither her ex-husband's betrayal nor her single-minded pursuit of her career goals made her cold or shut her off from humanity. Her heart was full and working overtime, making it oh, so hard to resist sharing some of her love with Cade, mystery man or not.

Loving people came naturally to her. Trusting wasn't so easy, but since she hadn't committed herself to Cade in any way, he hadn't broken any bond. With his eyes, with his words, with his touch, he'd promised only to pleasure her. And he had. Allowing the memory into her mind while in his room and with him so near caused a stirring deep inside her.

"You made it pretty clear yesterday that you weren't looking for something permanent," Cade reminded her. "Have you changed your mind?"

She shook her head, denying that she heard a hopeful lilt in his voice. She had to stick to her original plan or risk her career and her heart at the same time. "No."

If he felt any disappointment, he hid it well. "Then

believe everything I say to you. And when I touch you, know that what we feel is true.''

He stroked her cheek with rough tenderness. A fissure of pure need widened, cracking through Jillian's defenses like a fault line. He didn't want to lie to her again, so he remained silent on the topics he couldn't reveal. But his attraction to her was another matter. He would tell her about that. And he would show her, too.

Her choice.

''Just tell me one thing,'' she asked, trying to waylay the thrill of arousal simmering at precisely the spot where his fingers massaged her neck. ''The truth. What you're doing, will it hurt anyone?''

Jillian and her company had skirted a law or two in the pursuit of truth, but if Cade wasn't a cop—if her guess was wrong—she couldn't stand by silently if Stanley faced any kind of physical danger. Though her instincts screamed otherwise, she'd read enough case reports and mystery novels to realize that Cade might be working for someone from Stanley's relatively sordid past. He probably had enemies that cared less about Stan's fraud and more about revenge. Or about his millions.

Cade whistled and shook his head, drawing Jillian away from the conspiracy theories and international espionage fantasies that started to form in her head—which she apparently hadn't hid well in her expression. The minute he lowered his hands and braced them on her bare shoulders, massaging her into a rhythmic lull, Jillian's infamous ability to concoct worse-case scenarios ceased. Once again, he'd silenced her overactive imagination without knowing and, more than likely, without even trying.

''All I'm doing, all I plan to do, is watch Stan from

time to time. I will not be arrested for keeping a very close eye on my neighbor next door, and no one will get hurt.''

Jillian sighed, allowing his words and his fingers to work free the tension clutching at her neck and shoulders. He wasn't going to hurt Stanley. He wasn't a rival private investigator. She couldn't confirm any possible connection to the police department until she got a hold of Mick's contact there, who might at least confirm if Cade was on the payroll.

But until then, any other possibilities were too complicated, too dry and uninteresting compared to the pressure and passion Cade wove with his palms stroking her arms.

If she was a pushover, so be it. She was an aroused pushover with nothing to lose but her mind and her body to the erotic ministrations of a man who couldn't be any more honest with her than she could be with him.

"No arrests, huh? That's reassuring," she said. "And disappointing. I thought maybe things were going to get interesting around here."

Cade's chuckle turned to a growl as he pressed his lips to her neck. "If it's any consolation, what I'm thinking right now could not only get me arrested, it could get me killed in several conservative countries."

She slowed his attack with her palms pressed to his chest. Slowed, but didn't stop. He felt too good, too solid, too warm, to push away completely. His heart pounded beneath her fingers. His chest hardened as he took a deep breath and inhaled her scent. "Will whatever you're thinking win me my panties back?"

"Are you wearing any right now?"

She licked her lips. "What do you think?"

Cade didn't know what to think, except that in all his years of undercover work, this was the closest he'd ever come to telling a lover everything about his job, about him. She'd come here this afternoon having already caught him snooping, and apparently she'd formed several scenarios to explain his behavior.

But still, she hadn't been angry. She trusted him to answer the questions she posed as honestly as he could. She hadn't reacted with any of the ordinary, understandable emotional histrionics Marisel had hit him with the minute she had started to suspect that he wasn't who he'd claimed to be.

Amazing.

Jillian Hennessy was full of surprises. And she'd just upped his fascination with her to a dangerously high level.

Maybe Jillian could help him. Maybe she wouldn't care that he was an undercover cop who rarely stayed in one place for long—that he was only now learning the difference between the man he was and the men he pretended to be.

On his former cases, official operations where he'd spent months if not years working his way into whatever illegal enterprise he was looking to bust, he'd never been Cade Lawrence. He'd been Joe Dawson, safecracker. Mike Riley, car thief. Even Lanzo Diez, drug supplier. He hadn't been Cade Lawrence for a long, long time, except in the squad room where the men he worked with had sworn an oath to protect his life. When his cover was nearly blown last year and his real name discovered in his fiasco with Marisel Rocha, the daughter of a Miami kingpin, his superiors ordered his identity altered to a few basic facts, reducing his real name to little more than an alias. For the first time, this unofficial investigation allowed him to recreate Cade Lawrence, make him whoever he wanted him to be.

And right now, all he wanted was to be Jillian Hennessy's lover. The simple, overwhelming power of becoming only that scared the hell out of him.

A million rationalizations and possibilities played in his head while he told her the closest thing to the truth he could manage—that he couldn't tell her more than he already had.

"I think you are incredible," he said.

"Why?" She forced a laugh, but Cade knew she didn't find the question any more amusing than he did. His attraction to her was serious, compelling, in a way that went beyond physical lust. And it was unexplainable as well, since he knew that she was hiding as much from him as he was from her. Still, he cared about her. Wanted to protect her. Hated having to lie or twist the truth.

Maybe that was the allure. Since he'd gone undercover, he'd flirted with a lot of women with secrets. They knew private account numbers. Drug delivery schedules. The location of warehouses stocked with stolen loot. But none of them ever hid anything about themselves, mainly because there was nothing to hide. They were uncomplicated, willing pawns in a dark world of scams and cons and heists.

Though he knew little about Jillian, he sensed she would be no man's pawn. The secrets she kept were her own.

"You're sensual and sexy and smart."

"That's not so rare a combination." Her husky voice enticed him, along with the warmth of her breath against his neck. "I know lots of women who are those things."

"I don't."

"Then maybe you haven't been hanging out with the right people."

She didn't know the half of it.

Cade twined his fingers with hers and lifted her hands to his mouth. He rolled soft kisses across her knuckles, smiling at the peppery scent of barbecue sauce clinging to her skin.

He took a lick and hummed his appreciation of the spicy flavor, made hotter by the smoothness of her flesh. "I can't wait to taste that sauce of yours."

Jillian gently pulled her hand away. "You won't have to wait much longer." She swiped her panties off the telescope and shoved them in the pocket of her apron. With a quick glance at the clock, she twisted out of his embrace and turned toward the door. "An hour."

"You're leaving?"

She pouted, biting her lip at the same time. There it was. In her eyes. *The secret.*

"You don't want me to burn my dessert, now do you?" she asked, but Cade wasn't fooled. She had what she wanted—his admission that he'd lied to her about his job. And she now had her underwear back in her possession—the only proof he'd had that she'd been his lover, if only for one night.

"You're not the dessert?" he asked.

"I'm talking about the chocolate one baking in my oven. Come over early and I'll let you taste the fudge frosting before I ice the cake."

He shrugged, unimpressed. "I can name several

things I'd like to taste a hell of a lot more than any damned frosting.''

Her blue eyes widened. "I didn't say where the frosting would be when you tasted it, now did I?''

With that, she left. Cade didn't follow, waiting until he heard his front door open and close before he collapsed onto his bed, his mind a jumbled mess of disjointed wants. He wanted to catch Stanley. He wanted to go back to active duty. But he wanted Jillian more...and he suspected that the three wants couldn't coexist without destroying each other.

Rolling over onto his back, he tried to ignore the subtle scent of her citrus shampoo that still haunted his bed, though perhaps he conjured the smell simply from memory. He glanced around the room of a house that wasn't his and wondered who the hell liked so much light in a bedroom. Everything was white, from the painted brass bed to the walls and wood trim. He hadn't paid much attention to the decor when he'd moved in, more interested in the placement of windows in relation to Stanley's house. But now that Jillian had been here, now that she's left her sensual imprint on his personal space, he spent the next few minutes imagining her in the naked brightness, stripped bare, honest. Secret revealed.

Cade shook his head, wondering if whatever she wasn't telling him was even cause for his concern. Maybe something about her divorce? Maybe her job? Short of her being Stanley's accomplice in his fraud against the department, he couldn't imagine one thing she could tell him that would alter or ruin the intense connection he felt to her.

A connection that deserved his attention, complete and undivided, with no distractions from his duty to his job or his personal need to solve all his cases in record time and with kudos from the brass. Maybe after his investigation of Stanley was over, he could activate some of the vacation time he'd accumulated over the past ten years and take Jillian somewhere. Just the two of them.

No secrets, no lies.

Cade cursed out loud, wondering what the hell was getting into him. Here he was an hour away from a promising social interaction with Stanley and all he could think about was lying on some beach, preferably a nude one, with a woman who wasn't being any more straight with him than he was with her.

And the worst part was, he didn't see any possibility that the situation could change.

That wouldn't be an option until he caught someone, preferably Stanley, in the act.

JILLIAN STIRRED THE SAUCE simmering on the stove, wiping the sheen of perspiration off her forehead with an impatient swipe. She couldn't believe she'd left Cade's house like that. She'd wanted so badly to make love to him, to bury her secrets and lies in a thick cover of lust and desire, but when the opportunity came, she didn't take it.

Before she'd met Cade, her greatest personal fear revolved around her once again falling for a guy who turned her on, but who would ultimately trample on her heart. She'd been so careful, so reluctant, before Neal had seduced his way into her life. And then she'd committed herself to him completely, body and soul.

And he'd thrown her love away without a backward glance.

Now that she'd met Cade, a man who skirted the

truth with great reluctance, she'd learned another lesson. Secrets and lies, particularly to a lover, were probably wise when lust and desire were the only emotions involved. They protected the heart and kept the playing field equal.

But Jillian wasn't equipped for this game, at least, not anymore. She cared about Cade Lawrence. She admired him, respected him. All suspicions aside, she knew whatever he was doing watching Stanley was probably for a damned good reason and was probably more honorable than merely as a means to garner business.

He'd lied, but when confronted, he'd come clean. She thought she could wait a little longer until she did the same, but his touch, his kiss, convinced her otherwise. Before they made love again, she had to tell him about the equipment in her bedroom, particularly the tools she'd used to watch him. She didn't have to reveal whom she worked for or the entire nature of her investigation, but she had to at least give him the choice to forgive her intrusion into his personal space, accidental or not.

She owed him an explanation. If her lies invited his anger, she'd accept that. The time for skirting laws, particularly those of honesty, was over.

But how do you tell a man that you've been secretly, illegally and shamelessly watching him without ruining his trust and totally turning him off?

An idea mushroomed in Jillian's mind and, before she could deny the wicked brilliance, she pulled a notepad out of a kitchen drawer and started to write. How do you tell a man that you've been secretly watching him without turning him off?

Simple. By totally turning him on first.

11

CADE HELPED JILLIAN clear the table and followed her to the kitchen, allowing them a minute alone from Stanley and Donna for the first time all evening. The backyard gleamed from tiki torches she'd placed in a tight perimeter around the patio, the strong scent of citronella doing little to chase away the mosquitoes. After placing a stack of dishes in her sink, she reached up into a cabinet for bug repellent.

"Guess I should have brought this out earlier." She popped off the top, but scratched a swelling red mark on her bare shoulder before spraying some over her skin. "They're eating me alive!"

"Can you blame them?"

Cade placed his handful of dishes atop hers, then snagged her hand and pulled her close. With the kitchen lit only by a dim bulb above the stove, her skin soaked in the light from the moon and the fire shining in through the window. The cloying floral smell of bug spray might have turned him off if not for her own overpowering scent, an aroma his nostrils locked onto like a drug he was addicted to. He'd spent the last two hours acting as if he didn't want to lick away the dribble of barbecue sauce at the corner of her mouth, or suck the greasy spiciness off her delicate fingers. He'd eaten a full slab of ribs, a cup or two of side dishes and washed them down with at least three beers, but he was still starving. For her.

"We need to go back outside. I have guests," she said, making no move whatsoever to pull out of his embrace.

"I think Donna and Stan will appreciate a moment alone."

Jillian glanced out the window. "Unlike us, they don't seem to be having any trouble keeping their hands off each other."

Cade couldn't argue her point. Though Stan and Donna flirted a bit, they didn't seem to know much about each other at all. The upshot was that because of their lack of familiarity, the conversation over dinner had been downright enlightening. Donna had asked, with complete innocence, how Stanley's brother was feeling.

A brother! In every single background check and report he'd read, Stanley Davison was listed as the only child of Myrna and Stanley Winston Davison, long deceased. A family relation that close seemed so elemental, he wondered how the police could have missed it.

Stan had a brother. A sibling he didn't talk about, and judging by his brief answer and quick change of topic, one he didn't want to discuss in front of Cade and Jillian. Cade had been completely prepared to let the matter drop until he'd done some deeper digging into Stan's past, but Jillian had asked more. Good questions, too. And all of them woven in with tales of her own family so that they seemed totally natural and casual. Thanks to her chattiness, he'd learned that Stan's brother's name was Paul and that he lived mostly outside the United States. He had a lead. First thing in the morning, he was going to pull up Stan's passport and

see if any of his travels might direct them to Stan's
secret brother.

"I don't think Stan's had the opportunity to lick water off Donna's body yet," Cade answered. "But give
them time."

"Didn't take us much time."

"Some people are just naturally sexual."

Jillian pushed back from him a little. "Is that how
you see me?"

Cade couldn't believe she was asking for clarifica-
tion on a subject that seemed as obvious as the auburn
hair on her head. "Jillian, you are the most sensual,
most erotically aware woman I've ever met."

"So you're saying what?"

Cade chuckled and pulled her back into his arms,
loving the feel of her soft skin beneath his palms, of
her slim belly against his growing erection, wondering
how he'd survive without her once he finished this case
and went back undercover. His cravings for her tasted
so much more than sexual—more like the flavors a man
craved when he found a woman worth changing his
life for.

"You have a sensuality about you that is part of who
you are. It's the way you move, the way you look up
from beneath your lashes, the way you lick your lips
really, really slowly when you're thinking—which, by
the way, makes me crazy."

She sighed and Cade couldn't miss the distinct sound
of surrender in one musical breath. If not for the sound
of a light, rapping knock on the side door, he would
have started devouring her right then and there.

Instead, he pulled away when Stan cleared his throat.

"Sorry to interrupt," Stan poked his head in from

the doorway. "Donna wants to go down to Jimmy Mac's to hear the band. Want to come?"

Jillian glanced up at Cade, but he couldn't read her expression. She looked as torn as he was. He couldn't pass up another chance to socialize with Stanley, but neither could he deny his overwhelming need to be alone with Jillian right away.

She beat him to the punch. "Sounds great. Just give me a minute to rinse off these dishes."

"We can take separate cars. Why don't we meet you there?" Cade suggested. A few minutes alone wouldn't hurt, right?

Stan grinned and rolled his eyes at Cade. "Yeah, well…maybe you'll get there, maybe you won't, huh, buddy? We'll save you a table."

After Stan shut the door, Cade turned back to Jillian, intent on picking up where they left off. But with her arms crossed tightly over her chest, he immediately stepped back.

"That wasn't very wise," she said, her eyes serious and her mouth curled in a tiny frown.

"What?"

Her expression was no-nonsense, reminding Cade of his commanding officer. One image of Lt. Carmen Mendez, while not an unattractive woman, still knocked his amorous intentions down a notch.

"Stan just offered you a chance to hang out. Get a little closer to him. That's what you're trying to do, isn't it? Become his friend. Invade his inner circle, if he indeed has one. You didn't know about his brother, did you?"

Cade's heart slammed against his chest as he realized that Jillian knew more about him than she should, that she'd been watching him much more closely than a lover would, seemed more concerned with his motives regarding Stanley than a work-at-home researcher for some unnamed firm. The look in her eyes was too sharp, too focused, for her to not have some suspicion about what he was really up to.

"Did you?" she repeated.

"Know he had a brother? No."

Jillian pushed away from the counter, suddenly looking nervous, frazzled. She couldn't meet his gaze, choosing instead to glance out the window. "Cade, could you grab those glasses off the table and bring them inside? I need to get something from upstairs. I'll be right down."

She disappeared. Cade thought about following, but decided they both needed a minute to regroup. He knew he did. He walked outside, dumped the remaining beverages in the bushes and snagged four pilsner glasses with one hand after stacking the plastic water cups in the other. Jillian's reaction had totally thrown him for a loop and he suddenly realized why. She was acting like Jake. All the way down to the duty-first expression, the crossed arms, the deep voice. For the first time since he'd known her, Jillian had pushed away that sexiness he'd just told her was an integral part of who she was.

Had she been trying to prove him wrong? Tell him something? Show him?

He brought the glasses inside, rinsed and stacked them in her dishwasher. He did the same with the dishes, trying to figure out what she was up to, what exactly she might know about him and his operation. After several moments of mulling he realized she'd been upstairs for quite a long time. Too long.

Had she lit out? Or was she waiting for him upstairs? In her bedroom, perhaps? Something about this didn't feel like a seduction, but the hair on the back of his neck prickled only slightly, as if stirred by a cold wind rather than by his instinctual reaction to danger.

Cade dried his hands and walked through the darkened house to the stairwell.

"Jillian?"

He listened, but heard no response. No word, no rustle of movement. Houses like this creaked when someone walked. The sound of footfalls upstairs usually echoed to the lower floor. He heard nothing, so he called her name again.

The air conditioner kicked on but, otherwise, he was fairly certain that he was now totally alone in her house. He shifted to the other side of the stairwell and looked upstairs, catching a thin sliver of bluish light emanating from a slightly open door.

He automatically reached for his service revolver but, of course, he was unarmed. His weapon was locked up in his lieutenant's office. He cursed silently. Jillian might have a secret and might know more than she'd let on since they first met, but she wasn't dangerous. Cade had worked with enough truly lethal people to know the difference between dangerous and mysterious. His reaction had been instinctual, a natural response to the quiet darkness and her apparent disappearance—a disappearance he figured was as planned as the slightly ajar door he found at the top of the stairs, complete with a note tacked on the knob that had his name on it in dark, block letters. The paper fluttered from the cool air blowing from inside the room as he snatched it.

You've been watching Stan. I've been watching you. Time for the truth. The whole truth.

Cade pushed the door open.

He noticed her bed first, his curiosity quelled by the sight of her mattress made up and empty. But the bluish light overrode his inherent disappointment at not finding her waiting in her bed for him to join her. He turned and cursed, starting with an understated, "Holy shit."

He counted five monitors, two on each side of a large, flat television...then six when he saw the laptop balanced on the seat of a swivel chair. One, the top right, showed the interior he immediately recognized as Stanley's bedroom.

The other four screens displayed views of Cade's house. The twenty-five-inch monitor at the center displayed a fly-on-the-wall view of his bedroom down to the telescope in the corner and the icy white decor, now reflected in a silvery gray. All the lights were dimmed except for the glow from the bathroom. And a growing billow of steam.

And then, movement.

In the mirror.

Jillian.

Cade lifted the laptop, sparing a cursory glance at the operating instructions on the screen. His gaze immediately returned to the picture of Jillian walking from his bathroom to his bedroom, still dressed in her pale pink haltertop and denim shorts. He plopped down into her chair, starting when he heard the clank of his cologne bottles when she bumped into his dresser.

His house had been wired for sight. And sound.

She'd been watching him, all right. But why? And for how long?

Then she glanced up, directly into the camera. He couldn't imagine where she'd stashed the device. In the air-conditioning vent? A light fixture? Wiretap orders were hard to come by in the court system, so his experience with the technology was fairly limited to what he'd read about in magazines and collected on busts. Whatever she had installed was undoubtedly state of the art.

She picked up the phone he recognized as his and punched in seven numbers. He jumped when a cell phone perched on her VCR chirped, then he flipped the phone and pushed talk.

"How mad are you?" she asked immediately, her sultry voice accompanied by a surreal echo from broadcasting on both the speakers beside her computer and the receiver of the phone.

He hesitated, watching how she bit her lip and twisted a lock from her ponytail while she waited for his answer.

"I'm still in stunned mode. What is this about?"

She shrugged, but the movement was anything but nonchalant. "It started as a mistake. I was supposed to be watching Stanley, just like you. Your house was tapped by accident. But I've still been watching you, Cade. Since before we met. Since the night I moved in."

Cade swallowed, unsure of what his reaction should be. If anyone else had admitted to spying on him, he was certain he'd be furious. But Jillian? She'd already become his lover. She knew things about him more personal than what he did for a living or what he ate for breakfast. She knew how hard he liked to be stroked, how hot he became at the sound of her short, panting breaths and a litany of his name. The idea of her watching him was incredibly erotic. Mysterious. Downright wicked.

He was glad she couldn't see his grin.

"I can't believe I didn't know I was being watched," he answered, honestly more irked by his lack of scrutiny than the idea that his private life had been intruded upon. "So what did you learn about me?"

She turned away from the camera so he couldn't see her expression, and with the picture in black and white, he couldn't tell if she was blushing. But something in the tilt of her head told him her skin had just flushed a deep, hot red.

"I know you take your showers really hot."

He could barely see into the bathroom, but he could see the steam. "How far could you see into the bathroom?"

She removed the clip she'd worn to hold her mass of auburn hair away off her neck and shook the thick tresses free.

"Where's the laptop?" she asked.

He glanced down. "On my lap, where else?"

She laughed. "Put it on the desk. I've locked the controls to stay on your bedroom. The camera will respond to the touchpad. You can manipulate the camera's direction by just pointing where you want to go, what you want to see...and clicking. A right click will zoom in. Left goes out. Here's a test. Tilt the camera toward this mirror."

She moved toward his bureau and he did as she instructed, then zoomed in. He could see straight into the shower if the curtains were thrown back as they were now. Hot water streamed out of his showerhead.

"So you watched me shower."

"Yeah, though you do have a nasty little habit of closing the curtain. I also watched you eat. Doughnuts. I watched you work out. Tae kwon do. I even watched you sleep."

"Do I snore?"

She giggled. "Not a bit. You're incredibly still when you sleep, as if you're ready to pounce at any second. Now last night, you snored like a freight train."

"See what you do to me?"

The smile faded from her face. "What I did was invade your privacy. I'm attempting to apologize, explain."

Cade nodded, believing despite her secrets that her reasons for watching him, for watching Stanley, must have been justified, at least at the time. His instincts from the start had been to trust her. And his instincts were rarely wrong. "Good thing I don't have too many bad habits."

Her grin returned. "I tried not to look then."

"You saw me naked before you even knew my name."

She sighed and reached beneath her hair to untie the top of her halter. "Not fair, is it?"

Cade's groin tightened. Good Lord, was she going to strip for him? Shower for him? Let him watch her the way she had watched him?

Erotic possibilities flooded his mind, but before he surrendered to the pleasure and decadence she offered, he had to know one vital thing—if his dalliance with Jillian had compromised his case. He wasn't entirely sure that he'd stop now since what was ruined was ruined, but he had to know before this fantasy progressed.

He cleared his throat. "Who do you work for, Jillian?"

"You won't like my answer," she said, allowing the straps to fall forward. The clingy material hugged her breasts and kept her covered, but his mouth watered nonetheless. She unbuttoned the top of her shorts.

"Try me," he urged.

She walked slowly to his bedstand, clicked on the tiny lamp he kept there and took something from her purse. For a heart-stopping minute, he thought she was going to pull out a badge and identify herself as Internal Affairs. He and his superiors could be in some serious trouble if I.A. poked their noses into this unorthodox investigation. Instead, she pulled out a small box attached to some thin black wires. Without losing her top, she laid down the handset of the phone, popped off the casing, manipulated a few wires and then twisted a small device into her ear. She looked back up at the camera and grinned.

"Can you hear me?" she asked.

"Not through the phone."

"I didn't have time to wire your bedroom so I could hear you. I settled for the earpiece. I need both hands to show you how sorry I am for lying to you."

She unzipped her shorts and pulled open the material. A tangle of dark curls peeked out from the sharp V. She wasn't wearing anything beneath her clothes. At that moment, he immediately spotted the panties she'd reclaimed from him this afternoon, tacked onto her bedroom wall on the other side of the speaker. He snagged them down, not caring when he heard a little rip.

"You didn't answer my question," he chastised. "Or are you trying to distract me?"

She strolled toward the bathroom, glancing over her shoulder toward the camera. "Is it working?"

"Most definitely. Who do you work for?"

She shook her head. "One-track mind."

"A short detour. Tell me, Jillian. Let me trust you. Completely."

Her expression grew serious even as she licked her lips. "Let's just say that you're a cop and I'm not."

"You know?"

Her shrug was utter nonchalance. "It wasn't easy information to dig up. I don't even know if you're retired or on active duty or which division you work for. All my contact could tell me is that five years ago, a man named Cade Lawrence received an expense check from the city that pulled off a TPD account. Whoever erased your identity missed that one. Lucky strike for me."

"So you're not with Internal Affairs?"

She laughed. "Not literally, no. This internal affair is just about us."

With a hot cloud from the shower behind her, Jillian stripped off her clothes. For a brief instant, she glanced down, her eyes tight with shyness. But when she met the camera again, her stare was bold, strong. Her smile went from embarrassed to brazen.

"Tell me your secret, Jillian," he coaxed, his voice thick, his words catching in his throat as he realized how she'd exposed herself for him and only him.

"I told you one secret already. I've been watching you. Now it's your turn to watch me. Fair is fair. Then I'll tell you my last secret."

"By the time you're done, I may not want to know that secret. Is that what you're hoping?"

She popped the earpiece out and laid it on the corner

of his sink, shaking her head with an enigmatic smile. The device obviously wasn't waterproof. She said something, but her words were lost in the sound of the raging shower. Cade scrambled to figure out the command to increase the volume in time to hear her say, "...just watch me."

JILLIAN STEPPED INTO the scalding stream and held her breath, releasing the air in her lungs and all her inhibitions at the same time. She had hidden so much from Cade already, the least she could do—for him, for herself—was to be honest and open and brave about her fantasies.

Her eyes fluttered open and she glanced toward the air vent where she knew the camera had been stashed. Would he figure out how to zoom in? Was he still watching her or was he on his way over? For all she knew, he was dialing his superiors and planning to have her arrested for planting illegal wiretaps in the home of an officer of the court.

But as the hot shards of water loosened her muscles and fired her skin, Jillian decided she couldn't worry about that. Not now. Not when she had the opportunity to be the seductive, sensual, sexual woman that Cade believed her to be. Wild with wanting. Free to pursue her pleasures. To live out her fantasies. Just today, in her uncle's office, she'd learned that the outcome she'd envisioned with Mick's retirement had been an unrealistic fantasy that would not come true.

But her midnight fantasies? The notions she entertained only in the darkest night? Those she could beguile into reality.

Starting right here, right now.

She slicked her hair back from her face, letting the

saturated weight curve her neck so that her back arched and her nipples caught a few hot, wayward drops and immediately hardened. She wondered what Cade wanted her to do and wished the earpiece she'd rigged with the phone could withstand the shower's moisture.

But with the opportunity to join Stan and Donna essentially lost, Jillian saw no reason to rush. She lathered a cloth and smoothed the soapy foam all over her body. When she attended to her breasts, she made no attempt to hide their tenderness to her touch. She rubbed her nipples hard, imagining Cade in the shower with her. She dropped the cloth, plucked and cupped and caressed herself, all while staring straight through the stream into the camera.

This is what I want you to do to me.

She rinsed and turned off the water, wrapping a towel around her as she moved toward the bed. She palmed the earpiece, but didn't slip it back into her ear. After spreading a second towel over his comforter, she grabbed a tube of bath oil from her purse, her favorite scent called Citrus Delight, reminiscent of the lemonade that lured him to her house only yesterday.

She'd bought it at the drugstore across the street from where she'd left her car to be serviced, an impulse buy she'd hoped to share with Cade. And she would share it with him. Soon. But first, she was going to revel in the intoxicating power of driving him mad with wanting her. She unscrewed the top, imagining him shifting in her swivel chair, anticipating what she'd do next, his mouth dry, his heart racing.

She placed the opened tube on a pillow, then replaced the earpiece.

Glancing at the camera, she leisurely reclined on the bed.

"Are you still watching?"

The silence crackled. Her anticipation skyrocketed. Had he left the cameras already? Was he near? In the house?

"Cade?"

"I'm still watching."

"Good." She arranged the pillows beneath her head. "We've done a lot of rushing since we first met. I think it's time to slow down, don't you?"

"If this is your idea of slow, lady, then take all the time you need."

12

As he requested, Jillian took her time with the oil. Cade fought the instinct to touch the screen and trace the leisurely movements of her body as she arranged his pillows and towels for her ultimate comfort—and his ultimate torture. He tore his gaze away long enough to study the damned laptop and figure out how the hell to work the camera so he could zoom in and out at will and heighten the volume so he could practically hear her heart beating.

Or was that his?

The cop part of him, the aspect of himself he'd once believed controlled his every action, his every thought, took a fascination in the amazingly invasive technology she'd left at his fingertips. But the elemental male part of him craved nothing more than a closer look at the woman who was about to rub herself with oil and possibly, hopefully, manipulate herself into an orgasm—just so he could watch.

"Comfortable?" he asked.

She shifted her adorable backside, nestling into the fluffy terry cloth. "You keep your house a little cold." She opened her towel. He zoomed in, not for the effect of the temperature on her breasts—that he witnessed from a distance, enough to force him to slide the chair back from the desk and adjust the position of the laptop. But the camera allowed him to see the prickly gooseflesh on her arms. Amazing.

"I could come warm you up. You've shown me so much already."

Jillian's eyes darkened as she considered his suggestion, her lashes a thick veil. "I want you to warm me, Cade. But why ruin the fantasy so soon?" When she glanced up, he recognized the importance of her next revelation. "I've never done anything like this before."

"I didn't think you had. But why now? Why with me? A man who's lied to you."

She shook her head as she squeezed some oil into her palm, then rubbed her hands together lightly. "I'm not sure."

"Yes, you are." Cade balanced the laptop on the desk, pushing it far to his right so his view of her on the main screen remained unhampered. "Tell me, Jillian."

As she spread a thin sheen of oil over her feet and ankles, she snagged her bottom lip with her teeth. "You make me feel sexy. And I don't mean regular, everyday, woman-who's-desired sexy."

"You are sexy. I have nothing to do with that."

"You're so wrong." She tapped the earpiece, as if she wanted desperately to touch him, but this was the closest action. "Look at me, Cade. I'm so tempted to say that I can't believe I'm doing this..." she rubbed the oil higher, over her knees, then parted her legs just enough to tend her inner thighs, "...but I do believe it. For you, I want..."

"You want the fantasy." Inch by inch, her body glistened. Though she stopped spreading oil before she reached the curls at the base of her thighs, Cade saw how they formed tight, wet ringlets damp from her shower, from her desire. His hands ached to stroke her, his tongue to taste her. But he forced himself to speak instead, regardless that he had no moisture in his mouth. "I'm virtually a stranger, like the guy in the video. With me, you can be anyone you want to be. Or maybe, you can be who you really are."

She laughed, the sound a little too quick and too loud, as if his assessment was dead-on. She drew a line across her arm with the oil and spread the lubricant slightly rougher than she had before. "Oh, yes. Jillian Hennessy, brazen seductress. Shameless, wanton woman concerned with only her own pleasure."

"Exactly."

Jillian paused, hesitated, as if he'd somehow said the wrong thing. Damn! She was all those things—brazen, shameless, wanton—and more. Intriguing, sensual, mysterious. But she wasn't selfish. Oh, no. Jillian's seduction, even if she was the first to have an orgasm, was just as much about him as it was about her. About his fantasy. Hell, about every man's fantasy.

"Honey, you don't think your fantasy is just for you, do you? That you're the only one experiencing pleasure? Do you have any idea how hard I am?"

The admission stole her attention from spreading the oil beneath her elbow. Briefly, she touched the earpiece again. "How hard?"

Cade shifted in her swivel chair. He'd never wanted a woman more than he did right now. His erection pounded, his blood raged, his nostrils flared like a starving man chained inches away from a gourmet feast. He closed his eyes and forced himself to savor the moment. Once he went to her, joined with her, made love to her, she'd have to reveal her final secret—

the one that could potentially destroy the affair he'd come to value more than solving this case or returning to duty.

"I'm not going to touch myself, Jillian. Maybe some other time when you can watch me, maybe help a little. Right now I want to help you."

"How are you going to help me from all the way over there?"

"Why don't you keep going and you'll find out? I want to watch you come, Jillian. I want to watch you pleasure yourself. I want to talk you through it. And when that orgasm starts, when those tiny tremors are shooting like hot fire through your body and you can't see or think, that's when I'll show you how hard I am. Live and in person. How does that sound?"

She pooled another dollop of oil on her palm. "Like the ultimate midnight fantasy. Tell me what you want me to do."

"Lie back."

She followed his direction with deliberate, rhythmic laziness, as if she had all the time in the world when he knew for certain his desire wouldn't remain under his control for long.

"What does the oil smell like?"

She took a deep whiff and massaged the lotion onto her other arm. "Like oranges and lemons."

With her panties still clutched in his left hand, he rubbed the thin material between his fingers and then drew them to his nose. Her heady scent taunted him, even as he smoothed the silk over his cheek.

"Tell me what it feels like."

"Slick. Decadent." She squeezed a stream into her belly button and closed her eyes, her mouth parted, as she spread the oil over her stomach and hips. "Delicious."

"I know delicious. Oil your breasts."

She did as he asked, slowly, cupping and stroking and massaging until the light from the lamp shimmered over her skin. Her nipples shone like dark points, hard as he was.

"Your breasts are perfect. More oil."

She obeyed, placing drops on each nipple. "It's cold."

"My mouth won't be."

"I can hardly wait." She smoothed another layer around her areolas, plucking her nipples, playing with fire.

"Don't wait. Imagine my hands are your hands. Show me. And tell me, too. I want to hear you. Like last night."

She did as he asked, pinching her breasts until the pleasurable pain made her entire body jolt and squirm, until his body reacted the same way. He wasn't sure if she knew how her legs had parted, how he could see her, open and aroused and vulnerable to him, but he cherished this power like a once-in-a-lifetime gift.

Jillian had admitted that she'd wanted a fantasy. An erotic drama to call her own. He'd make sure she received this gift, for tonight, for forever, no matter how her secret changed them.

He pressed the record button on her VCR.

"Now, Jillian. You're almost there. I'm almost there. Cross the edge."

He watched her shaky hand slide down her belly, his breath catching as she drew her knees up and parted her flesh with oil-slickened fingers.

"Cade."

She spoke his name as she slipped inside and initiated the madness. He stood, bumping his knee into the desk, nearly dropping the cell phone. "That's right, sweetheart. Believe I'm there. Believe it's me."

He inched toward the door, watching, waiting, nearing pure insanity as he held on and held out for the precise moment to join her. The minute he left the monitors, he wouldn't be able to hear her anymore. Wouldn't be able to see her. He didn't want to miss one second of her climax, one instant of her surrender to the elemental lust coursing through her body. He lunged back at the computer and zoomed in on her face. Her mouth rounded in a sweet O as she panted and cooed. Her lashes fluttered as the quivers intensified into a clenching quake.

He'd never witnessed anything more amazing, anyone more beautiful. But he'd had enough of this closed circuit. He'd watch her come again, very soon. Close up.

Jillian rolled over, dragging a towel across her bare back as the tremors from her climax yielded to shivers from the cold air conditioner. She barely had time to register what she'd just done, what she'd just revealed, when Cade's voice taunted her over the earpiece.

"You're amazing."

She buried her face in the pillow. "Yeah, well, you're late. Where are you?"

Jillian waited for his answer, but all she could hear was a crackle of static and a distant jingle that almost sounded like keys in a pocket.

"Don't move," he instructed.

Jillian relaxed and remained still, not so much because Cade's deep, throaty voice echoed with natural command, but because her body was still shivering and limp from the combination of the piping hot shower and her sexual release. Yet despite her orgasm, her body still throbbed, still ached for more. She'd never associated shame with the art of going solo, but her fingers and her fantasies could never replace the reality of Cade inside her, joined with her, strong as steel, his loving measured, deliberate and skilled.

He was also incredibly crafty. She grinned into the pillow the minute she sensed that he'd entered the room.

"Can I move yet?"

"No." He still had the cell phone. His whisper was so soft, she only heard him through the earpiece. Her body instantly tensed. Maybe it wasn't him who'd come into the room.

"Shh. It's me," he reassured her. "I'm here. And I'm still watching."

She nodded, listening as she heard a drawer open… close. Then the closet door. Open…close.

"What are you doing?" She spoke loudly, her words muffled by the pillow, the pulsing between her thighs intensifying as she realized how prone she was, how exposed.

"Wondering if you'd care to live out one of *my* fantasies."

Still he whispered, his voice barely audible outside the range of the headphone.

"Fair is fair," she said. "Will I like it?"

"Sweetheart, if you don't enjoy yourself, I'm a poor excuse for a man. Close your eyes and hold still."

"But I want to see you."

She heard him flip the cell phone off just before he removed her earpiece. "You will soon enough."

Instinctively, she pulled back when she felt something slip in front of her eyes—something thin and soft, like a scarf, but stiffer. Like a tie.

"A blindfold?"

"Not exactly. I'm improvising."

She laughed lightly as he secured the tie with a loose but effective knot. "I thought tonight was all about watching."

"Who said that?"

She heard the rasp of his zipper, the rush of cotton over flesh and hoped he would soon be as naked as she was.

"Tonight is all about fantasies," he explained. "In the morning, you're going to tell me precisely who you are, who you work for and why you have Stanley Davison under surveillance."

"I can tell you now," she teased, knowing from the slight breathlessness in his voice that a full confession was most definitely not what he wanted from her right now.

"Sure you want to do that?"

She jumped and squealed when she felt a stream of cold bath oil splash right between her shoulder blades. "What are you doing?"

He answered with his weight on the mattress, followed by the warmth of his erection against her buttocks. With one finger, he drew a buttery line from the center of her back to the precise spot where the tip of his hardness nestled with her flesh. "You missed a spot."

OUT OF THE CORNER of his eye, Cade caught the flash of headlights shining up Stanley's driveway, then heard the slam of a car door. Jillian responded to the sound, emerging from his bathroom wearing nothing but one of his T-shirts to ward off the chill. He preferred keeping the room temperature low, especially when the pearled shape of Jillian's erect nipples pressed through the fabric and reminded him of how sensitive her breasts were, how responsive she became whenever he touched them, even lightly. He had a hard time concentrating on anything but the possibility of pleasuring her again when she slipped over to the window.

"Stan's home. Alone, I think."

"Poor Stan." Cade rolled out of bed, snagged her by the hem of the shirt and dragged her back onto the mattress. "However, since I'm not home alone..."

Jillian didn't resist his kiss, but she didn't respond either. Damn. It wasn't morning. He really didn't want to know her secret yet, but he supposed he didn't have a choice. Running from the truth had never been his mode of operation.

He rolled over and folded his hands beneath his head. "Okay, hit me."

She snuggled onto his chest and leaned her chin on her hands. "Ooh, now there's a fantasy I wouldn't think you had. You don't seem like a sadomasochist type."

"I'm not, but my constantly working, intuitive cop-brain tells me you're just a few minutes away from a confession."

She wiggled her eyebrows. "I don't know. I think you may have to work it out of me. What methods of interrogation could you employ, Officer Lawrence?"

"Detective Lawrence," he corrected, knowing she was fishing for information and not caring in the least. His cover had already been blown as far as she was concerned. He didn't see the logic in hiding his job from a woman who'd helped him live out one of his sexual fantasies.

Two, actually.

"Detective. Interesting you should use that word," she said.

"You're a P.I."

"Ever heard of the Hennessy Group?"

"Actually, no."

She smiled, her pride evident. "Good. Then we're doing our job. That's our operating name. We use it for corporate espionage and background checks, but cases that might come to the attention of the police are usually worked through several smaller investigative subsidiaries, mainly under the names of our employees."

"Why would you do that?"

She glanced up at the air-conditioning vent where he now knew for certain that she'd stashed the camera. "We don't really like to draw attention to ourselves."

"Yeah, those wiretap laws are a bitch, aren't they? Damned right to privacy. The way the courts take those invasions seriously, you'd think some dudes died to make that a constitutional right."

Jillian hardly flinched from his even-toned tirade. She was an intelligent, if not incredibly resourceful woman. She'd have to expect his response. "Spoken like a man with blue in his blood."

"I'd have a badge tattooed on my ass, too, but it would be hard to explain when I'm undercover."

He sat up and dislodged her comfortable position. Her pout was incredibly adorable and even more distracting, but he couldn't waylay this conversation. After yanking on a pair of gym shorts, he put some distance between them and leaned his hip against the bureau, his arms crossed. The tie he'd used as a blind-fold lay half on, half off the bed. His sheets sported dark spots from spilled oil and his comforter had some-how become a massive crumple on his floor. He had a damned hard time maintaining a serious comportment, particularly when she snagged the tie and started wind-ing it around her wrist.

"Undercover. That's why I couldn't find out any-thing about you. You must have worked a few really dangerous cases."

He nodded, but couldn't tell her anything more with-out possibly endangering her life. Some of the creeps he'd put in prison had long memories and a particularly sharp taste for revenge. Once he finished a job, the identity he created—the names, the disguises—imme-diately ceased to exist.

"Why are you watching Stanley?"

She grabbed a few pillows from the foot of the bed and slapped them up against the headboard. "I think for the same reason you are. To find out if he's faking his injury after successfully bamboozling over two-million dollars out of your bosses."

Okay, that response Cade didn't anticipate. Watch-ing the same man was one thing. But for the same reason?

"Hold on. You're working for the department?"

She laughed, then twined the other end of the tie on her other wrist. "Oh, yeah, right. They'd approve my methods? I don't think so. Actually, I'm not working for anyone. This investigation is a fact-finding mission. And if I get the right facts, the Hennessy Group could receive a rather large, rather lucrative retainer fee from First Mutual Insurance, the TPD's carrier, who has lost a great deal of money to various fraud cases in the past eighteen months.''

''Do they know you're watching Stan?'' Though First Mutual provided the liability insurance for the city and the police department, he couldn't see any reason why they'd be compelled to inform any officials of this private, off-the-record investigation any more than the mayor or the police chief had told anyone about his insertion. The Stanley Davison case hadn't exactly been landmark, but no one liked to lose, particularly to a cheat.

Jillian shook her head. ''I'm not really sure how much the insurance company knows. My uncle, Mick Hennessy, has contacts at First Mutual. He does the schmoozing. Knowing Mick, he'd whet their appetite with the possibility of gathering enough evidence to warrant a possible fraud charge. If nothing else, First Mutual will recoup some loss in publicity. Maybe teach a few potential fakers to stay clear.''

Cade could see the potential for good public relations, but if this Hennessy Group caught Stan in the act with illegal wiretaps and cameras, he couldn't be charged. In fact, Jillian's meddling could hurt any future fraud-charge prosecution. ''What you see with those illegal cameras isn't admissible in court.''

''No,'' Jillian admitted, ''but what I see with my own two eyes is, as is anything I get on film taken from my property, or yours, with the sound off, so long as I have your permission to be in your house. The cameras and taps give me an edge. That's my ultimate goal. The secret stuff is just a means to an end.''

Cade swallowed deeply, tamping down his urge to deliver a diatribe on the potential interference of private investigations into criminal activity. He didn't have the right. This wasn't a drug deal or a murder case and no official investigation of Stan's fraud had been brought before the state attorney.

They were, apparently, both after the same thing.

"Now, Detective Lawrence, why don't you tell me why *you* are watching Stan." She mirrored his staunch pose, mouth grim, but she managed to look playfully sexy in the process, particularly with the tie twined aound her wrists.

He closed his eyes. He'd already told her more than he should have and could face some serious repercussions if she leaked his investigation to the press.

"My presence here is voluntary. I was on leave following a shooting and the department has been under a lot of pressure to regain the public's trust. Stan was very convincing on the stand."

"I read the transcripts. Made the TPD sound like jackbooted Nazis, trampling him in their pursuit of a purse snatcher and then not only denying him medical attention, but preventing anyone from helping him."

Cade shook his head. "I know the policemen who worked that beat. They were young, a little inexperienced, but they aren't thugs. They claimed no one was knocked down in their pursuit and that they didn't even see Stan on the ground until after they'd apprehended the purse snatcher, cuffed him and read him his rights. Two witnesses testified on their behalf."

"And two other witnesses testified against them. It was up to Stan to sway the jury. He did."

Cade's eyes narrowed. "So why do you think he's faking?"

Jillian shrugged. "The man has a history of suspected fraud a mile long, none of which was admissible in court. The clinic where he receives his therapy is entirely legitimate, but his doctor...did you know he left the clinic? Went to Peru to study ancient healing techniques?''

''No way. Who does Stanley see at his appointments?''

''According to my sources, yesterday he met with a new therapist, wet behind the ears, overeager and, reportedly, intent on curing the world of all its ills. In other words, probably someone who can be easily fooled by a man with Stanley's history. But Stan wasn't too happy about it. His doctor paid off all his student loans and his mortgage before he left. Makes you wonder where he got all that money.''

Cade whistled, impressed that she had such useful information. ''Stan?''

Jillian shivered and stretched for the comforter, but the feathery blanket was out of her reach. He snagged the rumpled material and floated it out, covering her with warmth.

''Probably. We haven't found a paper trail. Yet. We can't even get access to his medical records. Well, we could,'' she admitted, biting her bottom lip as he sat beside her and tucked the comforter around her, ''but the risk isn't worth it. Our best bet is still to catch him lifting something heavy, running, doing some kind of sport activity that proves his so-called permanent injuries were overstated.''

''The state attorney could subpoena those records if a grand jury brings charges of fraud. Which they'll likely do, if I get legal evidence.''

''Gathering legal evidence isn't normally my specialty, but I'm willing to work on it.''

Cade smiled. ''You know your cameras and bugs

have to go," he said gently, regretting the loss to his sex life more than any loss to his case, or hers.

Her frown was only slightly genuine. "Oh, Detective, am I busted?" She leaned slightly forward, pressing close to him in a blatant effort to employ her feminine wiles.

God, this woman was incredible. He was going to have to fight damned hard not to fall in love with her, if he hadn't already.

"I'm not officially in a position to arrest you, if that's what you're asking."

"Damn. No strip search? No handcuffs?"

"Don't tempt me, Jillian."

"Why not? Without my techno-magic, I'm going to have to resort to more traditional methods of surveillance. A real old-fashioned stakeout. Might be more fun if we work together."

"I don't think my superiors would agree to that arrangement."

She slipped her hands, still twined with the tie, around his neck and pulled him closer. "No, I guess they wouldn't. I know for a fact that Uncle Mick's going to have a true Irish fit when he finds out I told you about our operation. We sign a contract swearing us to secrecy."

"Then why did you tell me?"

"The same reason you told me that you're an undercover cop on an unofficial assignment." She nibbled his earlobe. "Powerful, isn't it, this lust?"

Cade inhaled the mingled scents of citrus oil and woman, remembered all that passed between them over the past few days and knew there was more than lust between them. A lot more. Like respect, trust. She'd given him valuable information about Stan's doctor—

a real lead he could pursue. The least he could do was promise his silence. "Uncle Mick doesn't have to know. And neither does anyone at the TPD. Not so long as you use only conventional methods from now on."

"Conventional? All the time, or just when I'm watching Stan?"

She whipped her hands over his head and then backward, snagging her arms on the bedpost with his tie. The light in her eyes glowed with renewed desire. She swallowed, her smile small, her expression relaxed. He would keep her secret and she would reward him.

Cade tore the comforter off the bed again and turned the T-shirt she'd been wearing into a rag with one quick rip down the center.

"Stan who?"

13

IN HIS TEN YEARS undercover, Cade had lived in just about every Tampa neighborhood, which is why he knew there was a wine shop and deli bakery near Old Hyde Park Village that opened at four o'clock in the morning. They didn't normally serve customers until six thirty, but one of Cade's least dangerous investigations had helped the owner rid herself of a loan shark, so he figured she'd make an exception. He'd figured right. On his way upstairs to surprise Jillian, he stopped in his kitchen to grab a bottle of vodka, colder than an arctic wind, two fluted glasses and a paper bag from Lavinia's Deli Bakery with his favorite delicacy—real Russian caviar.

Well, the caviar used to be his favorite delicacy, before he met Jillian—before she'd revealed all her secrets, showing him nothing more rare or precious existed than a brave and honest woman. Still, he suspected he'd only tasted an appetizer of the true, complete woman she still kept tightly under wraps. He knew some of her sexual fantasies, but little of her lifelong dreams or how her past hurts shaped her into a woman so willing, so open, that Cade felt like the strongbox with the unopened lock. Through her, he'd discovered a few things about himself. He wanted to know more. But he didn't have the right to ask—not if he intended to leave her behind when he moved on to his next case.

When he entered his bedroom, she was snuggled deep in his comforter, her hair a wildfire of passionate disarray, her lips swollen and pink from his kisses, her skin still slightly flushed from their last round of love-making. His one and only tie still dangled from her wrist, draped across her pillow like a sleeping serpent. He'd denied her devilish request to swap the tie for his handcuffs, and wasn't the least bit sorry he'd insisted they improvise. While she might have indeed devised some wicked delights with his standard issue shackles, he couldn't bear the thought of touching her delicate wrists with the same cuffs he'd slapped on cursing criminals.

He'd spent the last ten years making these criminals his friends and confidants so he could learn their secrets and expose them to the law. So he could betray them for the greater good.

In all these years, he'd never once regretted his career choices, never looked back from the moment he was tapped straight out of the Academy to work undercover as a low-level street dealer in Tampa's party scene. His military-brat background made him adaptable and resourceful. With no real friends outside those he'd made in his Academy class, he could easily disappear from being Cade Lawrence and reappear as someone else, with no one to recognize him or contradict his cover story. Even his strained relationship with his father—a relationship based on two brief, cordial visits per year on Christmas and Easter—bolstered his position as the department's most reliable and effective mole.

He'd always taken great pride in his ability to be

someone else. Until now. Until Jillian. She was the first woman to seek out the real Cade Lawrence, to at least catch a glimpse of the man he suspected he'd lost long ago. And she liked what she saw. Wanted to know more about him.

Hell, so did he.

She stirred when he set the bottle and glasses down on the bedstand. She yawned, prettily covering her mouth with the hand still tethered to his tie. "You weren't kidding. You really do have a craving for vodka at four-thirty in the morning?"

Cade unscrewed the top of the bottle and filled the fluted vodka glasses Jake had given him to celebrate a particularly tough bust. At the time, he'd thought them the most impractical gift he'd ever received. He didn't need glasses of any type to enjoy his vodka and could make do with whatever was around if he had to share. Still, he'd carefully stashed the glassware in the guest room of Jake's apartment, where he kept the rest of his personal belongings. He had taken them and a few other mementos with him when he moved into this house, for the first time thinking he might want to unpack, settle in. Maybe rediscover the real Cade Lawrence and get to know him a little bit. Outside the squad room. Outside any official investigation.

Jillian had, unknowingly, helped him do that, but to what end? So far as he could guess, Cade Lawrence was nothing more than a shadow from the past. A boy who wanted to grow up to be a cop and nothing more. A man who might have been, if he hadn't been so many other people instead.

"I have quite a few cravings at this very minute, but I should give you a break. I've got some tomato juice and Tabasco sauce downstairs if straight-up vodka isn't your thing."

Jillian sat up, her mouth skewed in a wary smirk. "I've never tried it, so I can't say."

"Well, don't say until you've tried it with this."

He pulled a chilled tin out of the paper bag, one Lavinia had lovingly packed with ice to hold another tin of his favorite dark fish roe and a package of her homemade cream cheese. He broke a triangle from the deli's signature cracked bread and using his finger, since he'd forgotten to grab a knife, smeared together a helping of his best-kept secret.

"Have you tasted caviar before?" he asked.

Jillian accepted the vodka he offered, but looked over the caviar skeptically. "Not exactly an Irish staple food, but I'm pretty certain Uncle Mick served it at the Christmas party one year. I don't remember if I liked it."

"Just take a little nibble." He held the cracker closer to her lips. "I won't be offended if you spit it out."

She glanced up at him skeptically. "I'll try to control myself."

She took a tentative, but surprisingly generous bite. Her eyes widened as the flavors exploded, then the cheese did its work and smoothed out the briny taste of the sea inherent to this fine caviar. As she chewed, her features softened. She closed her eyes, surrendering to her senses as he knew in his heart she would.

"Now chase it with the vodka," he instructed.

She did so, moaning in delight as the ice-cold alcohol mixed with the flavors on her tongue. "Wow."

Cade popped the rest of the cracker in his mouth, chewed, sipped and swallowed. "Yeah. Worth every penny, isn't it? I don't get much of a chance to indulge on my cop's salary."

She nodded, helping herself to another cracker and slathering another layer of cheese and caviar just as he had, with his hands. The dichotomy of eating fine caviar with their fingers made the experience all the more sensual.

"If you ate it every day, it wouldn't be so special," she concluded.

He finished his vodka and refilled his glass. Something in her tone, in the quick flash of color in her eyes, reminded him that their liaison was supposed to be as limited as his access to his favorite snack. They'd made that deal long before he'd known she was a private investigator or she'd discovered he was a cop. The truth behind their professions should have acted like liquid cement, bonding them even more tightly to that decision to say goodbye without regrets.

But Cade wondered if he could still let go. Jillian was his one and only link to the man he abandoned in lieu of a string of aliases. She'd brought him back to the surface and he liked what he saw, wanted to know himself even better, but still not half as much as he wanted to know the woman who had set him free.

"Tell me why you're a private investigator." Cade licked his fingers clean before he shrugged out of his clothes and climbed back into bed with her.

She scooted over to make space. "My uncle brought me around the office after he noticed my keen interest in mystery novels. And my father, the movie critic," she said, reminding him that they'd discussed her parents briefly when they'd gone to dinner the night before, "used to complain to Mick that I'd always figure out the ending of movies about fifteen to twenty minutes in. Used to drive him nuts. I think he sent me to work with Mick sometimes so he could just enjoy his films."

"But you said you used to watch the movies with him."

She shrugged. "I got older. I learned to keep my mouth shut and appreciate other aspects of the film-making process beyond the plot."

"Why didn't you become a cop?"

Jillian looked at Cade, trying to decipher if there was more to his question than met the ear. She half expected her profession to erect some immovable barrier between them, yet so far he was taking her admission in stride. Even the part about her not-so-legal ways of watching. Once he secured her promise to cease and desist, he seemed to have forgotten the matter entirely.

"Patrick is a cop." She groaned at her mistake in tense, a variable that had recently turned her dreams inside out. "*Was* a cop. He's retired and bucking for my job. At least, the job I've wanted my whole life."

"Patrick?"

"My oldest brother. He headed up an elite homicide squad in Atlanta until six months ago. And even though he essentially ignored the Hennessy Group until now, Mick wants to bring him on and make him lead detective."

"The job you wanted."

Jillian didn't think the word *wanted* accurately described what she'd been feeling all these years. More like *coveted. Craved.* She recognized the emotion better now than she ever had before, thanks to Cade. He introduced her to the full breadth of true necessity and desire. And, yet again, his giving nature made her wish for something she couldn't have.

"Let's not talk about work," she said, helping herself to another sip of vodka.

Cade shook his head. "Sorry. All bets are off on that one. We've got to talk about work, yours and mine, before we can decide what to do about us."

Something thick lodged in Jillian's throat, and it wasn't anything salty or cheesy. "What about us?"

"You still willing to just let us go? Because we never put a real time limit on our deal. Common sense says that we'll be over when one of us gets the goods on Stanley. And if that's the case…"

"You're not a typical undercover cop, are you?"

"What?"

She scooted aside to pour more vodka into her glass, but she didn't return to her spot, needing a little distance from the suggestion in his voice.

She'd had no inkling, no idea that Cade would want to prolong things. She hadn't given herself the luxury to consider the possibility herself. She'd already broken a boatload of contractual rules just by telling Cade who she was, much less describing the full nature of her investigation. She's shown him their technology. Hell, she'd shown him how to work the cameras! That he was an officer of the law fractured a whole separate set of Hennessy Group policies. To be involved with him, she'd have to do so in secret and lie to anyone and everyone who was important to her—her uncle, her brother, Elisa. Everyone.

Or she'd have to leave the Hennessy Group. After all these years. All her hard work.

The thought caused her chest to constrict.

"You aren't working a nine-to-five beat," she went on, "pretending to be some lowlife a few times a week. If you were, I wouldn't have had such a hard time finding out that you were on the police payroll. You go in deep, stay for long periods of time and, unless I'm wrong, have few ties to the world outside."

Cade frowned, and though Jillian didn't remember seeing the expression on him before, she was certain she didn't want to see it again. His whole face seemed to darken, from his eyes to the color in his cheeks. "You just accurately described the last decade of my life in one sentence."

"Are you ready to change that?" she asked.

When he paused and looked askance, as if to honestly consider and perhaps give her a surprising, affirmative response, Jillian said the first thing that popped into her head. "Because I'm not willing to change what I want. And I can't be with a cop and still keep my job. Not beyond this case." Jillian forced herself beyond her regret—beyond the strong suspicion that she was making a huge mistake. "No matter how much I might think I want to."

Self-preservation and pure selfish stubbornness put the words in her mouth and she couldn't call them back, not even when she saw a flash of hurt skitter across Cade's face or when a trickle of moisture burned behind her eyes. He had another dressed cracker in his hand, but he tossed the delicacy into the paper bag and finished his vodka instead.

"I guess that answers your question, doesn't it?" he snapped. "But you've made only one assumption that's correct. I'm not willing to give up my job, not any more than you are. I appreciate your honesty, at least from this point forward."

"I never lied to you, Cade. I just wasn't always...literal. And neither were you."

"Yeah, well, that's in the past, isn't it? So where do we go from here?"

Jillian took his empty vodka glass and set it beside hers on the table. The chill inching up her spine had little to do with the temperature of either the drink or the air-conditioning. Cade didn't appreciate that she'd taken away his chance to respond to her question, and Jillian couldn't blame him. But she also couldn't bear to think about parting with the dream she'd worked toward her entire life. Yes, Mick said he wanted Patrick to take over as lead detective, but she hadn't had a chance to break this case yet, show him what she could really do.

She attempted to snuggle closer to Cade, distract him from the wall suddenly standing between them, but he didn't wrap his arms around her the way he would have before she cut off any chance of a relationship outside this undercover work. In the real world, the outside world—the world she lived in nearly every day of her life—Jillian couldn't fall in love with a man she'd see only a few days a month, and possibly, probably, in secret.

But for the moment, she could live in the fantasy. "We could go back to bed. Like you said before, what's between us here has always been honest."

He didn't look so sure anymore, and she couldn't blame him for that, either. With every second he took to respond, her own certainty slipped away. But, dammit, she'd worked her entire life, planned her entire life, in pursuit of the leadership of the Hennessy Group. How could she give that all up for a man she'd see only between cases? Then she'd also have Mick's stupid rule to deal with. Any relationship with a police officer would jeopardize her last-ditch effort to win control of the company after Mick's retirement—maybe even her chance to run the administrative side. She was so confused! She didn't know what she really wanted anymore—from Cade, from life…from herself.

"In bed, we seem to be more honest than I think either of us is willing to admit." Cade's body softened when he drew her closer. He clicked off the lamp and settled in, enveloping her in a warmth unlike any other she'd ever known. Jillian nearly protested and took back her words, denied her life goals. But she'd done that once for the sake of love, and while the men involved couldn't have been more different, the consequences to her would be the same.

Her sorrow caught in her throat. Her stomach rolled. For a minute, she thought she'd have to dash to the bathroom before she lost their intimate breakfast all over herself. But the nausea dissolved at the sound of Cade's low murmur.

"Let's grab some sleep," he said. "We've blown our cover with each other, so in the morning, we'll try to find a way to work this out. Together. And a way to solve this case."

"That's probably a good idea," she said, hating herself for agreeing when she wanted nothing more than to feel him inside her, perhaps one last time. Instead, she closed her eyes, wrapped her arm over his chest and inhaled, breathing in his scent, concentrating on the beat of his heart beneath her ear, desperate to imprint this moment into her soul.

Her heart nearly broke when he swept a tender kiss across the top of her head and drew her even closer in a tight embrace. "Not one of my best ideas, but it will have to do."

CADE WOKE ONLY TWO hours later, both grateful and somewhat miffed that Jillian had chosen this night to remain in his bed until well past dawn. Part of him needed some time and some space to determine what his next move should be. The other part of him wanted only to make the most of the time they had left.

While she showered, this time alone and without his watchful eyes to spur the activity into something more, Cade went downstairs to find the cat and to deliver his missed late-night snack. He was on the back porch rattling a bag of kitty treats when Donna emerged from Stan's house and waved hello.

"Sorry we didn't show up last night," Cade offered, hoping he hadn't destroyed his chance with Stan by bailing on his invitation.

Donna's grin brimmed with naughty speculation. "No, you're not. Hell, neither am I." If Cade didn't know better, he'd guess that old Stan hit a home run with his new girlfriend. Cade covered his surprise with a well-timed yawn. "But the band was awesome. We hit the late set. Next time, we'll make it a foursome. Talk to Stan when he gets back."

She pulled keys out of her pocket and proceeded to unlock the driver side of Stan's car, which Cade just realized he'd left parked in the driveway. How odd. Stan never left his prized Mercedes out all night.

Cade checked his watch. He found it hard to believe that Stan had awakened before him two days in a row, especially if he'd gotten laid the night before.

Unless he hadn't come home at all. Suddenly, Cade remembered hearing only one set of footfalls last night when he'd listened to Stan's car pull up. And he hadn't heard the garage door open. If he hadn't been so happily distracted with Jillian, he might have sensed that something wasn't right.

"Stan left town?"

"Yeah," Donna's gaze turned from sad to perplexed. "Wait. Didn't you know he was leaving? He told me he told you—that you'd agreed to watch the house for him if I kept the car. That's why he said he couldn't leave me the garage door opener because he'd left it with you so you could get his spare key in the toolbox."

Cade's lungs hurt from the sudden clench of muscles in his chest. "Yeah, right. I just thought he was leaving tomorrow, not last night."

Donna nodded, obviously buying Cade's forced nonchalance. "Me, too. But he said something came up and he had to leave early. Well, I guess I'll see you around."

She'd started the car and was backing up when Cade overcame his shock over Stan's sudden disappearance and dashed across his yard to wave for her to stop. Donna was, for the moment, his only link to Stan and his unscheduled vacation. Stan had most definitely *not* told him about any trip out of town any more than he'd asked him to watch his house.

"Sorry," he apologized when she rolled down the window. "I forgot. Jillian had wanted to invite you to lunch sometime. She was going to ask you last night, but..."

Donna smiled again and nodded, reaching into her purse to pull out a business card. Bingo.

"Tell her to call me at work. I have voice mail, so she can leave a message even if I'm not there."

Cade took the business card and forced himself to wait while Donna backed up and drove away down the street. Then he dashed upstairs and grabbed his cell phone from the bedstand. He had Jake on the line before Jillian came out of the shower, wrapped from head to knee in his towels.

"He's bolted. Stan. Ran out last night after hearing the band with Donna," he reported to Jake, staring into Jillian's eyes so she understood the gravity of the situation.

She cursed and threw off the towels, scrambling to find her clothes.

Cade had to turn away. Watching her dance around naked was way too much for his libido, even with a crisis on his hands.

"What do you mean, he's bolted?" Cade heard Jake swear at a driver while he undoubtedly maneuvered his car to the side of the road.

"I mean he's gone. I don't know anything and haven't had a chance to check around. Just talked to his girlfriend. She said he left me the garage door opener so I could watch the house while he was gone, using the extra key in the toolbox. He made it sound to her like we'd prearranged this."

"Damn. What spooked him?" Jake asked.

Cade glanced at Jillian, who had thrown on her top and shorts, but was still wrestling with her sandals. He had no idea which of them, or if either of them, was responsible for Stanley's escape, and figured blame didn't matter. First they had to find out if he'd left any clues behind. Then, they had to track him down.

"No idea," Cade said. He doubted Stan had found Jillian's equipment. Even though he knew now where she'd hidden the camera in his room, he still hadn't actually seen it with his own eyes. "I had dinner with him last night. He acted like my new best friend."

"I'm downtown. I'll be there in fifteen minutes, twenty tops. The traffic sucks. Don't go over to his place until I get there. He could have that garage door rigged to blow or something."

Cade laughed. Stanley Davison was a first-rate con artist, but demolitions expert? Not likely.

"I don't think that's Stan's style."

"You never know."

He disconnected the call just as Jillian was shooting out of his door and motioning for him to follow. She held her cell phone, which he'd discarded in his bedroom just before blindfolding her the night before, clutched in her hand.

"What happened?" she asked.

"No clue. Donna just left. Said Stan was going out of town and that I knew about it."

She stopped dead at the bottom of his stairs and he nearly tripped the rest of the way trying not to mow over her. As she dialed, she stopped him from going out the door.

"Wait, Cade." He closed the front door and decided he needed to do as she asked, if for no other reason than because he wanted to make her happy. Dammit, but he wasn't anywhere near ready to let her go, Stan or no Stan. She'd explained the policies of her uncle's firm, told him how hard she'd worked for the top spot despite her brother's recent expropriation of the CEO position. He desperately wanted to understand, but as an only child of a hard-assed father, the dynamics of a functional family remained beyond his grasp. If she wanted the job, she should either take it or quit. He saw no gray area, no questions. But she saw them and he had to operate with that in mind.

He had to show her he wouldn't betray her. Not like every other man in her life had—her uncle, her ex.

"Patrick, patch me in to Jase and Tim."

He watched her wait while her brother tracked down what he assumed was the tail they'd placed on Stan.

"They're in the office? Damn. What? Oh, no. No, everything's fine." Jillian pressed her eyes tightly shut and exhaled, driving all the urgency out of her voice. "Stan was just on his way out, but I forgot I have my car back. I'll tail him myself."

Her expression of nonchalance skewed as she listened to her brother on the other end of the line. "I can manage a simple tail, Patrick. No, Stanley doesn't usually go out this early. Look, I gotta run or I'm going to lose him. Yeah, right."

She clicked the end button.

"Why'd you lie to your brother?" he asked.

"Because if I didn't, he'd either pull my ass off the case and chalk the whole thing up to one of Jillian's whims or he'd rush down here and get in our way. In your way. My way. Who has jurisdiction here, anyway?"

Cade laughed. "Neither of us, I'm afraid. I wish I had taken ten seconds to think before I called Jake. He'll be here any minute."

"How by-the-book is your partner?"

Cade frowned. Jake Tanner practically invented the term, though he had been known to look the other way from a questionable decision so long as no one got hurt. But he wasn't willing to take a chance on telling Jake about Jillian's equipment, not unless he knew the matter would be ignored.

"Thinking about taking a peek into Stan's garage before we go charging in?" Cade asked.

"If you don't mind. I'd feel better knowing what was waiting for us inside. I've got this nasty little habit of always imagining the worst possible scenario."

Cade nodded. She most certainly did. She'd summarily dismissed the possibility of them having a relationship by focusing only on the potentially negative outcome.

Well, damn. Cade was an optimist. Chalk up one more new lesson he'd learned about himself.

"You go warm up your equipment. I'm going to take a look around here. Stan told Donna he left me the garage door opener. I'm going to see if that's true."

"Don't go pushing any buttons," she warned him as she scurried by, sounding way too much like his partner for his liking.

But he most definitely was going to push some buttons. Hers. Just as soon as they tracked Stanley down and put this matter to rest. Less than fifteen minutes into "the morning after" and Cade knew one thing for certain—Stan may have devised a perfect escape, but Jillian was going to be stuck with him for a long, long time.

14

"WHERE'S JAKE?"

Without looking up from her keyboard, Jillian asked the question the minute she sensed that Cade had entered the room. Though she didn't have the luxury of time to enjoy the added warmth his presence brought into the cold room or the dizzying thrill his scent alone shot through her veins, she did take a moment to wonder how the heck she was going to let this man go. They'd known each other for a tad over three days, became lovers less than forty-eight hours ago, and Jillian still wondered how she could possibly live without him.

She was in love with him. How or when she'd fallen, she had no idea, but she suspected that the first hint of the emotion came instantaneously, and was inextricably tied to the first moment she laid eyes on him from across the street. The minute she'd heard his voice, felt his touch, experienced the inventive, giving nature of his lovemaking, she was captured. And that he'd been willing last night to listen to her outline her goals and dreams, even pulling back so she could make her own choices, made her resulting admiration for him even more disastrous.

The muscles in her eyes tightened, protesting with involuntary constrictions that forced her to shut her lids until the pain passed. How could everything go so wrong so fast? First, she'd had to tell Cade she couldn't pursue their affair beyond this case. Now she knew she was in love with a man she couldn't afford to pursue. Was this irony? Payback? Full-fledged retribution?

She swallowed a long draft from her coffee while Cade read her screen from over her shoulder.

"Jake's downstairs checking out your video collection. He doesn't want to know what kind of magic you have up here that allowed you to tell us with one-hundred-percent certainty that Stan's garage wasn't wired to blow when we hit the button on the opener."

"What he doesn't know won't hurt him, huh?" Jillian asked.

"Won't hurt him...or you. What have you got?"

Jillian pulled up the window that showed the passenger manifests for the airline with nonstops to New Orleans. Cade had found the garage door opener in his mailbox, shoved in an envelope with a New Orleans Tourist Board return address. Stan obviously wanted them to find him or, at least, send them on some chase so he could escape for good. But he'd left a fairly simple trail for her to follow, booking the flight under his own name, though he had paid cash at the gate.

"Sure you want to see?" she asked.

Cade turned the laptop toward him. "No, but we don't have much choice. He's pretty much invited us to chase him." He frowned when Jillian pointed to his name on the screen. "And he isn't even trying to make it difficult."

"Maybe he didn't have time to get ID for an alias, though that should be easy for a man with his background. He may be taking care of that right now in Louisiana. This may be the end of the trail."

"Did you check his bank accounts?"

Jillian bit her lip, slightly amused by the way Cade slipped into her world so easily. Or maybe he was just comparing this investigation to an official one, where he would have the same access she enjoyed now, but with court-sanctioned approval. "We've been monitoring his account for weeks."

She made the mistake of glancing up to gauge his expression. It wasn't pretty. "Well, I wasn't actually doing it myself. Someone at the office was. Anyway, he's made no big withdrawals or significant transfers. But when the settlement was initially wired into his account way back, he made a huge withdrawal. Nearly half the total amount. We assumed he'd used it to buy the house, his car, the place in Long Island for his mother. Every other withdrawal since has been relatively small. A couple of hundred here, a thousand there. The largest was fifty thousand, and we never could find out what he used the money for."

Cade nodded, understanding at least why Stan hadn't just taken the money and disappeared like any other con man would. He'd worked slowly, purposefully giving the appearance of legitimacy to anyone who might be monitoring his spending habits. But why? A million reasons popped into his head, none that were any more than pure speculation. First, they had to deal with the verifiable information. If they found Stan, they could ask questions. And maybe, if he had nothing to lose, he'd tell them the truth.

"So he's going to New Orleans," Cade said. "Big city, lots of tourists in and out every day. Very easy to blend in. Did he book any hotels?"

Jillian shook her head and deleted the airline manifest from the screen. Stan had left on the first flight this morning. He was either already in New Orleans, or had hopped a flight from there, though she couldn't find any record of his name on any other airline. But if he still had a bulk of that cash left over, he could charter a private plane and go anywhere he wanted, practically without a trace.

"I can check some of the major chains, but there are a million places Stan could be, including well on his way to another country. Did he leave you any clues in his garage?"

After Jillian had used her hidden cameras to sweep the garage for any sign of incendiary devices or booby traps, Cade had asked her to disconnect her links.

She'd complied without arguing. The cameras had been convenient, but they were wrong. Not that she was suffering from any sudden case of conscience. She'd known the invasion was questionable from the beginning, but had let her goal to lead the company blind her from her better judgment. She'd allowed that for years and now, in the face of Cade's success at working within the law to catch criminals in the act, she couldn't ignore the fact that she had to do some serious thinking about her methods.

She glanced at the VCR tape she'd ejected, unwatched, from her secondary machine this morning, the one connected to the relatively legal camera she'd had Ted install last night while Stan and Cade were at her house enjoying a barbecue dinner. Relatively, because she had gotten more than a little distracted last night and hadn't had a chance to secure Cade's permission to have it on his property. With the lens angled toward Stan's bedroom and no sound capability, anything that camera caught would be, according to the law, fair game and completely useable in a court of law.

But who knew Stan would bolt before she had a decent chance to use it?

It had been her last chance to prove Stanley had acted fraudulently in his suit against the police and the insurance company. Something about her or Cade, or both of them, tipped Stan off and sent him running. Men who were innocent didn't run...and they most certainly didn't leave a teasing trail for pursuers to follow.

"Oh, Stan left us something quite interesting in his garage. Come see for yourself."

Jillian followed Cade downstairs, her eyes and mouth widening into saucers when she spotted a layout of 8 X 10, black-and-white glossy photographs on her dining room table. Pictures of her peering out of her window with binoculars. A snapshot of Cade poking through Stan's garbage. A clear shot of Jillian's junior detectives, Tim and Jase, tailing him on a busy road. Even a somewhat fuzzy but essentially functional photo of Jake making a call from his cell phone outside the Blue Star Diner.

Cade pawed through the dozen or so photos to find one of Jillian and Elisa getting out of her car outside the Hennessy Group offices, taken, no doubt, yesterday morning.

"Now we know why Stan reacted to your last name when you met. He knew he was being watched by one of your firm's agents, but not one of the owners." Jillian grabbed it, disbelieving that someone could have followed her without her noticing. *Owner, my ass.* She might have fired a junior agent for allowing such a breach of security.

"How'd he do this? I never even saw a camera in his house."

Jillian steeled herself against a strange, slithering shiver that ran up and down her spine until her nerves vibrated like a tuning fork struck hard against a concrete floor. She hadn't minded when Cade had watched her last night, particularly since she had orchestrated the whole event. But discovering that Stan had been stalking her every move, inside and outside her home and place of business...

She released a string of curse words that had both Cade and Jake fighting the urge to double over with laughter. There was that damned irony again.

Cade gave her a moment to calm down, then caressed her shoulder and pulled her close. "Turnabout isn't so fair, is it?"

She skewered him with the meanest look she could muster, and he backed off an inch or two. She wasn't stupid, damn him. She'd already noted the satirical implications of her being watched by someone else without her knowledge or consent. She didn't need him to point it out, even if she did deserve a little chiding.

Jake broke the tension by clearing his throat. "We figure he had an accomplice."

"Donna?" she guessed.

Cade shook his head. "I don't think so, but we can't rule her out. I got her business card from her this morning. Jake's going over to meet her now, see if he can't charm some information out of her. Point is, Stan knew we were watching him. Both of us."

"Then why run?" Jillian was no expert in the minds of criminal types, so she honestly hoped Cade had more insight than she did. Maybe if she gave herself a minute to regroup. Push the image of someone stalking her with a camera out of her head. "Why didn't he just wait us out? Eventually, both of us would have given up.''

"He didn't know that. We don't even know if he knew I was a cop or that you, as a private investigator, didn't have a high-powered, deep-pocketed client paying you to watch him for the rest of his life. Or maybe he just didn't want to take the chance at getting caught and being sued, possibly even arrested, for fraud. Whatever the case, he wanted us to follow him or he wouldn't have let us know where he was going.''

Jake pulled a folded manila envelope out of his pocket. "He left the garage door opener inside this. There's a phone number on the back. I already tried calling, but it's a public pay phone at a convenience store across town. I'll check it out after I go to the library, but I think it's a dead end. Maybe a number he used to contact his accomplice. But you keep this. I have the number and address.''

Jillian looked at the number as Jake passed it to Cade, itching to feed it through one of her encryption programs on her computer, run a nationwide search for the numerical sequence against all area codes in and out of the country. But she'd promised to behave herself, and after seeing the photograph of her arguing with her mechanic over the price of a new muffler, she vowed to keep to that promise for as long as she possibly could.

"So what do we do next?" she asked.

Cade took her hand and brushed a soft kiss over her knuckles. "Think you can use that computer of yours to make a completely legal reservation for two on the next flight to New Orleans?''

She snatched her hand away and gave him a playful slap. "We'll probably never find him.''

"Come on, Jillian. He wants us to find him. Besides, you haven't really seen me in action. Stand back a moment and observe the cunning expertise of one of Tampa's finest..."

She almost took a shot at his bravado with the question, "Tampa's finest what?" but instead she held her tongue, sighed, and walked toward the stairs to book the flight. Cade knew something. Something he hadn't shared yet. But he would, and Jillian decided he deserved to keep a secret or two.

He had automatically included her in the next step of this investigation, assuming she'd work with him willingly, as if they'd been partners from the beginning. She liked that feeling way too much to ruin it with grandstanding.

Let him surprise her. Maybe she could learn something from him, something she could use, something that might lessen her regret after she walked away from the sexual excitement and soulful freedom of her affair with Cade for her single-minded, boring, lonely life.

THEY STOPPED IN THE New Orleans airport long enough for Jillian to try the phone number, with a New Orleans area code, that Stan had written on the envelope. They hit pay dirt. A very nice, very young woman from Caribbean Travel answered and gave them directions to her shop on Poydras Street. Stan had obviously been in New Orleans long enough to secure fake identification, because none of the agents in the office recognized his name. They did, however, recognize the picture Cade brought, and after he flashed his badge, they immediately helped him and his "partner" learn that Stan had booked passage on a cruise ship that would leave the dock at nine o'clock tonight and would reach Cozumel, Mexico, the day after tomorrow.

"We should get on that cruise," Jillian suggested.

The woman shook her head. "I'm afraid he booked the last cabin, paid way too much and it isn't even a good one."

She wrote down the cabin number for them. They thanked her and headed out.

Jillian wasn't ready to give up, bitten by the game Stan initiated and more determined than ever to catch the mouse who'd slipped away. "We could hang around the dock. Maybe go flash your badge at the purser and see if they'll let us on board."

Cade hailed a cab, grinning. "Now, that would be a misuse of my authority, wouldn't it? A naive travel agent is one thing, but what if the purser isn't so gullible and realizes a Florida cop has no business searching cruise ships in New Orleans? They could call in the local cops, or worse, the Coast Guard."

"Oh, yeah. Sorry. This working within the law stuff is all kind of new."

Cade laughed, opening the door for her. "You'll get the hang of it. Airport, please," he directed the driver. "Too bad we can't hang around here a while longer. I know this bar at the end of Bourbon Street that makes these remarkable voodoo daiquiris. Mmm."

Jillian glanced outside her window, allowing the longing she felt inside to show on her face. She'd never been to New Orleans, but had read so many mystery and true-crime novels set here. How exciting it would be to explore the city with Cade, search out landmarks from her favorite books, maybe discover a few personal attractions with Cade.

"What if Stan doesn't even board the ship? What if he's just buying time to make a clean getaway?"

Cade drew her into his arms and Jillian didn't have the strength to protest. God, she loved the feel of this man's arms around her. She loved how he'd held her hand during takeoff, how he'd made sure she had one of those little airline pillows even though the flight lasted less than two hours. She loved everything about him, except his job—a job he undoubtedly loved as much as she loved hers. A job he was good at. A job that would keep them apart when he was undercover, just as hers would while she tried to search for her new place in the Hennessy Group hierarchy.

"If Stan doesn't show, we'll have a couple of days on a Mexican beach to soothe our battered egos," he assured her. "But I have a strong hunch Stan isn't just going to disappear without explaining his ruse. He could have too easily just slipped away without us ever hearing another word from him. Stan's a player. This is a game. And he doesn't like to lose."

Jillian understood that mentality, since it had been ingrained in her since birth. But she also realized that she'd worked very hard her whole life to handpick her competition in order to give herself better odds. She hadn't become a cop, an idea she'd toyed with, because then she'd have had to compete with Patrick. And now, here she was, fighting him anyway for the leadership of the Hennessy Group.

Good Lord, if she had one more bout with irony, she was going to puke. Instead, while the cabdriver fought traffic toward the airport, she settled into Cade's arms and took a catnap, content to dream about the sexy bikini she was going to buy at the first surf shop she found on Cozumel.

THEY'D PLANNED TO HOP A flight to Miami, laying over in Cancún and finally arriving in Cozumel, Mexico, the small resort island where they hoped to find Stanley Davison and discover what the hell he was up to. But first Cade called his lieutenant to request a real vacation. Since his current assignment was unofficial and teetering on cancellation anyway, Mendez approved his request, asking only for his promise that he'd return to active duty immediately upon his return.

Cade knew Mendez was curious about why he was leaving in such a rush and if the Davison investigation had anything to do with his departure, but the woman was a veteran detective with more hours on the beat than the current, politically appointed chief. She knew when to ask questions and when to trust her men.

Cade only hoped this jaunt around the Caribbean didn't end in a wild-goose chase, his time wasted searching for Stanley when he could be using the luscious island locale to seduce Jillian into rethinking her belief that they had no choice but to end their affair once the case was closed. He still didn't have a solution to her company policy problem, except that if she ran the company, she could change the unofficial rule.

But he hadn't yet solved the problem caused by his own job. Like the fact that he disappeared for weeks, even months at a time, often with no contact with the outside world other than Jake. So long as he worked the undercover beat, the real Cade Lawrence couldn't have much of a life.

Before Jillian, he'd accepted the high price his career demanded without question. But now…a normal, steady job with a daily schedule didn't seem so boring and predictable, not if he had Jillian to come home to every night.

With his mind and heart set on finding a mutually agreeable compromise, Cade had included Jillian, despite Jake's objections, in this last-ditch chance to find Stanley and catch him lying about his injuries. If they succeeded, she'd have a case victory to give her a leadership edge over her brother; he'd have, perhaps, one last undercover collar to bring his career to a close.

And even if Jillian didn't win the CEO post and he didn't make an arrest, maybe the surge of confidence from exposing Stan would give her the notion to quit and start her own firm. She could make her own rules, fraternize with whomever the hell she pleased. But Cade had no intention of voicing that particularly self-serving suggestion just yet. He couldn't dismiss the time and effort she'd already devoted to her company, pursuing her dream of someday taking over and running the show.

While he didn't fully understand her drive, having worked for someone else his entire life, he had to respect her choices the same way he had to acknowledge the limitations of his job. With Stan out of the country and no official investigation upon which to request either extradition or cooperation from the local authorities, Cade was pretty much along for the ride. But since Stanley had gone to such trouble to lure him to Mexico, Cade figured he had some payoff to look forward to, even if it was just confirmation that he'd been right about Stan all along.

Once in Cozumel, they'd checked into a large resort hotel, and while Jillian freshened up in the room after nearly thirty-six hours of plane rides and airport waits, Cade lingered around the bar and double-checked the cruise schedule. *The Starlight Princess* was set to dock first thing in the morning. He and Jillian had the night to themselves, maybe their last. And though they'd made love the night before in a hotel room in Miami, Cade had sensed a chasm widening between them. He guessed Jillian was trying to prepare him, and herself, for the inevitable break.

He had to put a stop to that right here, right now. He signaled the bartender.

"*Sì, señor?* What can I get you?"

Cade nearly ordered a bottle of vodka, but realized he'd already shared that most romantic scenario with Jillian, for all the good it did. He needed to whip up something special, something Jillian couldn't dismiss easily or forget. Ever. He already had one ace up his sleeve, a plan B scenario that was slightly over the top, so he decided to hold on to that idea in case his current one failed.

He resolved to try the traditional route. "A bottle of champagne, please. Two glasses."

"We could have room service deliver to your room," the bartender suggested.

Cade glanced out through the bank of clear windows on the beach side of the bar, counting on the dying sunlight to provide more atmosphere than some cookie-cutter hotel room with tropical prints on the bedspread. "No, thanks. But while you chill the bubbly, could you point me toward the gift shop?"

FIRST, THE FLOWERS arrived—a gorgeous bouquet of tiger lilies and birds of paradise in twilight orange and royal blue. A minute later, a woman from the gift shop brought up a Caribbean-styled sarong dress in nearly the same shades as the flowers. The saleswoman insisted Jillian put on the dress right away so she could show her how to work the ties. After convincing her that the dark swirls of red, orange and sienna didn't clash with her hair and fair skin and that the blue truly brought out her eyes, the woman presented her with an envelope containing a handwritten invitation from Cade.

Did I ever tell you about my fantasy of being stranded on a desert island? You see, there's this beautiful native girl, wearing a dress the color of the sunset...

The message ended there, but Jillian could fill in the blanks simply by going downstairs and meeting Cade. She closed her eyes and tried very, very hard to come up with a good reason to refuse. She was in too deep. Too far gone. She had to stop playing with fire, or she'd never walk away without suffering some serious burns.

"Too late for that, Hennessy," she told herself as she snagged a lily from the bouquet and arranged it behind her ear. "Might as well go for third degree."

15

"WHAT I DON'T understand is *why* Stanley bolted."

Jillian asked the question for the hundredth time in less than two days, trying desperately to change the tone of her evening with Cade before they reached their room. Cade didn't reply, but held open the elevator door and then took her hand and led her down the hall. They'd already finished off the bottle of champagne, walked down the beach marveling at the lush, tropical landscape, and eaten a delicious Mexican meal on the back porch of some local's beach house shack. They'd also had a deceptively innocuous conversation about their favorite romantic movies that seemed to be fraught with double meaning and wishful thinking. His favorite? *Casablanca*. The one where the woman walks away from her one true love.

Jillian had always hated that part.

And she wondered if Cade meant anything more by his movie choice. There was something in his eyes— a challenge—that tempered the assumption she'd nearly made—that Cade was willing to let her walk away, if that's what she chose.

Would he, really? And if he let her, could she live with that choice for the rest of her life? Unlike Ingrid Bergman's character, Jillian wouldn't be walking away for the sake of some vaulted ideal or greater good. If

Jillian left Cade, the only payoff would be for her job, where she was undervalued and unappreciated.

But Cade appreciated her. And he valued her enough to give her up, right?

The confusion spurred Jillian to rephrase her original query—needing to talk about anything other than what was at the forefront of her mind, heart and soul.

"I mean, what happened to make Stan leave after all this time?"

Cade slipped a key card out of the pocket of his newly purchased linen slacks. Worn with a Caribbean shirt sporting palm trees the color of his eyes and blue skies the color of hers, he reminded her of Don Johnson in the *Miami Vice* heyday. Only better. Jillian sighed, closed her eyes and allowed herself to babble.

"If Stan knew we were watching him, and he obviously did if he had those pictures, and he just needed some time to get his affairs in order before he ran, okay, I understand why he took off. But so far as I know, he didn't do anything to prepare for his exit other than his lies to Donna and leaving the photographs and envelope—and that was all last-minute stuff he could have thrown together in ten minutes. Something happened that made him run. It's as if he thought we were close to catching him. As if he'd done something to give himself away. I didn't have anything on him, did you?"

Cade frowned at her insistence on addressing this topic, but answered her question. "No. We were both too distracted."

"Distracted? We were both watching him, when we weren't, you know..."

Jillian winced. She'd somehow led them back to the theme she was trying to avoid. When they'd last made love in Miami, and it had taken all her strength and stubbornness not to succumb to tears sometime during the night. He was so tender, so loving. As in tune to her body as she was to his, and they'd barely been lovers for a week. They hadn't had to speak to express the emotion neither was willing to admit aloud.

They were in love. And yet, she was still willing to give it all up for some stupid job she'd worked for her whole stupid life. Only it wasn't a stupid job—it was her dream.

"But we did 'you know' the night before he bolted," Cade quipped. "If we had been watching Stan instead, maybe his hot night with Donna might have given us some proof."

Jillian waited until they were inside to voice her surprise. "What hot night? They acted like they barely knew each other when they were at my house."

Cade tossed the key card on top of the television and walked over to the sliding glass doors to pull back the curtains. "Apparently, your barbecue was one potent aphrodisiac for everyone involved. Donna didn't say so exactly, but she gave me the distinct impression we all got real lucky after dinner."

Jillian froze. Good Lord. She hadn't even…what if…oh…my…God.

"Are you telling me that Stan and Donna were doing the wild thing at the same time we were?"

"Probably more like during your little show in the shower. Though I dashed across the street at breakneck speed, I did notice that their cars were gone by then. It may have been quick, but Donna seemed more than satisfied. Why?"

Jillian couldn't speak. She couldn't believe she hadn't checked before they'd left the country, but she had a very strong feeling that Stan bolted because he knew he'd been caught in the act—the act of making love. Not necessarily something an injured man *couldn't* do exceptionally well, but if his actions were particularly acrobatic or required physical exertion he was supposedly incapable of, his unexpected and quick departure would make sense. She had to check.

"I have to call Elisa."

"Elisa? What are you talking about, Jillian?"

Jillian rummaged through her purse for her cell phone, cursing when she couldn't get service on the island. She grabbed the framed instructions for obtaining an outside line through the hotel phone and shook her head, refusing to answer until she had the number properly dialed.

"I think I know why Stanley ran. And I think I have proof. Legal proof that we both can use."

As SCHEDULED, *The Starlight Princess* docked just after sunrise. Though neither of them had more than an hour's sleep since Jillian's discovery, they waited just beyond the gangplank, next to a unmanned cart and awning where someone would sell *churros* and cold drinks later in the day. For now, no one was around except for the early birds disembarking the ship before breakfast. Cade didn't expect the late-rising Stanley for at least another hour, but he wasn't taking any chances. He may have been right about Stanley bilking the police, but he never would have guessed the man had such a taste for kinky sex. And he most certainly never thought he'd have to spend an evening viewing Stan in action, all while taking notes.

After arranging for Elisa to go to Jillian's house and replay the video while they watched via an Internet connection and a videocam, they only had the matter of finding Stanley to deal with.

Though neither Jillian nor Cade needed to confront him to make a case, both were too curious about his breadcrumb clues to just leave. They wanted to take this last chance to talk to him—and talking was all either could do, unfortunately. Cade couldn't make an arrest. Though he'd called his superiors during his first glimpse of Stanley carrying a not-so-light Donna to his bed, Lieutenant Mendez made one phone call, then nixed the idea of prosecution or even a civil countersuit against Stan Davison. He was gone. He had his money. Neither she, nor the police chief, nor the mayor for that matter, wanted to deal with the backlash of the police peeking into people's windows and catching them with their pants down—even if the evidence was gained legally.

They had had all the bad publicity they could stomach, though his boss had commended him for mounting a perfectly legal, perfectly inventive twenty-four-hour-feed video camera, with no sound, behind the vaulted eave on his second floor. And while Cade did hint that he wasn't entirely responsible for that trick, he didn't explain further. As expected, Mendez ordered Cade to prepare a report and make arrangements to be out of the rental house and back on the job as soon as he returned from Cozumel.

Jillian also had the evidence she needed to show the insurance company that she could deliver the goods on suspected frauds, but she'd asked Elisa to keep mum about her discovery until after she pieced together the last bits of the story. She was a P.I., not a bounty hunter. And with no prosecution forthcoming from the police, they had no reason to drag Stan home. Yet even as she paced in front of the *churro* stand clutching a manila envelope with printout images from the video, she didn't look half as happy as he expected her to be.

"We don't have to do this, you know," Cade pointed out for the second time in the last hour.

"You know you're as curious as I am," she answered.

"About?"

"Why he did it. Why he stayed so long and then why he ran, making sure that we'd follow."

"He's a greedy bastard. He ran a scam and won. He probably wants to gloat."

Jillian shook her head. "No, there's more to it. You read his profile. In his whole life, Stan never lived in one place for more than it took to grift some sucker. He never owned a house and he never had a girlfriend, at least, not one that wasn't in on his scams. Donna was a real person, kind of quirky, but still the type who lived on the up-and-up. I think Stan was looking to change his ways after the big payoff from the police suit. But something spooked him."

"He knew we were watching him. Maybe he realized that in the moment of passion, he'd forgotten to close the blinds."

"There's no way he saw that camera. It's one thing to catch me with my binoculars or to follow me to the office, but I'm telling you, my tech team is too good to get caught. Heck, they had your whole house done and you never noticed, Mr. Cop."

"Don't remind me."

"Why not?" she teased. "If not for those cameras, we might never have met."

"We met because of the lemon basket your pal stuck on my porch *by mistake*."

Jillian turned away, glancing once over her shoulder as a half-dozen tourists came off the ship. "I'd already decided to have an affair with you, even before you brought the basket to my house."

"Oh, really?" Cade surveyed the disembarking tourists and, certain none were Stanley, snagged Jillian around the waist and pulled her against him. "What was it you liked so much? My lean muscles? My tight butt?"

"Oh, yes. All that," she said with a sigh. "But I think the kicker was the way you stroked that cat of yours. A girl can learn a lot from the way a man pets his pet."

"You're a bad girl, Jillian Hennessy, you know that?"

Cade pressed Jillian closer when he heard someone tsk-tsking from behind them. "And here I thought I was the bad one."

Stanley—nearly unrecognizable with bleach-blond hair, blue contacts and a T-shirt sporting an irreverent "Big Johnson" double entendre—but Stanley Davison nonetheless.

"Nah, you're just a lying, conniving creep." Cade released Jillian, but kept her between him and Stan. He wasn't so sure he had the self-control left to keep from punching the guy in the jaw. One jab. Just enough to wipe that smarmy look off his face.

Stan's frown brimmed with mockery. "Aw, man, you wound me. And I thought we were well on the road to friendship."

"You thought wrong."

Jillian held her arm out to keep Cade from slipping around her, but she had no way of knowing that other than the instinct to break a little cartilage, Cade couldn't manage to drum up half the hostility he'd felt when he first accepted this assignment. He couldn't help feeling just a little grateful to the lying son of a bitch for bringing him and Jillian together, though he wouldn't admit such an illogical sentiment aloud. Unless, of course, the confession would somehow keep Jillian in his life.

"Okay, Stan. You wanted us to follow you. You left a trail with boulder-sized breadcrumbs. What did you want us to know? That you won? That your scam worked? That you'll be back? Because if you think you'll ever be able to jump back into your old life," Jillian said, waving the envelope in front of him, "you think again."

Stan snatched the envelope away, causing Cade to step forward. Stan held up his hand, then politely asked, "May I?"

Jillian silently gave him permission.

He pulled the printout, low-quality stills from the videotape and frowned.

Jillian reached across and tapped the pale image of Stan's scrawny butt. "Not exactly your best side, but no man with a spinal injury like yours could do the things you did in your bedroom a few nights ago. There's going to be a fraud case pending against you and—who knows?—maybe the insurance company will be pissed off enough to try and find you, even outside the country."

Stan sighed. Cade couldn't miss the melancholy sound, and judging by the disbelieving look on Jillian's face as she glanced over her shoulder at him, neither did she.

"May I keep this?" Stan asked.

Jillian hesitated, then said, "Sure. I have the original.

I'd offer to make you a copy of the tape, but I don't think Donna would be too pleased.''

"I never meant to get involved with her or to hurt her. I guess I was getting soft. But Donna didn't know anything about this," Stan insisted, focusing on Cade. "You know that, right?"

For an instant, Cade considered yanking Stan's chain, threatening to prosecute Donna as an accomplice if he didn't come back to the States and face the music, but two things stopped him. First, Cade had no illusions that a lying louse like Stan Davison would trade either his freedom or his money for true love. Second, he had no substantial proof to implicate Donna—a fact Stan undoubtedly counted on. The man was a creep, but he obviously wasn't stupid and knew his way around the law.

"So why'd you lure us here, Stan?" Cade asked. "You knew we were watching you. Did you figure we'd caught you with those, so you left town before we took you in?"

Stan folded the picture and put it in the pocket of his extra-long surfer shorts.

"I had no idea you had a camera aimed into my bedroom. Or that you were watching me that night after dinner. I wasn't the only one with the blinds open."

That he aimed at Jillian. She blushed deep scarlet, and Cade nearly stepped around her to bop Stan in the mouth. "Relax, caveman. I was too busy to watch. I brought you here to explain."

"Explain what? That you're a greedy SOB? We both knew that from the beginning," Cade said.

Stan shook his head and took a file folder out of the backpack he wore slung over one shoulder, making him look so much like a young college student cruising on spring break, Cade doubted he would have recognized the man if he hadn't stopped to talk to them.

"That's no secret to anyone who knows me. But until Donna slipped, no one knew I had a brother. No one. Not even my mother. He's my father's bastard kid. I only learned about him myself about three years ago after Dad got popped in a bad deal in Vegas."

Jillian accepted the file and opened it, turning the pages so Cade could read over her shoulder. There was a snapshot of a boy, about twelve years old, but she flipped it over quickly, without looking. Jillian wasn't an easy woman to manipulate. She knew her weaknesses and compensated for them—a fact Cade found both attractive and disheartening.

"What's wrong with him?" Jillian asked, her voice steady.

"What isn't? He's got MS, for starters. He also has bad lungs and a weak heart, but his life won't be so bad if he's in a decent place. Call me a softie," Stan said with a laugh, "but I couldn't let the kid rot in some public facility. A hefty hunk of the money is now in a trust in his name. The rest bought me this cruise and a small cottage on the coastline of a country with no extradition agreement with the US of A. In a few days, my brother will be moved to a private home run by his trustees, a delightful group of Carmelite nuns. So unless you want to go after a little sick kid and the Catholic Church, you'll forget all about me."

Jillian slapped the folder shut, and even though not an inkling of sympathy showed on her face, Cade knew she wasn't immune. Hell, he couldn't help feel sorry for the kid, disabled or not, just for sharing half his blood and genes with a creep like Stan.

"So this is why we came to Mexico? So you could

ease your conscience, convince us you scammed the taxpayers of Tampa for the sake of a sick child?''

Stan's grin revealed a fresh set of brace-straight dentures, one more change in his appearance that would ensure that he'd be very, very hard to find in the future. ''I don't have a conscience. I'm just hoping you'll both have one and leave the kid alone. As for the trip to Mexico, consider it my parting gift, along with my congratulations. I had the highest priced private investigator in town watching my back and you still managed to catch me.'' He patted the pant pocket that held the photo of him and Donna in flagrante delicto. ''Thank Donna for opening her mouth about my brother. If she hadn't, I might have stayed around long enough for you,'' he looked at Jillian, ''to reclaim all my money and you,'' he turned to Cade, ''to throw me in jail. You're a formidable team.''

With that, Stan strolled away, whistling.

''I hate losing,'' Jillian said, slapping the file against her thigh.

''Well, we didn't really lose. We just didn't win.''

Jillian turned and skewered him with her shock. ''I can't believe that's your attitude. Look at all the time we wasted!''

''I don't consider our time together wasted,'' Cade told her, his voice even, calm, surprising him because now that Jillian had all she wanted in her hot little hands, she still wasn't happy.

Women.

''That's not what I meant. I guess I still have enough to at least show the insurance company that their investigators missed some big stuff, even if they can't recoup their money. His brother. The doctor who left town. Donna. Even the videotape.''

Cade shook his head and started back toward the hotel. For the first time in his life, Cade didn't give a rat's ass about the case. He didn't care about going back to his superiors empty-handed or about being bested by a two-bit creep. He cared only about Jillian, and she didn't seem to notice.

"Wait! Cade!" She jogged to catch up to him just as he hailed a cab. "Where are you going?"

"Back to the hotel to get my stuff." He folded himself into the tiny back seat of the compact Volkswagen doubling as a taxi. He watched her face, saw the confusion. The fear.

The case was solved. File closed. The only thing left to deal with was the ending of their relationship...or not.

Her choice. Did she want him as much as he wanted her?

"I..."

"Decide, Jillian. My boss wants me back on the job, out of the house. Unless you give me a reason to hang around, I'm booking the first flight home. I've enjoyed being your diversion, your little meaningless affair. But I'm tired now. Either we move ahead, together, or I move along, alone."

16

WITH TOTAL AWARENESS of the irony yet again, Jillian watched from the window as a worker in dingy coveralls pounded a For Rent sign into the front yard of the house she'd always think of as Cade's.

She was such a fool. A certifiable idiot. She'd let Cade walk away all for the sake of a dream she'd known for weeks would never come true. And while her actions indicated that she'd chosen her career over a wonderfully sexy, giving man who had already proven he could make her fantasies come to life, the truth remained that Jillian had run scared. She hadn't expected to fall in love so hard, so fast. She hadn't been able to overcome her fear of pushing her goals aside for a man and grab the opportunity to cherish the other half of her own heart, the half that belonged to Cade.

So now, she had a new job, complete with the freedom to fraternize with whomever she damned well pleased, but no Cade. Though impressed with her report on Stanley and her assessment of where their investigators had missed some clues to Stan's fraud, the insurance company declined to either go after Stanley further or put the Hennessy Group on retainer. But by the end of her meeting with the Board of Directors at First Mutual, Jillian had wrangled an offer to train investigators and develop a program that could benefit the company and, eventually, be offered as a course to insurance companies around the country.

She'd found something to call her own, and Cade had been her inspiration. She only wished she knew where he was so she could at the very least thank him. At the very most, she wanted to wrap her arms around him, tell him she loved him and beg his forgiveness for letting him go when all she wanted to do was find a way to make him stay.

"You're sure this insurance thing is what you want to do?" Elisa asked, stacking the last of Jillian's videos in a lined box. "Seems to me you gave up rather easily on running Hennessy. Mick has years left until his retirement. He could change his mind."

Jillian watched, perplexed, as the man who just put up the For Rent sign at Cade's moved next door to remove the For Sale sign that had been posted at Stanley's. A few days after her return from Mexico, Donna had stopped by with a letter she'd received from Stanley giving her the deed to his house. Hurt and angry at his betrayal, she'd immediately put the place up for sale. Someone had apparently snapped it right up.

"Mick's not going to change his mind. I may not get to run the company, but I can at least run this new division. Patrick and Uncle Mick promised me free reign. And I'll be out in the field, working with investigators, doing legal surveillance, maybe catching a few frauds before they bilk the company out of millions. It's almost like being a cop."

Elisa grabbed the last handful of videos from the entertainment center shelf. "Except you won't have the pleasure of running into Detective Cade Lawrence in the squad room."

Jillian pushed away from the window, determined

not to look again for at least five more minutes. "No. I won't have that."

Elisa folded down the flaps of the box and stretched a length of tape to seal it, working so efficiently and quietly that Jillian thought she might go insane. She grabbed the box from her friend even before she'd finished marking it and lugged it to the pile in her front hall. She had to get out of here. Away from the memories. The regrets.

"You haven't heard from him, have you?" Elisa asked softly.

Jillian shook her head. She'd left three messages with Cade's partner, Jake Tanner, all unanswered, and decided this morning that enough was enough. She couldn't go chasing the man like some obsessed schoolgirl. If he wanted to talk to her, see what she wanted, he could easily find her. She didn't have the same luxury.

By the time she'd returned to the hotel in Cozumel, he'd left. She'd missed him at the airport and then had had to stay an extra day, alone, after the next flight out was cancelled. She spent the time thinking, realizing she couldn't let him go just because their relationship wouldn't be predictable. She'd be busy with her new career, too. Seeing Cade whenever and wherever his job allowed seemed infinitely better than not seeing him at all.

But by the time she returned to Tampa, Cade had moved out and left no forwarding address. Nearly a week had passed since then with no word from him, so she figured the time had come for her to go back to her old apartment and try to reinvent her life on her own.

"Hey, what's this?"

Elisa held up a video case. Jillian returned to the

study and examined the black, unmarked cartridge. She slid the movie out. No label. It didn't fit all the way when she tried to put it back in.

"I don't know. Where'd you find it?"

"On the table. It must have been under the box."

Jillian moved to slide the tape into the VCR, but the machine had been disconnected and repacked last night. "I'll look at it upstairs."

"Hasn't Ted taken out that equipment yet?"

Jillian only wished he had. She'd spent more time in the last few nights staring at motionless blue screens than she had sleeping. "They retrieved all the equipment from Cade's house and Stan's, but they had another job to do, so I told them I'd pack it up myself."

Elisa's brows disappeared beneath her curly bangs. "Ted's going to let you touch his babies?"

Jillian laughed. "Well, since I sign some of the checks that buy him those babies, he didn't have a choice. Look, Lise, you've been here all day. Why don't you take off? I'll finish up."

"You sure? You've got a lot left to do if you want to be out by tomorrow."

"I know. I just want…"

When Elisa held up her hands and grabbed her purse and keys without a word of argument, Jillian felt her heart lurch. She loved having someone who could fill in the blanks for her, understand when she needed some space, respect her dreams, no matter how narrow-minded and pie-in-the-sky. She hugged Elisa tightly, then watched her leave through the side door. Yes, she loved having someone like Elisa, but she loved Cade a whole lot more.

She spent another fifteen minutes packing her kitchen utensils when her cell phone rang. She scanned the LCD, but her phone didn't recognize the caller. Expecting a wrong number, she answered with a curt, "Hello?"

"Don't you like watching anymore?"

Jillian's heart froze. "Cade?"

"Here I leave you a fascinating, mysterious present where even the worst private investigator can find it and still you haven't watched."

Watched? *The video.*

"How do you know I haven't watched it?"

His chuckle was throaty and deep, the sexy sound immediately flaring the tips of her breasts and melting her insides into lava-hot lotion. "Because I'm watching you."

She shot toward her front window, but he stopped her before she touched the blinds when he said, "Oh, no. No peeking. What I want you to watch on that video is infinitely more interesting than some shady cop on a stakeout."

"Am I under investigation?" she asked, prolonging the conversation while she retrieved the tape and jogged up the stairs. Cade had called her. Cade was watching her. He hadn't written her off. She still had a shot.

"Sweetheart, with you, the word *investigation* could include some delicious possibilities."

She snagged her bottom lip as a thrill shimmied through her veins. "Is that good or bad?"

"Remains to be seen."

Jillian hurried to her room, slid the video into the machine and turned on the set. The blue screen changed to black, then a hazy gray. Sound lines distorted the picture. She adjusted the tracking in time to see herself nude on Cade's bed, a bottle of oil poised in one hand.

"You taped me?"

"Guilty as charged. Are you mad?"

Jillian fast-forwarded through her self-gratification show, stopping the action when she saw Cade enter the frame. She watched him stalk into the room and find the tie he used to blindfold her, watched him warm the massage oil she'd left on his bedstand before he slid his slick palms down her back. Her skin tingled, as if he was touching her again. The flesh between her thighs pounded, tightened. She propelled herself backward on shaky legs, collapsing onto the bed, since her chair had already been carried downstairs.

"So? Are you angry?" he asked.

"No, I'm fascinated. I'm titillated. I'm...sorry."

She heard a click and a full ten seconds must have passed before she realized he'd hung up. When she heard his voice again, he was standing in her doorway, dressed in faded jeans and a plain gray T-shirt, sporting a day's growth of beard and shaggy black hair that desperately needed a cut.

He was gorgeous.

"Cade..." She moved toward him, but he stopped her with his hand.

"No touching, just looking."

He tilted his head toward the television. She glanced back in time to see Cade adjust the pillows on his bed, placing one beneath her belly just before he drove her mad with slick fingers and a warm tongue.

She didn't have to watch. She remembered each and every sensation and wondered if his showing up, teasing her with the video, meant she still had a chance to relive those feelings again. And again. Forever.

Her skin flushed. She couldn't help the heat suffusing through her, some from embarrassment and some from lust.

But mostly from love. The kind of love that made a woman do the stupidest things for the smartest reasons.

"What if I don't want to watch?" she asked with mock defiance.

He dug into his pocket and pulled out the same bright red tie he'd used that night to bind her. "I have my ways of coercion. And I still have those handcuffs you were begging me to use."

"Then why didn't you use them on me in Mexico? Convince me that I was being an utter fool for letting you go?"

Cade glanced down, but he couldn't completely hide the tiny grin that told her he was pleased to hear her voice her regret. "You had to learn for yourself. You had to make the choice, Jillian, with your eyes open, with your future in your control. If not, you'd spend the rest of your life wondering if I was any better for you than your ex. You couldn't make choices about your career just so we could be together. You had to follow your dream."

"You figured that out before I did," she lamented.

He shrugged. "I didn't have a lifelong desire to cloud my judgment."

"I still work for the Hennessy Group," Jillian offered, not wanting him to think she'd given up entirely. "but I'm starting my own division. Corporate training for insurance investigators."

"I heard."

"From whom?"

"The same person who let me into your house while you were taking a shower this morning."

Elisa.

"You've been in the house all day and I didn't know?"

Cade's grin was pure sin. "Well, I didn't become a crack undercover cop by being bad at my job."

A chorus of oohs and ahs from the videotape machine verified he was good at quite a few things under the covers. Jillian searched fruitlessly for the remote. She couldn't concentrate with Cade looking all sexy on one side of the room and images of him making love to her on the other. And she had to concentrate. At least until he stripped off her clothes and provided the live reenactment she so desperately craved.

"I thought maybe that's why you didn't answer my messages." She tore the comforter away and dug under a pillow. "That you were on assignment again."

"I was. Funny, but I couldn't seem to focus on the guy I was supposed to be. In the last few weeks, I finally met the real Cade Lawrence. I like him. I think he needs to get out and about more often, so I told my bosses yesterday to transfer me out of the undercover squad. I'm just a regular cop now. No hidden identity, no big secrets. I even bought a house."

She remembered seeing the For Rent sign, so her hopes that he'd purchased the house across the street, the house where they'd made such sweet, seductive memories, faded as quickly as it popped into her head. Then she remembered the quick sale of Stanley's house next door.

"You didn't! You bought Stan's house from Donna?"

"More square footage and much better landscaping. No pool, though. We'll have to fix that, don't you think?"

"We?"

Cade pulled her remote control out of his back pocket and pushed the pause button, freezing the frame just as they were hitting the orgasm portion of the tape.

"I didn't come back to torture you with that tape, Jillian."

"It is torturing me. You have no idea how much I want you to make love to me right now."

"Watching us make love makes you hot, huh?"

He stalked toward her slowly, tossing the remote and his cell phone on the floor as he took her hands and twined her fingers with his, tugging her close and nibbling her neck.

"Maybe my air-conditioning isn't working again," she suggested, certain the temperature in the room had just shot up into the nineties.

"Maybe you're a shameless voyeur. Or maybe you're just wearing too many clothes."

"Maybe…"

They were naked in an instant, but Jillian stopped Cade before he could press her onto the bed. Yes, she wanted to feel him inside her more than she'd ever wanted anything else in her entire life, but first, she had to tell him everything. No more secrets.

"I love you, Cade. But I want more than just an affair, more than just moving in together and living some fantasy for a little while."

He combed his fingers into her hair, tugging her head back so he could penetrate her desire-clouded gaze with the purest expression of honesty she'd ever witnessed in her life. "I love you, Jillian. You helped me find myself, helped me realize that I'd buried myself so deeply in my job, I didn't have any dreams of my own. Nothing. No goals beyond staying alive and bringing in the collar. You don't know what a precious gift you've given me. And one precious gift deserves another.''

He kissed her softly, then picked her up and laid her gently on the bed. He didn't join her immediately, but strode across the room, retrieved the empty video case, then knelt at the bedside.

"Your investigative skills are slipping just a tad."

Jillian remembered having trouble sliding the video in all the way, so she dug inside until she felt something taped into the bottom. Something metal. Something round.

A sob caught in her throat. She tugged, releasing a thin band of gold inlaid with an exquisite emerald, four diamonds and eight tiny opals filled with red fire.

She looked up at him, needing to hear the question, hoping with her whole heart she'd have the composure to reply.

"Marry me, Jillian."

He took the ring out of her quaking hand and slipped the gold band onto her finger, kissing her knuckles gently while he searched her eyes for her reply.

She managed to swallow and release her trapped voice. "I will marry you, Cade. If you promise me one thing."

"One thing? Sweetheart, you become my wife and I doubt there's anything I'll ever be able to deny you."

His confession tweaked the part of her that was inherently wicked, the sensual, sexual part of her Cade had awakened, the part she knew she'd never lose so long as this man was in her life. She'd only wanted to make him promise to return to Cozumel for their honeymoon and enjoy the romantic setting they'd missed before, but his willingness to please her cooked up a better idea.

"Even if my request includes the use of your handcuffs? You were awfully reluctant to use them on me last time I asked."

Cade dashed to his jeans, pulled the silver fetters out of his back pocket and quickly clicked one around her wrist.

"That was before I realized I could bind you to me forever."

Jillian pulled Cade down until his nude body covered hers with a heat that seared her straight to her soul. "You don't need handcuffs for that, Cade."

She closed her eyes, luxuriating in all the soft, smooth, hard, hot sensations. The cold steel dangling from her wrist. The fiery feel of his lips on hers.

"Then what do I need them for?"

Her mouth dried as she reached around and clicked the other cuff on his wrist. "I don't know. I just thought it might be fun to see if you could do anything inventive with me chained to you, naked."

His eyes darkened with sensual challenge and Jillian knew she'd be the most sexually satisfied woman in the world, as well as the happiest, thanks to Cade. "Just watch me…"

What is your secret fantasy?

Is it to have your own love slave, to be seduced by a stranger, or to experience total sexual freedom?

Enjoy all of these and more in Blaze's newest miniseries

Heat up your nights with...

#17 EROTIC INVITATION *by Carly Phillips*
Available December 2001

#21 ACTING ON IMPULSE *by Vicki Lewis Thompson*
Available January 2002

#25 ENSLAVED *by Susan Kearney*
Available February 2002

#29 JUST WATCH ME... *by Julie Elizabeth Leto*
Available March 2002

#33 A WICKED SEDUCTION *by Janelle Denison*
Available April 2002

#37 A STRANGER'S TOUCH *by Tori Carrington*
Available May 2002

Midnight Fantasies—The nights aren't just for sleeping...

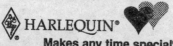

If you enjoyed what you just read,
then we've got an offer you can't resist!

Take 2 bestselling love stories FREE!
Plus get a FREE surprise gift!